From the library of
The Book Fairies
... to read and pass on...

PLACE FOUND	READER	DATE	THOUGHTS ON THE BOOK

#ibelieveinbookfairies www.ibelieveinbookfairies.com

THE NEEDFIRE

THE NEEDFIRE

MK HARDY

SOLARIS

First published 2025 by Solaris
an imprint of Rebellion Publishing Ltd,
Riverside House, Osney Mead,
Oxford, OX2 0ES, UK

www.solarisbooks.com

ISBN: 978-1-83786-295-5

10 9 8 7 6 5 4 3 2 1

A CIP catalogue record for this book is available from the
British Library.

Jacket illustration © Holly Macdonald
Designed & typeset by Rebellion Publishing

Printed in the UK

CHAPTER ONE

AT FIRST, YOU *take it as you find it. You live in caverns and hollows. You pluck fruit and pull roots and hunt.*

You survive.

You make marks on rock. You plant seeds. You fell trees and build shelters. You tan hides and knap stone.

You burn.

You bend beasts to your will and reshape the land beneath your feet. You raze dense forests into rolling fields. You turn flood plains into cities.

You dig.

Peat and coal, stone and iron. You hollow mountains with gaping pits. You riddle the earth with holes. You fill the air with smoke.

You consume.

※

THE HOUSE CLUNG to the very edge of the point, a squat brown limpet on an iron grey cliff, looking half-minded to jump. The sea beyond roiled fitfully, near-black beneath a dirty white sky, the clouds an expressionless sheet. Somehow, there was no horizon, sea and sky fading one into the other.

It was not raining, but it was wet. After only a few moments in the open air a film of mist settled on Norah's skin, biting at her lips, nose, ears. The hired carriage ejected her unceremoniously, luggage and all, at the bottom of the winding driveway, and it was a long, tense few minutes before a small horse and cart clattered into view from over the rise. It was clearly for work rather than transport, open-topped and drawn by a large bay draught horse. Driving it was a broad-shouldered, light-haired man of around her own age, who greeted her with a barely perceptible chin tip as he reached her.

"I'm sorry to trouble you," she said as soon as he was in earshot. This looked like a man who probably had a hundred other things he ought to be doing. "I would have walked, but…" She gestured. Her life, such as it was, fit into two portmanteaus. Small in the grand scheme of things given her thirty-two years on the earth, but too large to haul up a hill by herself.

He gave a shrug as he reined the horse to a halt, and then swung down from the cart with an easy grace. Any hoped-for introductions were not forthcoming. He hefted the cases into the back of the cart, and Norah was left to scramble up onto the seat herself, catching and ripping her skirt hem under one short heel in the process. She bit back a curse, reeling at a sudden wave of fatigue.

Yesterday had seen a full day's travel from Glasgow to Inverness through a steady downpour that seemed somehow bleaker and more oppressive than the precipitation she was accustomed to in the streets of her home city. Today's journey—six hours on the train and then another two in a rickety carriage—had left her wrung-out and ready for a warm hearth and a soft mattress. The hand climbed up beside her and directed the cart up the hill, and she had no choice but to face it fully: Corrain House.

Her new home.

It was perhaps an hour 'til dark yet, but the winter-weak sun hung low by the time they reached the house, the cloud cover casting its sickly yellow-pink hue over land and sea alike. To the west was barren coastline as far as the eye could see:

treeless scrubland that seemed to absorb what precious little light fell upon it, to gobble it up into the winding crevasses between its slumped hills. The land fell away sharply into the water as though cut off, as though God had decided *'enough'* and scooped it away leaving blasted pebble and bitter water behind.

The house stood broad and square. No cheerful crenulations or towers here, just a big hollow box: brown harling and dull slate. She stared up and its rows of smoky windows stared balefully back.

"It's bigger than I pictured," she remarked to the man—gardener? fieldhand?—as he lugged her cases up the steps. He grunted and paused to rap the front door, whose rough-hewn wood must've taken a journey much like her own to get there.

"Gie it time," he commented. His voice was lighter and higher than she would have expected, almost musical. "It will soon feel small enough."

He didn't wait, setting off back down the hill without another word. Norah watched the low-lying mist swallow his retreating form. Behind her, muffled footsteps in an echoing hall, heavy, disused bolts drew back, and one half of the big front doors groaned open wide enough to reveal a pale, angular face and the darkest eyes she'd ever seen.

"Miss Mackenzie."

She nodded, struck into silence. She couldn't shake the feeling that she had shifted a boulder and found something underneath, bleached from lack of light, too isolated to know fear. She eventually found her voice. "Yes, that's correct. I hope I'm not intruding." As soon as she said it she regretted it; how could she be intruding? Was this not to be *her* house now?

The woman didn't answer. She pulled the door open further to emerge fully into the early evening air. Her dress was brown or black, her hair brown or black. The dying light and the drab landscape sucked every other colour from the world. She was not wearing a uniform. Housekeeper, then, not maid.

Between them (Norah quietly noted that the housekeeper did not even make a token effort to prevent her from doing her share) they dragged her luggage a final few feet inside. The front hall was somehow at once cavernous and enclosed, an oppressive collage of dark wood and ageing wallpaper, of candle smoke and damp.

She could feel the housekeeper's eyes on her and was almost afraid to look back. "You'll want tea." Her voice had that same melodic up and down as the man with the cart, a warmth and colour at odds with her monochromatic appearance.

"Yes, that would be lovely." Before she could even turn she heard the housekeeper's footsteps echo away, and had to decide: follow her, or try to find a reception room on her own? The hall loomed around her, the dimness a physical weight that slumped her shoulders and set her head pounding. No, she'd wait for the proper tour before venturing unaccompanied into the house. With a speed she told herself was alacrity, and not trepidation, she followed.

The kitchen was along a narrow corridor and down a half-set of stone stairs. Larger than back home, though still smaller than Norah would have expected given the size of the house, it looked to have changed little in the past couple of centuries save for the two modern ranges crammed side-by-side at the far end of the room, only one of which appeared to be burning. There were no other staff to be seen, and the housekeeper herself attended to the pot warmer where a large kettle sat at the ready.

With the other woman's eyes now elsewhere, Norah finally felt safe to watch her in turn. Her body was lean like her face, though not in a way that would be considered fashionable— too tall, too strong, shoulders too square beneath her dark cotton dress. She moved with a restrained economy that gave Norah an involuntary pang of envy and frustration: her mother would approve. *It's even in the way you walk, dearest, as if the air itself is in your way. Nobody finds that attractive.* As the 'steel-engraving lady' with her dainty features and consumptive figure became evermore popular, so Margaret Mackenzie's dissatisfaction with her sturdy, full-figured daughter had deepened until Norah felt she could barely stand or sit without eliciting a disappointed tut.

Only once the tea was brewing in its pot did the housekeeper seem to notice that she had been followed, and Norah spotted the tiniest ripple in her placid exterior, a moment of hesitation. The knot in her stomach loosened. Behind those unfathomable eyes this woman was as uncertain as she was about how they should behave, what they should do next. The empathy flooded through her, and she made the decision for them, moving to sit at the large kitchen table, as close to the range as she could get.

"You'll have some too," she said—instruction or invitation she wasn't sure. After all, the other woman had the pot.

Two cups of tea were poured. The housekeeper sat. It seemed an aeon before anyone spoke.

"I hope your journey went smoothly, my lady."

"Yes, it passed easily enough. It's quite remote here," Norah said, and immediately pressed her fingertips to the teacup, the heat radiating its scorching reprimand. She held them there until she could take no more. "I mean to say that I don't think I registered quite how far the country extends beyond the bounds with which I'm familiar. I know some families travel up north to lodges and retreats quite regularly, but I've never had the pleasure. Until now."

"I don't think you'll find many families repairing to this part of the world for leisure, my lady."

'My lady' again. It was very strange to hear. Still, there was little point in pressing for 'Miss Mackenzie' given how short-lived the epithet was to be.

"No, perhaps not." Would anybody make the journey to see her here? Her mother found travel to be altogether too taxing, and her friends, well. Perhaps they were all glad to see the back of her. Norah pushed those thoughts aside, refocusing on the woman here in front of her. "Have you lived here all your life, then? In the area, I mean."

The housekeeper inclined her head. "More or less."

"Well, that's lucky. I'll have no lack of local knowledge as I settle in." Norah gave a manufactured smile, lifting her cup to her lips for a polite sip. "May I ask your name, Mrs…"

"Gunn."

"Of course." Despite the dark, probing eyes and sombre nature of her companion, Norah found her tensions seeping away. The dread that had settled over her upon stepping into the house seemed like a distant memory now as she sat in the pleasant warmth radiating from the range. It was an old house, yes, but it had its charms; she was sure she'd soon grow fond of its dark patterns and lofty, cavernous rooms. Any foreboding she had felt was nothing more than weariness and nerves. She took another sip. "After this I should like to freshen up, I think—and perhaps a wee rest before dinner."

"Oh, my apologies, my lady, I thought you knew… his Lordship's already at the kirk. W—he thought, under the circumstances, that you would not want to spend a night unmarried under his roof."

Norah's hand shook; tea quaked out of her cup and splashed the dusty front of her travelling frock. "So soon? Not that I object, mind, I just… thought there'd be more time to get my bearings."

Gunn tipped her head to the side. "The banns were posted for today. Of course, I'm sure the minister could be persuaded to amend the date on the papers…"

"No, no, I'm sure it's fine. I'm here now, we might as well. No sense in wasting the minister's time." Norah hoped she sounded upbeat, practical, but her voice was too high and thin to be truly convincing. It was as if the earth had begun to pitch and tremble beneath her just as she'd started to find her feet, and try though she might, she couldn't quite steady herself.

"Would you like to change? It's a short walk but you'll want good shoes—it'll be dark soon."

Norah looked down at her dress: tea-stained front, the hem rent with a jagged tear, dust all along her skirts. She had finer gowns with her, though they'd be crushed by their time in her portmanteau and wanting a proper airing and pressing before they'd be fit to wear. She had no compunctions about the pomp and circumstance afforded to her by the rather odd situation, but even so, she'd had expectations. She'd imagined trips to the village where she'd be fitted for a wedding dress; nothing grand, mind, but something fresh for this new chapter in her life. Instead it seemed she was destined to start it looking like a bedraggled orphan; hardly anybody's idea of a blushing bride. Perhaps it was fitting. "No, I think I shall go as I am. My shoes are sturdy enough, and as you say, it's getting dark. We mustn't waste time."

"As you like it."

GUNN ACCOMPANIED HER alone, and indeed Norah saw no signs of any other living soul as they prepared for departure, closing and shuttering the range and locking up the house. The air was chill, the ground crisp. There'd be a freeze that night.

The kirk was nowhere and then suddenly right before them, the mist parting to admit them into its waiting open doors. They had only walked back down the driveway and partway along a side path, though with the thick mist and the light fading fast it felt as though they had left the house far behind nonetheless. The building was broad and squat and harled just like the house, and it occurred to Norah that they had probably been built at the same time. It was built for practicality rather than beauty, a far cry from the delicate spire and stained glass of St John's back home. Still, the unadorned windows glowed from the light within, and at the sight of it some warmth returned to Norah's belly. She had chosen this. As strange as it was, this was her will.

They stepped from the falling blanket of night into the church, lit with candles and sturdy lamps along its nave. The interior was dressed sandstone, muting the glow of the flames and capturing what little warmth they radiated. Standing at the altar was a man so like the housekeeper that had greeted her that she had to glance between them just to believe her eyes. He had the same dark eyes set in a face of sharp angles and planes, the same broad shoulders and straight-backed bearing. And he looked at her in the same peculiar way, as if suspicious of her sudden arrival despite the fact that it was he himself who had asked her here—he who had arranged for them to meet like this, in a church, first setting eyes on one another minutes before exchanging eternal vows.

The minister was a slight and unassuming sort of character with steely hair and a narrow, pinched face, fully a head shorter than her fiancé. He was drowning in his vestments, which were a spartan affair and clearly made for a much larger frame. He was the first to break the silence by clearing his throat. The sound echoed around the chamber, impossibly loud.

"Gunn." Norah fancied the minister did not like the taste of that word in his mouth and her mind began to spin stories as to why. "And you must be Miss Mackenzie. It's good to meet you at last." He did not speak like Gunn or the man with the cart. His speech was clipped and monotone, though still a little unfamiliar to Norah's ear. An east coast lowlander.

"Good evening, Reverend. I must thank you for coming all the way out here to perform the service—I hope to be able to visit your church one day soon, and meet the families who attend." She couldn't shake the feeling that she was being hidden away; why else have the service here instead of in the village? Was he *ashamed* of her?

"Indeed," replied the minister with a smile, though it was close-lipped and didn't reach his pale eyes. "I was sorry to hear that his lordship's health would prevent him from attending, as indeed it has these past few years." The tone was significant, and Norah turned to scrutinise the man by her side all the closer, but then Gunn spoke up.

"Ah, there you are, Jamie." Nobody else had noticed the light-haired man letting himself in. He was wearing a flatcap now, and a threadbare jacket instead of his earlier coat. "Miss Mackenzie, I believe you met earlier: Jamie MacCulloch is our groundskeeper." The man tipped his head in greeting again, but didn't move from his post by the door. Gunn turned her gaze back to the minister and lifted her dark eyebrows. "Are we ready, then?"

"Please." It was the first word her fiancé had spoken, and it nearly made her jump out of her skin. His voice was deep and yet thin, scratchy, as though he used it little. "Begin."

What followed was a perfunctory ceremony made all the stranger by the dead silence around them.

There were few bodies in the church to muffle the sound, and so the minister's voice reached every corner where it hung, expectant and ringing with judgement. Norah fixed her gaze on his face, suddenly unable to look at the man beside her as their fates were woven together by fiat of God and His representative here on earth.

What had she expected? That she might set eyes on her fiancé and find the pit in her stomach miraculously vanished? That he might be a guiding light in these damp and dreary environs? She had never thought as much consciously, but it seemed she must have hoped it, for as the minister pressed onward and she mechanically followed his instructions to turn and face her groom, she was gripped with a sudden and all-consuming terror. She had made a dreadful mistake.

It was not sentimentality that made her quail; she had never dreamed of her wedding as some little girls did, so a perfunctory ceremony in her travelling clothes was as favourable as a cathedral filled with well-wishers—perhaps more so, given the expectations that would place upon her. No, her dread stemmed from a far more mundane source: the dawning realisation that she was surrounded by strangers, for despite the dozens of letters they had exchanged, Lord Alexander Barland regarded her with nothing but mild chagrin as they recited their vows. No one had challenged the banns because she knew no one here, *was* nothing here. She was completely and wholly alone.

The staff were their witnesses (Norah chided herself inwardly for her mild surprise that McCulloch signed his name and not an 'X'). The minister presided over the whole affair with that same pinched-face expression, clearly under sufferance, though whether due to the obviously unromantic technicalities of this union or being dragged away from his manse on a Saturday evening was hard to say. Comfort, when it came, was from an unexpected source: as Norah looked up from signing her own name, her eyes met those of the housekeeper, standing in front of the pews, still in her coat. Gunn favoured her with a grim, tight-lipped smile, and for just a flicker of a second, Norah perceived something real behind her unmoving gaze. Not sympathy, exactly, but not its sanctimonious cousin pity either. She glanced from Gunn to her new husband, two straight-backed peas in a pod, and her heart sank again. There was no such secret warmth in his eyes.

It was properly dark when they emerged from the church into frigid air. The clouds were too heavy for stars and even the waxing full moon was a hazy smudge. The land sloped steeply off to the north and Norah knew the sea was spread out forever beyond, but it was gone now, nothing but the path before them visible in the fog.

"Stay close." It was Gunn and not the baron who'd fallen into step at her elbow, and she was perversely relieved. She had to keep from moving closer still, her body hewing to Gunn's out of cold and not a little apprehension.

"Is this normal? That the fog should be so low and dense?"

"Sometimes." A pause. "Often, in the mornings and at night. In the summer it usually burns off during the day."

"I'm beginning to think arriving in the summer would have been a far wiser choice," Norah said with a rueful shake of her head. "The dark is…"

"You don't have the dark in Glasgow?" The tone was even, flat, and yet Norah thought she could hear the tease in it.

She ducked her head, holding back a smile of gratitude at this small gesture. "Not like this. At ho—in Glasgow the dark is always softened by the streetlights, the lamps shining out of people's windows. It never feels truly dark, even in the dead of winter."

"Well, it will never feel truly dark by the middle of summer here, so you have that to look forward to."

Norah hadn't thought about this; hadn't thought about many things to do with her new life, it seemed. She considered it now, the fact that they found themselves so far north that in winter, the sun barely deigned to come near at all, its absence casting the world into perpetual dimness. How did the plants and animals grow in these conditions? How did the *people*?

At length, Gunn cleared her throat. "You did not bring a lady's maid," she said. "Are you accustomed… will you be requiring my services?"

"Oh." She hadn't seen any other servants in the house, it was true, but then, she'd barely spent ten minutes inside before being whisked off to the church. She'd assumed—hoped—that there'd be a lady's maid already in position, since her mother had steadfastly refused to let her away with the one they had 'shared' for the past year or so. In truth her mother had kept the poor girl so busy that Norah had taken to seeing to her own needs rather than require the girl to work twice as much for paltry pay. She'd gotten proficient enough at most tasks that she wouldn't feel the lack of a maid now, even if it was unexpected. "I'll manage just fine, thank you. I'm sure you have enough to be getting on with, anyhow."

"There's plenty to do, right enough. Careful—" The last utterance was accompanied by a firm hand on Norah's elbow as her footing betrayed her on the steep root-laced path. For a moment everything seemed to tilt, and vaguely Norah pondered that if the light could forsake them this far north, why not gravity as well? But then her boot settled more firmly on the ground and Gunn pulled back her hand, and the world righted itself once more.

The housekeeper's next breath came out with a *whoosh*. "There's a steep drop to your right," she said. "Mind yourself."

Somehow Norah knew better than to look down. Sometimes one didn't have to see the fall to know it was real.

They arrived back at the house a few minutes later, the stillness broken only by Gunn's key scraping in the lock. Norah heard a crunch of gravel behind her and had to fight the urge to spin round, her nerves taut as an overtuned fiddle. A moment later her husband moved past her through the doorway, a dark figure swallowed by the dark house. A hand on her arm again.

"I'll show you to your rooms. You can rest before dinner."

BOTH MCCULLOCH AND her new husband were gone again, snuffed from existence by the haar and the quiet and the dark of the house. Norah was taken aback by her husband's disappearance—surely he would want to speak to her further, welcome her to the house? Gunn reassured her he would rejoin her soon enough and then led Norah up two boxy little stairwells and through straight, narrow corridors to her room—or 'rooms' as Gunn had more accurately put it, for there were several interconnected chambers for sitting, dressing, sleeping. Though it was more space than she'd had at Westbourne Gardens, the rooms themselves were smaller than she was accustomed to, with lower ceilings and darker decor. Everything was grand after a fashion, but outdated and run down, the old-fashioned four-colour wallpaper peeling at the edges, that ever-present aroma of damp hanging in the air.

"Would you like some hot water brought up, my lady?"

"Please."

Gunn nodded and melted back into the doorway; Norah tried to shake the feeling that perhaps she was still there, in shadow, watching her. To take her mind off this she began to move purposefully about the room, inspecting the windows, holding up a hand to test the draught. The panes radiated cold but she could feel no gusts of wind whistling through, thank God. She tugged the curtains across anyway, keen to make the room feel cosier and more homely. The brocade fabric was stiff under her fingers, reluctant to shift. It wasn't until she grasped it with both hands and pulled, hard, that the curtain followed, the runners screeching a protest at the movement. The sound scraped along her very marrow.

By the time Gunn returned she had pulled all the curtains and unpacked one of her cases; the puff-sleeved dresses and stiffly ribboned hats looked strangely out of place here, colourful adornments pasted in from another, gayer album. The housekeeper eyed them, her expression unreadable.

"There'll be a bell for dinner—I've checked it can be heard from here. Will you be needing escorted back or d'you think you can find your own way?"

"I might as well begin as I mean to go on," Norah said. "Though if you ring and I don't appear in good time, do send someone after me. Just follow the sound of the wailing," she added, grinning.

"Wailing? Why w—" Gunn caught herself, blinked. Her pale brow unfurrowed. "Ah, *your* wailing. Right you are."

"Thank you. For... your patience. While I settle in."

A slow nod. "That's my job, my lady."

"Yes, of course. Well." Norah wasn't quite sure what to do now—for as long as she could remember the staff had just moved through their house and their lives in perfectly choreographed harmony, familiar enough with their moods that they could predict her mother's requirement for a glass of sherry after a particularly animated visit from her closest confidante, or Norah's desire to be undisturbed when she was deep in her sketchbooks. She hadn't really thought about how to negotiate these ins and outs with a new staff—even a staff of one, as it were. She was desperate for even a hint of kindness but knew the mistress of the house should be decisive and proper. Should she be presenting Gunn with a list of errands and housework, setting a new schedule now that she had arrived? If only she had paid more attention to the logistics of running a household; if only she wasn't so very alone.

In the time it took her to grapple with this new hurdle Gunn once again excused herself into the shadowed corridor, and in her wake, silence swallowed Norah whole.

CHAPTER TWO

Tuesday, November 12th, 1889
10 Westbourne Gardens, Glasgow

Dear Lord Barland,

Please forgive me for the forward nature of my communication, and for the suddenness of its arrival. You do not know me, nor I you, but I found your name among my father's correspondences and I am writing in the hopes that we may strike up an arrangement.

I will be frank. My father died this September past, of a sudden and incurable illness that robbed him of his faculties, but even before that it transpires that he had conducted himself in business with a recklessness that has left the family accounts overdrawn and our prospects grim. Your company holds the largest share of my father's debt, for it seems in his role as broker for Barland & Co. he repeatedly and knowingly oversold to buyers while pocketing a cut for himself—though I am sure I do not need to explain the intricacies of these dealings to you, who will surely be more familiar with the ins and outs of the business than I.

We do not have the funds to repay this debt or the wherewithal with which to procure them. If you decide to pursue this debt, as is your right, you will bankrupt us and likely leave myself and my mother destitute. I am not accustomed to begging, Sir, but in this I must break *the habit of a lifetime to entreat you to show mercy on two women who were completely unaware of this man's dealings.*

In return, as things stand I can offer only my undying gratitude. However, I am an educated and capable woman with—God willing—decades of good health ahead of me. Though it is not the future for which I was prepared, I now have every intention of entering a profession as soon as my mother's health allows me to leave her side. Most likely I will become a governess, or tutor young women in painting or literature. At such times as I secured a position I would of course make arrangements to begin repaying our family's debt to you from my wages.

It is my fervent hope that this letter will not fall upon unsympathetic ears. If you desire a confirmation of my good character and standing, inquiries can be made to Mr and Mrs Peter Sinclair of 6 Goldsmith Terrace.

Yours respectfully,
Miss Norah Mackenzie

SHE HADN'T MEANT to lie down, much less fall asleep, but the dinner bell jarred Norah awake from a fitful slumber. She couldn't quite remember her dreams, but as she rose and approached the mirror it warped and shimmered for a moment, like water disturbed by a cold wind. She blinked, and then all she could see was the disarray of her hair, the pattern of the counterpane imprinted on her flushed cheek.

She dressed quickly and simply for dinner, in one of her darkest gowns—anything light or floral felt entirely inappropriate to the setting. Finding her way to the dining room was easier than she had feared—though the house was not laid out in an intuitive way, all the doors to other rooms were firmly shut, and so she only had to follow the narrow corridor to eventually find herself back in the main hall. From there she followed the faint glow of candlelight until she was standing in the doorway of the dining room, skewered by the gaze of her husband.

He was handsome. Tall, stone-cut, austere. She had pictured him greyer, older—it should have been a pleasant surprise to find him closer to her age perhaps but instead it just added to her disquiet. Everything was just a wee bit squint, somehow, off-kilter. This weird, square box of a house with its narrow hallways and its peeling wallpaper, its skeleton staff, its silent master. It was not a home. It was a tomb.

Her seat was at the foot of the table, the other end from her husband. A glass of red wine awaited her and she could scarcely conceal her relief.

"Corrain House is quite unlike anything I've seen before," she ventured after a moment of dusty silence. "Perhaps you can remind me of its story, so that I can begin to know it better."

Lord Barland's Adam's apple bobbed beneath pale, close-shaven skin. He opened his mouth a crack but no sound came out. Instead, her answer came from her periphery.

"It was built in the seventeenth century."

Gunn stood in the doorway, a large tray in her grasp, a tureen of soup balanced atop. It was as though she had just appeared there, framed in dark wood at the threshold of the chamber.

The soup was a vegetable broth. To Norah's pleasant surprise it smelled good.

"It was the clan seat for a minor chieftain—a MacKay. He went bankrupt in eighteen ten, and the baron—well, he wasn't a baron then, of course—bought the barony."

"Yes, I see." Norah nodded as Gunn moved about the room, watching the other woman's confident bearing, the way she seemed to fit among the dark portraits and narrow chairs. "And it's been in the family since."

"That's right."

Norah knew the rest—or some of it, at any rate. The man sitting opposite had been more forthcoming in his letters than he was here, in person, and was quite open on the topic of the estate in the past seventy years. The estate had been a small going concern in the kelp industry before its collapse, and from then had farmed sheep. From her own investigations in Glasgow, Norah strongly suspected that the land was more millstone than asset, and that the Barland ironstone mines were heavily subsidising the family seat.

She had hoped that the topic of the house would elicit some of the openness that had been present in his letters, which, while not quite veering into the territory of loquaciousness, had at least given her hope that she would find a companion with whom conversation would be easy. Not so tonight; the baron spooned his soup in silence, eyes fixed on the flecks of green and orange floating in his bowl. With a sigh Norah emulated him; if she was not to nourish her soul tonight then at least her stomach might benefit from the repast.

The main course was mutton with vegetables, and was again excellent. There was no pudding. After they had eaten (and in Norah's case imbibed fully two nervous glasses of wine), Barland stood. He inclined his head, and, with that same stiff, hesitant intonation as back at the kirk, as though speaking was a conscious physical effort for him, he said, "I'll be in my study. I have work."

Norah fought to untangle the meanings and implications behind this simple utterance. He had known she was coming—indeed, had planned their nuptials to take place that very night—but had not spared himself a night from his responsibilities. Was he so disappointed in her that he was already aching to be free of her company? She was a touch too short, she knew, for fashionable tastes, and of course she was plump and plain to boot. Her eyes were an indeterminate hazel, her hair an uninspiring brown which lay too straight for current styles and too tousled for sleekness. She had never intimated she was a beauty, but perhaps his imaginings had built up a picture to which she was a pale comparison.

She darted a glance at the half-empty wine bottle on the sideboard and nodded, looking back to her husband. "Very well."

He took his leave, and for some minutes, Norah sat entirely alone at the table, just her and her glass of wine, the dishes already removed by the housekeeper. The room was cold—not so much as to induce shivering, but enough to be uncomfortable without the distraction of a hearty meal. Above her, the dark wood panelled ceiling pressed downward, growing ever lower until she felt she was staring directly into the lifeless eyes of the leafy faces carved into its borders.

"I thought you might like to see the library."

This time Norah did give a start, and her frayed patience wore through. "Will you refrain from sneaking up on me like that," she snapped, twisting her napkin tightly with both hands as the housekeeper emerged from the doorway at the other end of the dining room. "Perhaps your master prefers you to be unobtrusive, but I do not. I like to know who I'm in a room with." The last sounded thin and sulky to her and she straightened, trying to look—even if she did not feel it—like the mistress of the house.

Gunn's dark brows twitched slightly. "My apologies, my lady. Would you like me to announce my presence in some way, or merely attempt to make more noise in my entrances and exits from rooms?"

Norah knew she should chastise the housekeeper for her cheekiness, but it was a blessed relief from the low-hanging dread that had settled over her during dinner; she could not help the rueful smile that overtook her. "Surely in this house the hinges must make an awful noise if left unoiled. Some benign neglect should do the trick."

Rather than answer this, Gunn returned to her earlier question. "I've made up the fire," she said, "in the library.

I can show you the way. We wouldn't want you reduced to wandering wailing from room to room."

With a final sip of her wine Norah pushed back from the table and stood, clinking the glass down with some resolve. "No, particularly once you've heard my singing. Lead on."

Gunn kept up a quiet narration as they wove through the silent hallways, pointing out this sitting room, that gallery. Norah felt tiny in the huge, empty house, an ant on a flagstone.

"It's not raining—well, not properly. We'll cross the courtyard."

The word brought to mind greenery, benches, perhaps a refuge from the oppressive atmosphere of the house itself. After less than a day it was folly to yearn for an escape, and yet Norah's steps sped up as they stepped through to the courtyard.

But if she had been hoping for an oasis, she was to be sorely disappointed.

The cold hit them in a wave as they opened the door—as cool as the house was, it was nothing to the sharp chill of night. The air was still, and even here a haar hung low to the ground, swirling around their feet as they stepped onto the flagstones.

The moonlight barely reached them here, and so it took a moment for Norah's eyes to adjust and begin to make out the mishmash of shapes dotted about the courtyard. It had been a garden. The remnants of it were discernible in the squat misshapen bushes and overgrown stoneware planters. It smelled of loam, and of decay.

At its centre, where one might expect to see a fountain or statue, there instead loomed a twisted mass of ancient wood, a gnarled, grasping shape like a giant pair of worn, arthritic hands raised in desperate supplication.

Norah felt as much as heard Gunn's breath, and so when she spoke it was not a shock. "She's a rowan," she murmured. "Been here as long as the house. Maybe longer."

She could picture it now—the young tree, its leaves fringed

and delicate, its berries red as a brand, standing on the edge of a cliff, buffeted by the coastal winds. Slowly the house rose up around it, circling closer, ringing it in stone and iron. Untouched by wind and straining towards the weak northern sun, it reached and twisted for the sky.

Leaves no longer lush but desperate, seeking.

Berries dropping on flagstone and meagre soil to shrivel and die.

"I've never seen one like it," Norah replied, her gaze still fixed on the tree. If she strained she could hear a faint moan, high pitched and pained, as if someone was trapped inside the whorl of bark and wood. Gunn shifted beside her and she realised with a start that it was only the wind high above them, rushing across the opening of the courtyard on its journey out to sea.

"There's a walkway round the edge."

Past broken pots and errant climbers, across cracked flagstone, they crossed—or rather circled—the space, and Gunn opened a stiff door on the other side.

The library was a large north-facing room at the back of the house, almost the mirror of the dining room they had left. Heavy curtains cloaked its tall windows and three sides of the room were lined with bookshelves from floor to ceiling. Gunn had made a fire in the hearth, and indeed a wave of warm air washed over them as they entered the room. In the shifting golden light, surrounded with the smell of paper and leather, Norah was almost able to forget for a moment where she was. She was cast back to her father's study, the pleasurable evenings she had spent curled up on the rug with a notebook and pencils while he worked.

"It's lovely," she said, turning a smile on the housekeeper. "How did you know I'd like it?"

A pause. Then, "Surely anybody likes a chair by a fire. I thought you would appreciate your own space, as his lordship does his." The room was not well lit so it was hard to say for sure, but Norah thought Gunn's eyes slid away from hers as she spoke.

"I'm sure I will," Norah said, resolute. "Thank you, Gunn. You may go."

The housekeeper hesitated. "Will you be able to find your own way to bed?"

The last thing Norah wanted was to return to that cold, dark room, to wait in uncertainty for her husband to join her—or not. It would almost be preferable to spend the night wandering the halls like a spectre. "Your concern is admirable, but I assure you, I shall be fine."

"Then I'll see you in the morning—make sure the guard is in place when you leave if the fire's still going. Please. My lady." If Gunn was embarrassed at forgetting due deference, her pale, angular countenance did not show it.

"Of course. Good night."

With a nod Gunn withdrew from the room, casting one last backwards glance at Norah that she felt as much as saw, the dark gaze almost a physical weight on her skin. And then she was gone, and though the weight did not lift, Norah could at least turn her attention to the hearth and the task of warming her hands with its glow. The cold had crept in through dinner, and the trip across the courtyard hadn't helped; her fingers felt as if they were cored with ice. She stepped closer to the fire, skirts whispering across the heavy rug, and waited for the fire's warmth to thaw them.

It really was a lovely room, even lit as it was only with firelight. The hearth was wood set into the stone of the wall, and as she stood before it her eyes wandered across the carvings, flickering and lit from below. There were curling vines and flourishes, shells and spirals, the handiwork at once crude and intricate. Norah leaned closer, wondering if the serrated leaves along the mantle were those of the rowan, like the one in the courtyard. The carvings came together in the middle in a whorl of woodgrain, and it was only once she had drawn her eyes across it several times that she resolved the face in its midst, surrounded by fronds and leaves which spilled across its chin and cheeks and into its open, gaping mouth. She started back, trying to shake the feeling that the lifeless eyes were following her.

In her desire for distraction she moved to the nearest shelf, fixing her gaze on the spines and picking each gilded title out in the flickering firelight. To her mild disappointment—though little surprise—the library did not appear at first glance to be a particularly up-to-date collection. The *Encyclopaedia Britannica* dominated one section—the 1817 edition with its enormously thick volumes and its old-fashioned typesetting. The spine cracked alarmingly when she retrieved a volume and flipped it open, and she feared that they had been left so long to moulder that they were no longer fit to be read.

Replacing the volume, she continued her perusal, moving slowly around the room, sometimes reaching out to trail her fingers along the shelves and the books within. Old though they might be, no dust rose at her touch. Gunn kept the house well, a fact which gave Norah some comfort. While the other woman was obviously perplexed by Norah's appearance at Corrain House she did not seem hostile; setting herself against the housekeeper would have created no small amount of tension in what was otherwise one of her only refuges from the isolation of her new situation.

When she came to the section of shelves split by the window, she paused. She could feel the cold emanating from it even through the thick woven curtains and she knew she ought to keep moving, but something fixed her to that point, the chill seeping back into her bones. The curtain was a dark, heavy damask, and she almost expected it to crack beneath her fingers like the book did as she gripped its edge and pulled it aside.

Behind it was blackness.

A knot of fear tightened in her throat. She knew it was the haar, the fog obscuring moon, land and sea alike, the candles and fire inside too dim to illuminate beyond the window. And yet there was something about that unfathomable dark that tapped into an ancient part of her, a Wrongness that could not be reasoned away. She let go of the curtain and stood back, too quickly, almost stumbling. The curtain fell back into place without a sound, without a ripple, immediately looking as though it had never moved.

There was nothing outside this house.

The longer Norah's thoughts lingered on this the more her heart fluttered, a moth battering itself against the cage of her chest. It was a childish fear, this dread in the face of darkness, one that hadn't plagued her since she was very young and quite naive. She knew that the world went on beyond Corrain House, logically—waves crashed against the shore, the stars wheeled overhead, and all around life crept onward—but that logic was slippery to grasp and impossible to hold onto. Once again she turned to books for refuge, selecting one from the nearest shelf and carrying it back to the hearth. The slipper chair set beside it was more comfortable than it looked, and as she flipped to the first pages of the book the warmth once again crept over her, soothing her and banishing the cold, dark thoughts of before.

The book was not a 'book' at all, per se, but rather a folio collating a sheaf of cheap broadsides. They were hand bound—rather inexpertly, in fact, the sheets loose and prone to tearing where the threads weakened their edge. Someone in the past—some decades ago if she had to guess from the typesetting and the quality of the paper—had been a collector. The folio had opened to a page with a long leaf that was folded up in half. Flipping the page down, her first sight was a woodcut illustration of a man and woman in a leafy clearing. They looked away from one another, clearly at odds. The title read 'An Advice to Married Women'. What followed was a (rather inaccurately typeset) ballad.

Now you married women all,
Your attention I do call,
And a good advice ill give you I am thinking,
For the husband I have got,
He Was once a drunken sot,
Till the money that he earn'd went into drinking

CHORUS

You married women all,
Pray take my advice,
When your husbands drunk in bed they are snoring,
In the Blankets sew him right
And lay on with all your might,
Till he swears he'll join tea-total in the morning

He stripped the house quite bare,
Of the Bedstead, stools and chair,
And in rags I was ready for flying,
When I saw my dismal state,
Then I cursed my wretched fate,
While the children for bread they were crying

Norah pressed her lips together, a quiet 'mph' of a chuckle echoing around the empty room. Ironic that she should turn to this page, though the predicament of this poor wife was rather closer to her mother's than her own.

One night he came home late,
In a beastly drunken state,
For the coat off his back, he had druuk it,
When he tumbled down in bed,
Then a thought came in my head,
For to sew him quite tight in the blanket

With the leg of an old table,
I laid on while I was able,
While Barney for mercy for roarin,
He cried, Biddy dear, stop, And ill never drink a drop,
Forll go and join-total in the morning

From our home that weary night,
Cold poverty took flight,
Now in peace and content we are living,
Like our neighbours now we are seen
On the Sundays neat and clean,
And a little in the bank we are saving

Norah flipped the folio closed and let it drop into her lap. So much for escaping into a book. Pinning a man down and beating some sense into him was all very well in a few stanzas of doggerel but the reality was quite different. As far as had been apparent in life, the late John Mackenzie's abuse of his wife and daughter had amounted to only benign neglect. It was only once he was in the ground and his estate audited that his sins emerged.

The fire spat a glowing ember onto the hearth, catching Norah's eye. She watched it pulse from yellow to orange to red, and then black, a wee spot of negative space on the grey stone. Before her eyes, the spot grew, tiny tendrils of soot spreading out like roots, dividing again and again into a dense, crisscrossing network until at its heart the black spot began to grow larger, covering the hearth, the rug, creeping up the fireplace and walls. It would soon reach her, its darkness all-consuming and inescapable, and her heart seized in her chest as she found that she could not move, and yet even as she opened her mouth to scream, tasting the soot snaking past her lips and down her throat, a tiny place in her mind called out to it, welcomed its promised oblivion.

Norah started as the folio slid off her lap and landed on the floor with a thud. When had she drifted off? The fireplace glowed low and cold, the room darker for it. She could no longer make out the ember on the hearthstone. She pushed to her feet, unsteady, the world around her still shifting back to normality. No doubt it had been a fancy born of fatigue; the journey had been more gruelling than she had expected, and the brief doze before dinner had only taken the edge off her exhaustion, and the dark, close walls of Corrain House were enough to drive even the most sober mind to strange chimeras under those circumstances. Why, the carvings on the hearth alone were like something straight from her nightmares—enough. Time for bed. Dreams could not hurt her, and a good night's rest would solve all the world's ills.

CHAPTER THREE

THE MORNING BROUGHT light and a resigned acceptance. Norah had hoped that with the day she would find a renewed sense of rightness, a settling of the shifted pieces of her life into a new and satisfactory pattern. Though the thin light pushed through the windows and showed the intricate designs on the bedroom wallpaper and her embroidered bedcover in all too much detail, she found no such clarity within her own self.

She hadn't been sure her husband would join her the previous night, given his immediate departure from her after dinner, and duly he had not. It was becoming clear that he did not intend to. She should be—she was—relieved, not to be obliged to share a bed with a man she knew even less well than she'd thought. And yet with the relief came a deepening of the emptiness she'd felt since she'd arrived. Longer, really. Since Isa. Since Father.

Perhaps her headstrong choice to come here had been a gamble, a desperate attempt at righting what had gone sour and wrong in her life. Her father had left their house in disarray: accounts overdrawn, letters of debt piling up on his polished mahogany desk. He had made these choices for himself, heedless of the impact it would have on his wife and daughter, and Norah wondered if the looming burden had ever given him pause or if he had blithely ignored it, preferring to enjoy the fruits of his deception.

Isa too had chosen her own course, knowing and pursuing

that which would bring her happiness without accounting for Norah's wishes. It was her prerogative, of course, and Norah couldn't deny that it seemed to have brought her joy, but it had driven a wedge too deeply, too irrevocably to ever withdraw.

None of this had been her fault—at least, that's what she told herself in the solitary, quiet moments when she reflected on what had changed—but it was left to her to remedy nonetheless. Perhaps it was watching her father, Isa, even her mother that had led her to choose to run to Corrain—a selfish and impulsive decision that seemed to have brought nothing but disappointment to all caught up in its wake.

Gradually a waft of steam at her bedside attracted her attention: a small teapot sat on the table, its burnished side reflecting her sleepy countenance back at her as she blinked and shifted into a sitting position. Gunn must have brought it before she woke; the thought of the sombre, silent housekeeper hovering over her as she slept made something inside her shiver.

There were no clocks in here—she had a little pocket watch, but she had forgotten to wind it last night and it had stopped around five o' clock in the morning. Though she had nothing in particular to do, it was disconcerting to be unmoored in time, much in the same way the sight out the window last night had left her feeling that this whole house was outside of the world itself.

Resolutely she turned her thoughts towards productivity; she would banish these silly apprehensions soon enough through industry and exploration. Of course she felt isolated and off-kilter—she had only just arrived, and the circumstances had been unusual, to say the least. But it was no more unusual than any number of young women who found themselves in new households, in new cities, in new marriages, and time and time again they adapted and flourished. She would be no different.

Tea first, then she would dress and familiarise herself with her new surroundings. There was solid ground to be found here, she was sure of it.

THE HOUSE LOOKED different in daylight—far from the intimidating expanse of corridors and doorways Norah had navigated the night before with only a candle to light her way, the anaemic beams through the curtains showed it to be tired and meek, the floorboards refusing to creak beneath her feet for fear of—what? She shook the silly thought off and turned her attention to her route.

As in any home of such magnitude her best hope, she knew, was to familiarise herself with the art. The hallway off which her bedroom was located was mostly hung with thick, dark tapestries, which left the air feeling odd-smelling and grimy in spite of the fact they were recently dusted, just like the library. The main corridors leading to the large central stairwell were punctuated with dour landscapes for the most part, just barely breaking the maroon monotony of the old-fashioned wallpaper. In the stairwell landscape gave way to portraiture and the occasional pastoral scene: sheep, cattle, farmland—Norah even spotted one rendering of the kirk where her nuptials had taken place the previous evening. The squat building peered back at her from the gloom, rendered in the same murky halftones she remembered, more bleak than bucolic. Apparently even an artist had not the capacity to introduce colour to this mist-grey edge of the world.

As she descended the final flight of stairs she found herself staring at an increasingly familiar face. The largest canvas in the building, it seemed, was given over to the baron himself—or rather, one of his forebears. The plaque on the heavy gilt frame read 'Lord William Alexander Barland, 8th Baron of Corrain'. Her own Lord Barland's grandfather looked a few years older than her husband in his portrait, and wore his side whiskers longer according to the fashion of the time, but the resemblance was obvious in the pale face with its sculpted cheekbones and straight, sharp nose. It was dated 1812, two years after Barland's purchase of the estate.

The portrait of the baron was flanked by mounted stag heads: dozens of them. Seeing them now, Norah marvelled that they had escaped her notice the previous evening, for they were hard to miss, most of them at least ten-pointers and crowded either side of the painting in a forest of bony prongs. The grotesque display was all the more ridiculous for the fact that they could not possibly all have been locally shot: there could be few deer roaming the barren, exposed scrubland and coastline of the Corrain estate. She had not even begun to think about redecoration of the house before now, but getting rid of this wall of death immediately became item number one on her brand new list.

In the dining room a spread had been left out, presumably for her. Rolls, sausages, eggs, thick slices of ham and yellow wedges of smoked haddock sat atop a tray, each crowded next to each other, their juices intermingling and puddling. It had probably been appetising when it had first graced the table, but she must have slept later than she thought, for the sausages were cold, sitting in a disc of their own congealed fat, and the eggs filmed over with a rheumy membrane. The sheen on the ham reminded her of the beetles she had seen at the Kelvingrove, pinned and spread under many gawking eyes. She had always expected them to twitch or shudder as she stood over their cabinet, the light catching the oily blacks and greens of their wings, making a blade of the small silver pins stuck straight through them.

Norah swallowed down her disgust and took a roll from atop the floury pile, adding butter and jam and wishing she had a cup of hot tea to wash it down—she had resisted the urge to bring down her bedside tray but was now regretting it. She'd hoped for something like the usual cosy scene at

Westbourne Gardens—her mother propping up one end of the table, adding far too much sugar to her tea and nattering away about this or that, Fletcher pottering at the sideboard, refreshing the pot at every opportunity and polishing it in between. But if her husband had been here at all he left no sign of it, and the silver teapot at the edge of the table was cold and smudged.

The tea at her bedside had at least been warm. Gunn knew she had overslept, and yet had left this grim tableau for her to find. Well. That was fine, she thought, and then stopped herself. It was in fact not fine. She was the mistress of the house, and it was inexcusable for her housekeeper to leave this stale and fragrant spread out to rebuke her, as if she had any right to shame Norah for sleeping late, for not adhering immediately to the house's routines and patterns. She could have woken her, could have helped her into her stays and stockings and dress instead of leaving her to struggle alone, but instead she had only left the teapot at her bedside, doubtlessly expecting it, too, to grow cold and chiding. Norah could not let this stand; she would have to reprimand Gunn and ensure that the behaviour did not continue. She could almost hear her mother's voice in her ear, instructing her to 'nip it in the bud', and a flush of anger and embarrassment spread over her cheeks, staining them with heat.

She set out to find the housekeeper, a task that soon proved more difficult than she had foreseen. Though it looked relatively plain and symmetrical from the outside, Corrain House's interior was unpredictable, with hallways that bled into one another confusingly. It didn't help that everything was so *dark*, making it hard for Norah to pinpoint landmarks that might help her place herself in this new landscape. She had been wandering for some time in what she hoped was the direction of the kitchen when she came upon the very woman she sought, moving whisper-quiet through the heavily carpeted corridors. Upon seeing Gunn Norah's ire nearly abandoned her, but she screwed it to the sticking place and drew her shoulders back with a gasp. "Gunn. There you are. About this morning—"

The rebuke died in her throat as she took in the housekeeper's appearance. Gunn had stopped mid-stride, her dark skirts bunched up in one fist, exposing sturdy brown boots. Tucked beneath her other arm was a jute sack filled with firewood. Her sleeves were rolled almost to the elbow, hair escaping from its utilitarian bun. Her bare arms and face were streaked with soot and shining with sweat. Even in this state it was impossible not to draw a comparison between her and Norah's husband—both dark-haired, pale-faced, lean and striking.

Gunn lifted her dark eyebrows. "My lady?"

The heat in Norah's cheeks flared again—shame, this time, instead of anger. Gunn was the only servant in the entire house, wholly responsible for its running, and here she was about to berate her for leaving the breakfast things out a bit too long. The housekeeper seemed to sense it, too, her gaze pinning Norah to the floor like the beetles had been fixed in their cabinet. "I normally rise much earlier," she stammered, resisting the urge to twist her hands together in consternation.

Gunn blinked slowly. "Your time is your own, my lady." She adjusted her grip on the sack, her arm corded with long, lean muscle. She carried some strength in her slim frame. Norah's blush deepened. "Is there anything else?"

"No, I only wanted to inform you that I will be walking the grounds this morning." Norah hadn't planned a walk, was barely dressed for one, but the words tumbled off her tongue before she realised what she was saying. "Nothing formal, only I wish to familiarise myself with my new home. Are the boundaries clearly marked?"

"Marked?" Gunn sniffed. "I supposed they're marked well enough. Our boundaries are the water. Rivers to the east and west, and to the north, the sea."

Norah nodded, the rushing of the water rising in her ears until she thought she might be swept away right then and there. "Very well. I shall be mindful."

The housekeeper inclined her head, apparently taking this for a dismissal, for she hefted the sack beneath her arm once more and strode off past Norah down the corridor without a backward glance. She did call out, though, as she went.

"Take care on the coastal path. The haar's not lifted yet."

THE DAMP SOUP that fell upon Glasgow on dreich days was a grimy, greasy fog that left a thin film of oily residue on skin and clothing, rendering its people as soot-caked and stained as its sandstone edifices. This haar, this sea mist, could not be more different: briny and bitterly cold, it had rolled in straight off the water to hang a crisp white sheet before Norah's vision that shocked her lungs the first time she breathed it in. She feared that whatever her intentions she would not see much of the grounds this morning.

Still, she pushed on through the mist, enjoying the squeeze in her lungs and the cold stroke of droplets upon her cheeks. Out here it was easy to put Corrain House and its strange inhabitants to the back of her mind—not forgotten, not at all, but distant, innocuous. The movement felt good as well, banishing the strange unease she had felt that morning in favour of robust exertion and tingling limbs. Norah traced the humps and hummocks of scruffy turf with her steps, her boots coping admirably with the uneven ground.

What she *could* see through the haar was unremarkable: grass, rock, and pale, crusty lichen. This was no bustling homestead, no lively farm with waving fields of wheat or barley, no. She thought she might have heard the bleat of a sheep over the distant waves, but if there were any livestock nearby she certainly couldn't see them. She had a moment of merriment imagining the fluffy animals melting into the fog, subsumed into the damp white, but the longer she lingered on the thought the more unsettling it became.

It was hard to gauge how far she was walking with no distant landmarks to aim for, so it took her quite by surprise when the family kirk loomed out of the fog to her right, nestled on its wee plateau hewn out of the hillside. She'd retraced her steps, then. She remembered the previous night, Gunn's warning—*There's a steep drop...* The ghost of a firm hand at her elbow sent gooseflesh prickling up her arm. She shivered, and flipped up the collar of her coat.

Though it was a Sunday, the kirk appeared silent and empty, and it occurred to her that it was not used at all except by the family—and from the minister's cool tone she suspected they found little need of it. Perhaps that was why it was so spartan in appearance, bare and undecorated inside and out. Or perhaps that was just how churches were up here.

She half expected that the door would be unlocked, and yet she did not try the handle, instead pacing out its perimeter. The ogival windows were high up on the exterior walls, pointing heavenward, sills above head height. They were diamond paned, and entirely absent of colour. They were not completely unadorned, however. As she squinted to see what she could inside, her view was marred by markings on the glass. At first they seemed to be just random scratches, but as she stared she began to make out the loops and curls of messily scrawled handwriting. The more she stared, the more she saw crammed haphazardly into the lower half of the warped leaded diamonds. She couldn't make out any complete words from down here, and she resolved to look more closely when she was next inside. Not today. Today, she knew, crossing that threshold would at once transport her back to the previous evening's nuptials, and she had no wish to pick back over that event in her mind's eye.

She supposed she could seek out MacCulloch, request that he take her into the village so that she could attend the

Sunday service there. But she reckoned it to be nearly noon and the minister clearly already viewed the residents of Corrain House with no small measure of disdain. Arriving late—assuming it wasn't finished long since—would only tar her with the same brush. Next week, she promised herself. She'd go to kirk, show herself to be a faithful member of the flock, the minister would soften to her. And she'd have at least one ally in this barren tract.

A motion out of the corner of her eye made her suck in a startled breath; she had not expected to see anybody else on her expedition. Turning, she realised that the movement had come from within the church, as if her imagining a service had somehow conjured one into being. A candle flickered in the window, and she could make out one figure, then two, then three, not seated and praying but roving past the windows in a restless cadence. Something in their movements put her in mind of cattle, penned and pacing. Norah frowned, unsettled, and approached, but by the time she was close enough to peer inside the figures were gone, and the church was empty. As, of course, it had always been, filled only by a trick of the light and her imagination.

She did not walk much further that day—the path continued on downward, presumably eventually reaching the village, but now that she remembered how dangerous this route was she didn't have the stomach to continue. By the time she got back to the top of the trail the wind had whipped up and the haar was clearing, parting in front of her in low-lying ribbons to reveal the house up ahead. It appeared as sturdy and rooted as it had the day before, as if reminding Norah it would stand there long after her ill-fated journey north had run its course.

THE AFTERNOON PASSED uneventfully; Norah ate a small meal alone in the dining room, attended by Gunn, and then continued unpacking and arranging her things. Though the room was hardly overly furnished it still held enough wardrobes and drawers for the modest amount of clothing she had brought. She placed her toiletries on the vanity, spending overlong arranging them just so. Her mother had made noises about buying her a new, silver-plated set, the type Norah had admired as a girl, all filigree and shine, but they both knew the household didn't have the funds to justify such an expense, and so she had brought the same hand mirror and brush that she'd had since she was a child.

Then of course there was the thick leather folio containing her sketchbook, writing paper, and assorted correspondence she could not bear to part with. Her stomach twisted with a complicated mix of discomfort and anger when she happened across it. It seemed like a different woman who'd carefully saved and stored the letters from her now-husband. What an innocent she was, what a child, to believe those letters contained even the tiniest insight into the character of the man! His first letter, the reply to her humiliating opening gambit, had been a perfunctory missive expressing sympathy at her situation and intimating that she and her mother should take whatever time they needed—within reason— to arrange their affairs before writing to arrange a schedule for repayment. But somehow Norah's letter thanking the baron prompted a further response, and another in turn, and in time she had taken to enquiring each day whether there might be any mail for her, while her mother looked on in a combination of hope and envy.

Saturday, December 21st, 1889
Corrain House

Dear Miss Mackenzie,
   I hope this letter reaches you in good health.
   You have been much in my thoughts this past fortnight, and I have found myself returning to your last letter,

poring over its contents for further insights into your wellbeing. Though I'm glad you have such close friends in the Sinclairs, I detect hints that their acquaintance can cause you occasional pain also. It is no doubt bold of me—perhaps presumptuous—to even guess at your innermost thoughts and feelings based only on written correspondence, and yet here I am doing just that. I hope you will forgive the insult, if insult there be.

On a day such as this, at the turning of the year, one tends to take stock—to look at one's situation and ask the question: where am I? How far have I come? How far have I yet to travel? Who are my companions on this journey?

This year, as in the many years before it, I survey my situation and find it decidedly lacking. I have no close family, no friends, little other than matters of business to occupy my mind or stimulate my imagination.

And yet, as I put pen to page to write to you, Miss Norah Mackenzie, I find that as I ponder the future, it is perhaps not so bleak as it was on this day one year ago.

I'll close here, lest I frighten you.

Yours,
Alexander Barland

It was the first letter he had signed with his Christian name, the 'A' in a sharp-peaked block capital style rather than rounded cursive, split in two on the downstroke by the cheap dip pen nib that was apparently his tool of choice. At the time, she had taken this to be significant. In a tiny corner of her heart, it had felt like a promise.

CHAPTER FOUR

NORAH WASN'T USED to quiet meals. Her mother was more than content to fill any silence presented to her with all manner of speech—gossip from the friends that came to visit, lamentations at the day's broadsheets, and of course a steady stream of censure, fault-finding and admonishment at Norah's comportment and her general existence. When she managed to escape to Isa and Peter's the repast was far more pleasant, buoyed along by gentle intellectual sparring and no small amount of laughter. That wasn't to say there wasn't the occasional stony silence, when Isa's temper had left both Norah and Peter studying their cutlery with apparent fascination, but those storms quickly passed, banished as easily as they were summoned—until the final one had broken, at least.

The cloud that hung over the dining room of Corrain House was far more persistent, weighing Norah down as she dissected the food on her plate into ever-smaller morsels. Her husband sat across from her at the long table, pushing his own meal about with a knife as if measuring the seconds until he could excuse himself. She felt a dull ache in the pit of her stomach that had nothing to do with physical hunger and pushed herself straighter in her seat.

"I thought perhaps I might go into the village, next Sunday," she announced. "That is, if the kirk on the grounds is to remain unused for such occasions."

Her husband lifted his head to look at her but said

nothing. It was, as usual, Gunn, hovering ever present in the background, who cleared her throat.

"It's entirely your choice, of course, my lady. But you might not find the service in the village to your liking."

"Whyever not? Is it in Gaelic?" Norah frowned in bemusement—she knew that Gaelic speakers were not so prevalent here as they were further west and would not have expected so many here that they ran the services in the tongue.

"Eh, no, my lady, but it is a Free Kirk, and I think you'll find it very different from what you're used to in the city. I'd suggest having MacCulloch take you to Thurso if you'd like to attend a Sunday service."

"Surely it's important for the lady of Corrain House to be seen in the village," Norah said, addressing her words not to Gunn but to her voiceless husband. There was an edge to them, a challenge: surely it was important for the *lord* to be seen.

Her husband did not blink. His mouth opened and closed again, once, before he finally seemed to find words. She was struck once again by the timbre and tone of his voice, the effort it seemed to take.

"You must do as you wish."

It was nothing. Less than nothing, a refusal to imbue the reply with anything nearing personal opinion or sentiment. Norah's fingers curled around her fork. "I imagine I must," she muttered. She did not ever wish to wear the mantle of nagging wife, but perhaps that was the only way she might elicit a reaction—*any* reaction—from her indifferent spouse.

A silence followed. Then, in a conciliatory tone that only *somewhat* bordered on patronising, the housekeeper spoke once again. "Perhaps it would be of benefit for you to see Corrain for yourself," she said. She pronounced it 'Corrin', with a short 'ih' and Norah's stomach twisted in embarrassment that she had been placing emphasis on the second syllable this whole time, and rhyming it with 'stain'.

"Would you like me to arrange for MacCulloch to take you tomorrow?"

It was sooner than Norah had planned, but perhaps that was for the better. "Yes, do. I look forward to getting to know the people of the town."

The look Gunn shot her at this was almost sympathetic.

WHAT NORAH HADN'T realised, what didn't sink in until she saw it with her own eyes, was that Corrain was not a town. It was barely even a village. What the map called 'Corrain' was in fact a miserable row of subsistence smallholdings clinging onto the coast for dear life.

"We'll need to walk from here," MacCulloch said, pulling up the open-topped cart at the top of a steep track. No haar today; the wind had changed and picked up and the view down to the shore was clear, the air fresh and scented with seaweed. The track was winding but well-worn, grooves from years of hand-pulled carts ground away down its length.

Norah picked her way down with care; she had worn one of her nicer dresses, hoping to present a proper picture of a baron's wife, and it wouldn't do to arrive covered in dirt and debris after putting in that effort. Effort which she was now regretting as they neared the village and she was faced with the ragged stone buildings and meagre vegetable plots clustered like barnacles on the craggy coast. There were perhaps two dozen of them, a mix of red-tiled roofs and slate, and the small windows were shuttered tightly. No windows or doors faced the coast, instead they were carved into the east or west of the buildings, and as they made it to the bottom of the path Norah suddenly saw why.

There was nothing between the crofts and the hungry sea. It stretched out to the horizon, grey and shifting, its waves churned by the wind and tide into frothy peaks. A slip, a stumble, and the unsteady-footed might slide right into its depths. The gable ends of the tiny homes lined up like jagged, uneven teeth.

There was no bay here. To the west the land curved and rose sharply into cliffs, and Norah could see a steep, narrow path climbing upward that must be the other end of the one she'd now taken twice, leading to the wee kirk and then Corrain House itself. To the east, a narrow breakwater jutted out into the waves. There were a few rowboats on the beach but no sign of anything larger, or even of a proper jetty. There was not a soul in sight. Norah turned to MacCulloch in confusion.

"I thought fishing was the main source of employment here," she said.

The groundskeeper snorted. "Aye but… no' here," he said. "The men fish fae Scrabster. They're gone for days at a time. Weeks, in good weather."

Norah frowned, turning back to the sea and squinting at the horizon. She had no reason to disbelieve MacCulloch, but there were ships there—boats, really, small dinghies clustered under the low, scudding clouds at the edge of the sky. They were too far away to make out any crew but she could *feel* them, the ache gripping their muscles, the uncertainty of each step. "Then what are those?"

"Eh?" MacCulloch turned, and she raised her hand to indicate the vessels. As her hand swept over the horizon they seemed to vanish, leaving the skyline as empty as a freshly cleaned slate. "What's that?"

"The… there were boats, just there. I saw them," Norah said, feeling her cheeks go hot as he looked back to her. "A good half-dozen. Fishing boats."

"No, you won't see them here, there's nothing worth fishing this far along." MacCulloch smirked. Norah opened her mouth to protest, but what was there to say? There were no boats to prove her point, only a flat grey sea. "Oh and there's the kirk," he said, gesturing to a building at the near end of the row, larger than the rest, the only one with a tiny round window on its gable end. "Gunn said to make sure you saw it."

There was something in his singsong tone, just a hint of mockery, of smug satisfaction, that made Norah want to slap him—and Gunn. Of course Gunn wanted her to be sure to see this house of worship even smaller than the family kirk, the church she had expressed her foolish desire to attend. Right now she would be chuckling away at her chores, picturing Norah's embarrassment that what she'd imagined as a small but active little fishing village was in fact a string of dour, shuttered boxes teetering on the very edge of a world only reluctantly tolerating their presence.

With a defiant clench to her jaw, Norah forced one foot in front of the other toward the row, rounding the kirk to approach the nearest home. Its front door was closed, but a slow drumbeat of metallic scrapes and thuds drew her to the tiny garden plot alongside, where a short, wiry woman was wrestling with a curious tool as big as she was. It had a long, curved shaft, with a metal-bladed foot. The woman worked backwards, grunting with the effort of forcing the blade into the earth, then leaning almost her full weight upon it to lift a furrow. The ground appeared hard and gritty, a far cry from the rich, dark earth of the paintings that adorned the hallways of Norah's new home. The woman was so intent on her task that Norah was almost upon her before she looked up in shock, speechless at the sight before her.

"Good morning," Norah said, imbuing the words with a confidence and cheer almost completely absent from her internal resolve. "I'm M—I'm Lady Barland, newly come to Corrain House." The crofter said nothing, betrayed nothing with her weathered features besides weary resignation. If she felt anything about the new lady of Corrain House it was buried deep. Norah tamped down her rising unease and pressed onward. "I was admiring the gardens of the village—tell me, what are you growing?"

The woman frowned in bemusement, looking at the hand-ploughed furrow between them, and then back to Norah. Of course. There was nothing growing. It was February.

"What an interesting contraption," Norah ventured then, her chance at making a good first impression was rapidly slipping beneath the nearby waves. "I've never seen one before. What is it called?"

Another *chnk* of blade into tight-packed soil before she got a response. "Cas-chrom." She stressed the second syllable—cas-*hroom*—with a light whisper of a 'ch' in the front of her mouth.

"I see." She heard a snicker from behind her; MacCulloch, no doubt amused at her paltry attempts to play-act the lady of the manor. He wasn't wrong, however much it stung. Norah was making a fool of herself. "Well, I won't keep you any longer. Thank you for your time."

Hoping that her cheeks looked merely wind-flushed, Norah eyed the beach again, with its rowboats hauled up onto the narrow band of grey sand, loosely moored to the cleats that lined the edge of a narrow stone walkway running the length of the row. The tide was ebbing, the steely water peeling back to reveal a broad bank of rock, wrinkled and cracked like old, weathered skin. The strip of sand drew her eyes along it like a trail of silver: it continued to the west, she saw now, at the foot of the cliff. It sparkled with invitation. She could think of nothing she wanted more in this moment than to escape both MacCulloch and the evidence of the desperate existence eked out in the long shadow of Corrain House.

"I'm going for a walk," she said, gesturing along the beach. "Alone. You can leave—I'll walk back along the cliff path, past the kirk."

MacCulloch frowned, "Ma'am, it's not—"

"I know how tides work," she snapped. "I have hours, do I not?"

"Aye, but—"

"I also have a pocketwatch. Credit me with some common sense. I'm sure you've got work to get back to."

MacCulloch's grey eyes narrowed, and though he did not shrug, she watched his broad shoulders slump as though he had. "As you say, ma'am. I'll let them know to expect you later on."

Norah hadn't been walking long along the shore in front of the cliff when she began to regret it. The wind blew wet and icy off the retreating waves, biting to her bone, and though her boots were sturdy enough her legs soon tired of toiling over the wet sand. She contemplated mounting the rocky band bordering the beach, but its jagged cracks and uneven surface spelled a twisted ankle, she was sure of it.

Dismay seeped through her, weighing her down like the water that wicked up the hem of her skirt. Each decision she made, though intended to assert her independence and gain the respect of those around her, only led her further into isolation and misery. She had a sudden aching urge to be back home in Glasgow, curled against Isa by the fire or even listening to her mother's clucking and tutting over tea. How fortunate she had been to be there, surrounded by those she loved and who loved her in return, if perhaps in ways more stifling and overwrought than Norah would have preferred. Her desire for liberation from the messy tendrils of affection and the assumptions of belonging and control therein had led her here—an empty beach, washed with salt.

Could she make something of the new stage on which she found herself? Create a place for herself in the house on the cliff, coax allies out of her sullen and silent companions? She would have to try, or resign herself to a lifetime of scouring winds and withering looks.

Step after step she trudged, her skirts growing ever heavier. Ahead, something curved out of the sand: a hulk of pale, bleached bone and jutting ribs. What at first looked like the ribcage of a massive sea beast resolved as she grew nearer into wooden strips and spars: a wreck. Her pulse skipped, and she picked up her pace, stumbling across the sinking sand to the remnants of a small sailing vessel. The entire back half of the boat was missing, the remaining hull half-buried, creating a waterlogged pool where the sand had drifted. A few feet of mast jutted up out of the water, weed and barnacles climbing its length. They ended a bit above her head height and Norah shivered to think that a few hours from now, almost the whole wreck would be submerged, only the mast tip visible.

Her fingers traced the pitted wood, wary of splinters yet drawn to the rough surface all the same. How many waves had crashed against these planks? How many hands had gripped that guard rail? Her stomach twisted, and she chided herself for the moment of romantic fancy. This boat had met its end, either against this cliff face, or before then, out at sea. The hands that had hauled its ropes belonged to dead men. She closed her watering eyes against the wind as it blew a sudden, sharp blast into her face that filled her senses with brine and seaweed, brothy and astringent, and a sudden wave of utter exhaustion washed through her.

She cast her eyes heavenwards, and it was not paradise she saw but her very own self-made hell: above her at the top of the crag, butted up against its very edge, loomed Corrain House. This was the rear of the building, the north facade. Its dingy edifice gazed out across the water through monotonous rows of dark and shuttered windows. Her eyes were drawn to the right hand side: those were the windows to the library, her quiet refuge. But then something else caught her notice.

At the base of the building, where cut stone met sheer cliff face, there ran a network of deep cracks and buckles. The stone was worn and delaminated, the rock beneath it crumbling and concave, harrowed away leaving the foundations exposed and jutting over the edge. Norah's heart rose into her throat. She had never thought, sitting in the corner of the library with her book, that she was so precariously positioned. What could have done this? The tide line was well short of the clifftop. Surely the wind could not wreak such damage?

Norah turned her eyes away from the sight with a shudder. With every passing day she felt the freedom she desired drift further from her grasp, elusive and shifting. She longed to be home. But home was three hundred miles to the south and over a mountain of irreversible decisions, so she instead turned her steps towards Corrain House.

CHAPTER FIVE

FACED WITH GRISTLY sausages and deflated eggs for a third morning in a row, Norah came to a decision. She'd risen early that morning and yet the dining room was empty, and she had no desire to sit alone among the smell of grease and wood polish while she ate her toast. If she was going to be left to her own devices for breakfast, well, then, she'd have the meal she wanted rather than someone else's assumptions about her desires.

Though it had felt labyrinthine that first evening, the house was not so difficult to navigate now that she had begun to get a feel for the shape of it. The building was a rectangle wrapped around its enclosed courtyard, with an asymmetric wing off to one side that housed the kitchen, stores, stables, and somewhere, Norah assumed, the servants' quarters. Dining and large receiving rooms to the south, library, study and smaller rooms to the north, it was straightforward enough once one had their bearings.

Momentarily torn whether to seek out a more palatable meal or an argument with her absent husband, Norah's stomach won out, and she made for the kitchen she'd invaded on that first bewildering day. She smelled her quarry before she saw it, the familiar, inviting smell of warm oatmeal. Someone in this house was eating porridge for breakfast, and she meant to join them.

Norah's first look at another human being all day was the sight of Gunn's back half, her front half almost entirely inside one of the ranges at the back of the room, skirts pooled on the floor and the worn soles of her boots on display. A large pot—large enough for several days' worth of porridge—sat atop the cooker that did *not* currently have a woman half inside it, unwatched and unattended, but presumably not forgotten.

She could have cleared her throat, summoned the housekeeper from her work to serve her, but the lady of the manor was an ill-fitting mantle. Better to shed it and help herself and hang whatever judgements it brought down on her head.

The bowls were kept on a shelf above the sink, standing neatly along with the plates and mugs that made up the rest of the crockery, as well as the well-polished copper pots not currently in use. There were two stacks; Norah eyed them for a good minute before realising one column contained the chipped and cracked pieces, while the other held those as-yet-unmarred. She supposed this was Corrain House's version of tableware for the guests. She selected one of the chipped bowls and scooped a healthy dollop of porridge from the pot, smiling at the familiar sticky *plop* it made. As before, her tension seemed to ebb the longer she was in the familiar warmth of the kitchen, which made the spike of surprise all the more sudden when she turned to find Gunn kneeling beside the range and staring up at her with an inscrutable expression.

"I, eh… fancied a bit of porridge," Norah said, fingers curling to grip the bowl to her chest. "Please, don't let me interrupt."

Gunn, ever-unfazed, took only a moment to recover her voice. "By all means, help yourself," she said, in a tone that wasn't hostile, but wasn't entirely kind, either. "You're lucky it's fresh, mind." She nodded to the hefty pot. "I'll be eating that for days."

Norah couldn't help the chuckle that bubbled up. "If you think I'm a stranger to days-old porridge then you'll have to readjust your assumptions. I never cut it from a drawer, but I became quite adept at making it stretch for days on end for frugality's sake." Her mother had thought meagre meals at home an acceptable sacrifice in order to keep up appearances in public life—no doubt hoping Norah's figure might also benefit from the reduced rations. "At any rate, I'd prefer aged porridge to cold sausages any day."

The housekeeper lifted her eyebrows just slightly, then placed hands on thighs, and pushed smoothly to her feet. "I'll fetch us some milk."

Us. It set a warm little flicker alight in her stomach. She was to sit down with company to eat—*real* company, not her forever silent husband.

Perhaps it was this company that made the first bite taste so satisfying, though it was as simple as a dish could be and still be called that. It was salty, of course, but not the briny salt of the sea, nor the bitter salt of the tears she had shed in the night, but a comforting and familiar tang on her tongue. She eagerly scooped up another bite, the spoon scraping against the bowl, and the sound made her flinch reflexively, expecting a sharp rebuke from across the table. None came.

Gunn ate quickly and in silence, as though she viewed her need for sustenance as an inconvenience more than anything else. When she rose with her empty plate though, she returned with tea, pouring cups for them both.

"MacCulloch tells me you made it down to Corrain."

Norah scrutinised Gunn's expression for any hint of mockery or amusement, but saw only mild curiosity. "I did. What little there was to see."

"It's a quiet spot, right enough."

"That's certainly an accurate description. It was still as death. MacCulloch said all the men were away fishing, that they go for weeks at a time."

"That's right. It's about the only way to make a living up here these days."

"But surely with all this land…" Norah arrested her reply when she realised she had no real understanding of how the land around them was put to use. "There are sheep," she said eventually, furrowing her brow. "Could the families not be brought on for their care and rearing?"

A patient smile. Gunn shook her head. "All the sheep farmers up here are incomers. From the borders, mostly. Or the north of England. And even then…" She tutted, took a sip of her tea. "Well, sheep are not so profitable now as they once were. Much of the land is being put over to deer stalking now—not here, mind—we haven't the terrain for it. But elsewhere."

"And the soil won't farm." She remembered as much from the letters—Barland's descriptions of the stark landscape, the wind that scoured every dip and rise. It had seemed almost romantic at the time, the baron and his manor standing stalwart against the elements, but she was beginning to see the truth of it: that the rock, the land and the open sea, they were more than a match.

"Not anymore, no. There were runrigs on the estate—you can still see them, from higher ground—and did MacCulloch show you the kelp kilns? No, I suppose he wouldn't have thought of it." Gunn had been staring thoughtfully into her tea, but now she looked up, right into Norah's eyes, and Norah felt a frisson jolt down her spine. "We've left scars all over this land. Our rigs and furrows. Our bothies and kilns. Our dry dykes and cairns. Everything fails. You have to wonder when we'll learn."

Norah blinked in confusion. "Learn what?"

"We're not wanted. We don't belong here."

Though Norah knew it was meant more broadly, she couldn't help but feel the statement was directed at her—*interloper, trespasser, outsider*. Worse still, there was no venom in Gunn's voice, just a weary certainty. Norah set down her cup with a clatter and muttered an apology as she brushed her hands over her skirts. "The skies don't look at all friendly so I must pass the time indoors today," she babbled.

"I think I'll set up my things in the library—my easel, I mean. Don't worry about me interrupting you any further; I'm quite self-sufficient."

"You can interrupt me whenever you please." Gunn's lilting accent made the words sound almost playful, and Norah yearned to respond in kind. But of course, she was the lady of the manor. That was what the other woman meant. Nothing more.

IT TOOK TWO trips for Norah to lug her painting supplies to the library from her bedroom—one for the easel itself, and one for the brushes, paints and palettes that had made up almost half of one of her cases. She was hardly a talented artist—her mother had frequently commented in surprise that practice was normally known to lead to *improvements*—but she was glad she had brought the painting kit all the same as the skies outside continued to darken with rain.

As with most hobby artists, she took her inspiration from the things around her; back in Glasgow her canvases had been replete with attempts to capture the sheen of lanternlight on wet cobblestones, domestic scenes with crisp napkins and merrily-flickering fires, and half-finished portraits of those nearest and dearest to her. She always abandoned them somewhere around the eyes, unable to make them look convincingly alive and vital. Peter used to compliment her work, chide her for being hard on herself. Isa, rather more sensitive perhaps given she was often the subject of Norah's failed attempts, had once teased that perhaps she needed to render her subjects in full Venetian mask.

Rather than try to reproduce MacCulloch, or worse still, her husband, she instead settled for attempting to recreate the landscape she had spent the past few days exploring. The initial strokes came easily enough, but after blocking out the basic shapes and geometries of the sky and cliffs she became preoccupied with mixing her paints to capture the exact shades of the landscape—the dingy white of the clouds, the faded parchment of the grass. Her palette became a sepia mire as the greys and browns, greens and blues eddied and crested beneath her brush, subtle hues slowly merging into one muddy, indeterminate paste.

Eventually she sat back, staring down at the palette as a wave of fatigue washed through her. She felt as drab and lifeless as the gobs of paint before her, swirled around until there was nothing good left, no use except to describe some grimy shadows or a stagnant puddle. On the paper the bare strokes of her sketch dried, going from glossy streaks to matt until it too was flat and uninspiring.

She swivelled in her seat—a stool she'd relocated from her bedchamber—her attention pulled to the windows at the end of the room. She'd set up her easel with the light at her back, and a good distance away, but now she pushed to her feet and closed the distance to the windowsill. Beneath her, she knew now, was a sheer drop. She was foolish to be afraid—the house was not about to collapse into the sea with no notice—and yet her pulse thudded in her neck as she remembered the sight from below of the house jutting out over the cliff's edge. Looking down, she saw only water—she had to twist her head and press her cheek to the pane to catch a glimpse of what she thought was the mast of the boat below. She would have to do something about the precarity of the manor's position, lest its decay catch them all by surprise. She didn't know the first thing about reinforcing a building, but just the idea was enough to energise her, sending a frisson of excitement fizzing through her.

Struck by the image of the dark spar rising from the churning sea, she peeled her cheek from the window and hurried back to her supplies. She didn't pause to stretch a new sheet of paper, too gripped with sudden fervour to bother with such delays. Instead she flipped open the nearest sketchbook and seized her charcoals, dragging a stick across the page to bring the waves and foam out of the fibres and into being.

Furiously she worked, the beach a flat wash of grey, the ship and its bones no longer pale and colourless but smears of darkest grey jutting from the sand. Though she normally prided herself on the delicacy of her sketchwork there was nothing dainty about this; it was as dark and relentless as the rain that suddenly hurled itself against the window, a staccato warning. She sketched as though she could exorcise the image of the wreck from her mind by committing it to paper, and when a fat tear fell upon the page she didn't stop, just smeared it with her thumb across the page, sand and sea rendered in salt water and ash.

It was unrecognisable when she'd finished. She had marked out the shape of the boat over and over again until it had become a black smudge at the centre of the page. The water was a damp smear. The cliff was a looming scribble carved so deeply on the paper that she'd broken several sticks in its creation. But her mind, at least, was calm.

That night at dinner Norah was all smiles. She ate her meal appreciatively—more mutton and root vegetables in an indeterminate, though delicious, brown sauce—and carried on a mostly one-sided and cheerful conversation with her husband. He did not seem surprised by this; indeed, he did not react much at all, merely grunting in response to her questions and focusing his gaze on the plate in front of him as if it held more interest for him than her attempts at communication. Norah was well-used to conversing with someone who wasn't listening to her side of the dialogue, though, thanks to long hours at her mother's side, and carried on regardless of his lack of engagement.

She made it through the meal in giddy anticipation, and when the last of the dishes had been collected she cleared her throat, noting that Gunn had paused on her way out the door, her attention piqued perhaps more than Barland's.

"I have been thinking," Norah said, "about how I can help improve things, now that I am here and more or less settled. I know your business takes a great deal of attention and effort and I have no wish to interfere with that, but I believe that those pulls upon your time may have allowed a rather more serious problem to go undetected in the management of the estate. The cliff that underpins Corrain House is dangerously eroded, and I am certain that if left unattended it may well lead to a disastrous outcome, as a house as large as this one must have solid foundations upon which to rest. Therefore it is my intention to employ a crew of workmen to investigate the extent of the damage so that proper repairs can be made—for the safety of all who dwell here, and those who might follow."

She wasn't sure what she expected by way of response from her husband. She braced for resistance—talk of available funds, perhaps, or a questioning of her own ability to manage such a project. She had considered her arguments carefully as she descended the stairs that evening—the structural repairs could not wait, not given the apparent rate of erosion, and Norah had been much involved in the running of her family home in the months following her father's death. The counters sat at the tip of her tongue, ready to deploy. What Barland did, she would never have foreseen.

He looked at Gunn.

More than that, he looked *to* Gunn. His face was a picture of bemusement, the man rendered at a total loss by this pronouncement from his wife.

The silence, punctuated only by a muffled ticking from the grandfather clock in the front hall, was eventually broken by Gunn.

"Perhaps his lordship would like some time to consider what funds might be available for such an endeavour?"

Norah recognised an instruction phrased as a question

when she heard one, and her mind began to race. Why was Barland deferring to Gunn? Every fibre of her being ached to confront them both, right here and now, to demand answers. But such a diversion might derail her plan entirely, and she needed this. She needed something to be within her control.

"Very well," she said, staunchly refusing to look in the housekeeper's direction, her gaze fixed on Barland. "But I would urge you to make available whatever monies we are quoted. The foundations are in danger of being laid entirely bare on the north-east corner. If you would like to join me on a walk along the beach to see from below—"

Barland flinched. "That will not be necessary." Again, it was Gunn who spoke, taking a single step forward in Norah's periphery. "His lordship will have thoughts on this tomorrow."

Norah nodded, finally turning towards the housekeeper, acknowledging her at last. She could feel the gravity of Gunn's gaze and tried to meet it with a weight of her own, stalwart and unmoving. If only the other woman would break, just once, so that Norah could see what lay behind the mask, could start to uncover the nest of secrets that lurked within the silences. But though Gunn was pale and obviously fatigued, she would not be broken. It was Norah who looked away, and though she consoled herself that she might still get what she wanted, she could feel her hard-won authority slipping between her fingers like grains of sand.

No matter. No matter. She would not be swayed on this. She would have her way, help would come, and she would save this ailing house from crumbling earth and greedy sea.

CHAPTER SIX

LIFE AT CORRAIN House settled into a routine of sorts—there was nothing easy or relaxed about it, but somehow it made the days pass more easily knowing the patterns of the house and its inhabitants. Norah rose and took her breakfast in the kitchen, with Gunn, which truth be told might have been the best part of the day. It was just porridge and pleasantries exchanged over tea, but it was the closest Norah felt to normal since arriving there, even on the awkward occasion when a woman and a wee girl knocked at the side door with a basket of eggs and caught her there at the kitchen table with the housekeeper. It didn't help that Norah, keen to present an air of normality, rose and followed them out the door afterward as if escorting an honoured guest. She was interested to note the woman make a small cross in the air before herself as they left, making for the cliff path back to Corrain. Curious though she was about what might prompt this—whether the house had some sort of reputation—Gunn was already inside and did not see the gesture, and Norah, not wanting to sound foolish, said nothing.

She knew her mother would be tutting over what she perceived as Norah fraternising below her station, but her options were limited, and she couldn't help but feel Gunn was glad of her company as well. The housekeeper was reserved but not unfriendly, and on occasion Norah even managed to coax a smile out of her, though it was quickly subsumed like a beach cast in shadow by a cloud passing in front of the sun. Gunn was austere and striking; in proper society she would have earned no small amount of admiration and admirers, despite—or perhaps because of—her aloof nature. Norah could not help but feel a flicker deep within, hot and hungry, every time Gunn's dark eyes met hers, and she knew it was more than camaraderie that warmed her through. It had been months since Norah had enjoyed any touch or affection and she was starved for it, but her appetite would have to remain unsated, her need unfulfilled. That the one woman she was to have any regular contact with should be Gunn—Gunn with her steady hands and her sure gait and that slight twitch of her eyebrow when she was amused or annoyed—that was a cruel irony indeed.

She had enquired with Barland whether he would accompany her to church in Thurso; Gunn had conveyed that he would not. Thus it was that Norah was the single occupant of the carriage that departed Corrain House on Sunday morning.

The vehicle's appearance in front of the house took Norah by surprise—she had half expected to find herself travelling to Thurso by cart. Indeed, it was very apparent that the carriage had not been in regular use in some time, its interior upholstery worn and dated, and smelling faintly of a mixture of damp and vinegar. The same draught horse that had brought her to the house was hitched up front; there were no high-stepping carriage horses hiding in the stables, it seemed.

MacCulloch was in the driver's seat, of course, his feet braced against the footboard.

"Are you missing church in Corrain for this?" Norah asked, concerned despite her general dislike of the man.

He snorted, scuffing a muddy boot on the footboard. "I'm no' fae Corrain. My family's a' fae Halkirk, on the river."

"Oh. What brought you out here then?"

A shrug. "Didnae fancy working in the distillery, smelling

like mash a' day." Norah caught a glint in his eye; that wasn't the full story. She raised her eyebrows politely, inviting him to go on. "Wanted tae make something of myself, and heard they'd lost their help at the big house here. Came alang to see if I'd fit, and what d'you know. Here I am still." This was the most the young man had spoken in the days Norah had known him—apparently MacCulloch was most at ease when talking about himself. The pieces slotted into place—the attitude, the swagger. He'd stepped in when the Barlands were in need, and aimed to make a name for himself from it. She wasn't sure being groundskeeper on a remote property was the best way of achieving that dream, but she supposed opportunities were hard to come by here in the barren north. "Well. I'm sure that was very fortuitous for all involved." She waited a moment longer but he made no move to step down and help her into the carriage. With a sigh, Norah bundled inside, her fist wrapped around the door handle like a vice as they jolted down the drive. If she reached Thurso with any teeth still in her head it would be a miracle.

Weary from a long day's travel, Norah had paid precious little attention to her surroundings when making this trip in the opposite direction just over a week before. Though she felt scarcely more awake now after an increasingly typically fitful night's sleep, she nevertheless watched the world go shakily by outside the window. The road—narrow, but serviceable—took them inland at first, the slate-grey sea disappearing behind the rise of the scrubby brown clifftops that characterised the locale. To the south, the land stretched away forever in waves, an ocean of pale grass and dark, bare heather as far as the eye could see. She felt a sudden pang of longing for the green rolling glens and rugged peaks of the Trossachs and the Isle of Arran where she'd spent so many happy childhood holidays. This barren and unforgiving terrain felt like another world.

At length, the land dropped down to the north and the sea hove in sight once more, little inlets and bays eating away at the flat coastline. Then, very suddenly, the buggy was thrown into woodland. Barring the dead rowan squatting in the courtyard they were the first trees Norah had seen in a week, birch and Scots pine as welcome as water to one dying of thirst. When they emerged, it was into farmland, the scrub and heather and whins somehow gone, replaced with dry dykes and fields of glorious green. They passed a smattering of homes, then a small graveyard and a handsome kirk painted a fresh, bright white. The carriage slowed to allow the passers-by to walk alongside safely as the folk of the village made their way to service, and the whole scene was such a welcome return to normality, to real life, that Norah almost banged the roof of the carriage and demanded MacCulloch stop and let her off to attend church right here.

If Norah squinted she could almost be back in Ayrshire: the rolling hills, the green fields, the small stone cottages dotting the lanes that radiated out from the track road. It was such a stark contrast from the landscape they had left behind that her head began to spin and she sagged, overcome, against the windowpane.

Once they passed through the village the carriage sped up, and Norah had to sit back lest her skull be jolted against the window and cracked like an egg. Perhaps it would serve her right, for her childish fantasies of fleeing back to Glasgow were nothing more than that: empty-headed dreams of a girl too scared to face up to the choices that had brought her here. She could no more flee than she could keep the sun from setting, no matter how she might long to drag it above the horizon for just a few moments more.

The remainder of the journey cut a path through farmland—some ploughed and ready for sowing and some scattered with dirty white sheep, all standing with their backs to the wind, grazing fitfully. The sea came in and out of view several times, but Norah fancied she could feel it regardless, pressing to her left side, cold and unforgiving. The wreck loomed in her mind's eye.

Thurso was quiet today, far more than when Norah had arrived on a Saturday afternoon, when the harbour was a hive of activity and the road had been crowded with wagons, mostly carting flagstones back and forth, into town from the quarry to be dressed, and then onwards to be sold.

St Peter's Church stood at the end of the main street in the town; a handsome, broad-set building with a sturdy square clock tower housing its bells, which pealed now in welcome. The sound rang through Norah, clear and sweet, and she unknit her fingers from their tangled grip on her skirts as the carriage slowed to a halt. She was not as devout as some, but the sight and sound of the kirk was a salve to her worried soul all the same.

MacCulloch descended from the driver's seat to open her door, which surprised her. She wondered if Barland had given him strict instructions to treat her as befit a lady of the house now, or if he possessed a heretofore unforeseen respect for tradition. Whatever the case, she was glad of it as the eyes of the other churchgoers turned her way, much as she was glad of having dressed in one of her nicer gowns for the sojourn. A fine wool muslin in dark blue, the cuffs and collar were a lovely patterned floral lace which Norah always worried made her hands look even more plump than they already were.

The congregation of St Peter's was a mixed bunch. Some were well-heeled and clearly affluent, and others were more simply dressed, the two groups moving in their own flocks, one smaller and more colourful than the other, like peacocks among hens. Norah clutched her hymnal and psalter to her stomach, trying to still its sudden writhing. Of course she would be stared at. No doubt some would even know who she was, whether by recognising the carriage or merely having read the banns in the local papers. Would she be welcomed into the fold, or rejected as an outsider? Would curiosity overwhelm insularity and suspicion? From what she knew of the folk she thought of as 'her mother's sort' back home, the question balanced on a knife's edge, and her own behaviour could tip it in either direction.

She fixed a smile upon her lips: not too wide, but not too tight, either. Her cheeks would be flushed, she knew, but there was nothing to be done about it now. At least her hat and hair would be more or less in working order—thank goodness for a closed cab carriage. Spine straight, chin lifted, she started down the path, bestowing what she hoped was an appropriately cordial but not too familiar smile and nod to any who met her eye. For one so inclined towards friendliness it was difficult not to press herself upon the nearest knot of people and offer introductions, but she knew that any hint of desperation or vulnerability would invite a metaphorical knife in her side.

This concern was presently replaced by another as she approached the large double doors where the minister stood to greet his flock. Dwarfed by the gothic arch of the portal that framed him was the diminutive figure of the very man who had sealed her fate a week before in the wee family kirk on the hill. He recognised her too, his lips thinning to a line as she approached.

"Lady Barland. Welcome." It somehow sounded more like admonishment than greeting.

"Thank you, Reverend." For a moment Norah allowed herself to fantasise about how it might feel if she truly *were* welcome here: the minister clasping her hand, the murmurs around her warm instead of admonishing. A dream within her grasp, or yet another flight of fancy? She could not say. "I look forward to meeting the congregation, and the guidance and wisdom of your sermon."

This seemed to mollify the man somewhat, and he inclined his head. "I was not sure we would see you here," he said. "I have not seen your husband these five years I've ministered here."

"Yes, I did request he accompany me, but…" She could not be too frank, could not expose the rifts in her situation to this near-stranger. She smiled and fluttered a hand. "He is a busy man."

"Indeed, well. It is good to see you—and in daylight, no less."

The church's interior was much like its facade—charming and tasteful and larger than she might have expected for the size of the town. Rich, dark wood rose up in strong trunks supporting the galleries to either side of her, and though there was not a scrap of stained glass to be seen, the window at the far end was large and multifaceted. There was no organ, of course, but that was still a novelty even at St John's. It was not terribly surprising that the community here were not yet inclined towards such indulgences.

Norah took a seat near the front of the pews, as seemed appropriate—it occurred to her that it was entirely possible the Barlands had family seating reserved for the barony, but she didn't dare enquire. MacCulloch hung behind as they entered, surprising Norah by sliding into a pew further back rather than leaving. The minister began promptly once the congregation was settled, blessing the proceedings and delivering some dry intimations regarding local goings on—the local market, a Bible study group, an afternoon tea collecting charitable donations. Norah fought tears at the sheer normality of it: the litany of trivia, the whisper of gowns and paper and quiet sighs. Even the hard wood beneath the too-thin cushion padding the pew upon which she sat was a balm to her raw nerves. Norah was not a woman of faith, particularly—the moral absolutes and strictures of religion ran too contrary to her nature for that. But there was a welcome familiarity to this that was profoundly reassuring after the quiet, lonely strangeness of the week past, with its shifting shadows and silent souls and spectral ships on an endless, empty sea.

The singing was a mix of psalms and hymns, as she'd expected, though her hymnal was too new and some of the psalm tunes different from the ones she knew. The lack of organ lent a slight air of chaos to the chorus, its pitch and tempo shifting at the whims of the strongest voices. The service was in English—not surprising from what little Norah knew of the area. Indeed, the history she'd read the other night had suggested the region's cultural roots were more Norse than Gaelic.

As sermon and readings and hymns gave way to the benediction and the congregation began to make their way out, Norah was once more at sea. Back home of course she would be at her mother's side, and therefore immediately swept off to the hall for tea and cake and endless gossip. Here she was left to make her way out alone, trying to spot MacCulloch's sandy hair among the sea of Sunday bonnets.

It was then that she became aware that conversations were taking place pertaining to her presence. This awareness came mostly in the form of chatter that fell abruptly silent as she passed nearby, but one group of well-heeled women around her mother's age seemed completely oblivious to who might hear them, even the subject of their discussion.

"…pected, would you credit it?"

"Well where else would she go? And after all Lord William did attend here; it's just his son who's…"

"He was always a funny one, that boy. Peely-wally. And too quiet."

"Mibbe his wife's a talker—Glaswegians are ay running their mooths."

Norah pushed past a cluster of biddies, none of whom were trying very hard to hide their scrutiny of the kirk's newest arrival. Her cheeks began to prick with heat, but she knew speaking now would only prove their aspersions true. She moved on.

"It'll take more than talk to save that estate, he's run it into the ground."

"Aye, maybe…"

"*Oh wheesht wi' your devil nonsense.*"

She almost stopped in her tracks—of all the rumours she had expected to encounter, this did not number among them.

"*I'm only saying, there's ay been something not right about the Gunns. Their women are too canny, if you get my meaning. The old baron should never have let one into his house.*"

"*Och away—he'll have thought he had to. I've heard the daughter's the spit of him.*"

"*Rubbish, who'd know that? Who's seen her?*"

"*Just saying what I've heard!*"

Norah's cheeks were burning anew as she fled through the bustling crowd, suddenly in desperate need of some fresh air. It was not a complete surprise, as such, that there was gossip about the baron's father and the Gunns. Even Norah had seen the resemblance between the housekeeper and her husband as soon as she had observed them side-by-side; it would take a far less observant soul to miss the implications. She had tried not to dwell on it too much, or the unseemly implications of their resemblance. The Barlands would not be the first family to have an arrangement of this sort; illegitimate children emerging from liaisons between the master of the house and his staff were all too common, and some tried to escape the scandal by keeping them close. Even so, the thought of such intimations being a matter for open discussion among these strangers brought a sick feeling to her stomach, as if she had watched the older women turning over a corpse and prodding at the maggots squirming there.

She spied a familiar stoop-shouldered figure at long last and strode towards him, putting all disgust and humiliation from her face as best she could. MacCulloch was surrounded by a small knot of men—friends, or family perhaps, from the nearby Halkirk? "I am ready to depart," she informed him tersely, and though the groundskeeper smirked he stayed thankfully silent, merely peeling away from the group and bobbing his head down the path. Norah knew she should stay and mingle, but dread of the gossip that would follow her quick departure was quickly drowned out by a sudden wave of fatigue. Listlessly she climbed back into the carriage, ignoring the way MacCulloch's fingers lingered just a moment too long around her own, and as they set off she slumped back against the moth-eaten cushions, pushing everything from her mind until there was nothing but the rattle of the wheels and the grey of the flat and empty sea.

CHAPTER SEVEN

Friday, January 3rd, 1890
Corrain House

Dearest Norah,

I trust you will not take it as admonition when I tell you that your last letter has left me deeply conflicted. Your proposal—if I may call it such—struck longing and foreboding into my heart in equal measure.

From your very first letter I have found myself captivated by your wit, intelligence, and decency, and this correspondence has brightened my otherwise drear existence considerably in these, the darkest months. I have never sought a match, but if I had, I could not imagine a better one.

But even as I dream of a life in your company, I must confess that as perfect a life partner you might be to me, I would not be such for you. I am a quiet man, not an adept conversationalist, and prone to fits of what might be called melancholia. I rarely leave the estate, and its workings keep me occupied much of the time with book-keeping and other such duties. I am also of an age and demeanour such that I have no desire to have a family— when I die it is my intention that my younger brother and his heirs will inherit (though whether they see fit to relocate back to Scotland from Georgia is another question entirely). I have the impression that you believe yourself to be of a similar mind, but Norah, are you quite sure? I fear your life here at Corrain House could be a very lonely one, and I a disappointing husband.

You have spoken of your age, and also of your reputation. I will not ask what you mean by the latter, though I confess to having an inkling that I shall not commit to paper. I do wonder whether you have ever spoken to Isabelle Sinclair about me. I wonder what she would have you do. I pray you do not make a hasty decision that you have cause to regret based on a desire to escape a situation that could be resolved in a less extreme manner. Shame is a miserable incentive, Norah, and one I hope you are free from. It is my fervent belief you should feel none. I hope you take this to heart. I hope I have not overstepped.

While I do not want to insult you by doubting your motives, I cannot help but wonder whether your age would feel so advanced, or your reputation so precarious, if your family's financial situation did not weigh so heavily upon you. Let me therefore remove that burden. Today I have sent notice of cancellation of the money owed to Barland & Co to your family solicitor. Your debt is settled. I shall not hold it against you for a moment if I never hear from you again—though I dare to hope that I will.

Yours,
A

UPON ARRIVAL BACK at Corrain House Norah felt unmoored, stuck between the two worlds like a fly in amber. She could not help but feel that the biddies in town knew more about the Barlands and their history than she did herself: a singularly isolating sensation. In their correspondence Alexander had related his grandfather's history—the wealth he had built through iron mining, his purchase of the house, his death when Alexander was a young boy—but had said little of his father, the ninth Lord Barland. As someone with an admittedly complicated relationship to her own father's legacy she had not pressed the issue, but now she wondered just what she was missing in her ignorance. If the gossip was to be believed, the ninth lord had invited scandal on at least one occasion. And where there was one, there were always more.

As Norah drifted into the main foyer, working a crick out of her neck, the stags stared down at her from the stairwell, glassy eyes flat and judgemental. Norah shuddered, her gaze drifting unbidden to the portrait of the original Lord Barland; Alexander's grandfather. She hadn't remarked on it before, but the lack of his father's portrait stood out now, though there was nothing so gauche as an empty space on the wall to mark its absence. Still, she could feel it, a dark cloud hanging over the hall, permeating the rugs, the wallpaper like so much tobacco smoke.

Ignoring the disapproving stags, Norah climbed the stairs, one hand trailing along the banister to steady herself. The first-floor corridors were, as far as she could tell, a completely average width and height, but the dark furnishings and heavy carpet made the walls and ceilings feel closer, more oppressive. The small side tables and classical gilt vases would have been the height of fashion fifty years ago but now spoke only of a space forgotten, left behind. It was her job, she knew, to fix this, to bring Corrain House into the current decade with the correct fabrics and appropriate furnishings, but she found herself less concerned about such superficial matters than uncovering the truth behind the Barland family's secrets.

Norah lost track of how long she drifted through the halls, climbing up and down the stairs and squinting at paintings in an attempt to find the portrait she sought. There were endless landscapes—idyllic renderings of what she could only assume were the English countryside, as well as canvases full of sweeping Highland glens. She understood why there were no depictions of the immediate surroundings, stark and windswept as they were, but it still lent an air of isolation to Norah's search. She ached for the scenery depicted in these frames, lush greens and clear blue skies, even if in truth they were as foreign to her city-born bones as the North's desolate coastline.

She found she could not look too long at the still lifes: fruit and flowers kept just on the cusp of decay, animals forever mired in thick strokes of oil. The technical accomplishment was overshadowed by the sick feeling they brought to her stomach, and she made absent note of the worst offenders; she would tell Gunn to remove them when they next spoke.

And then, just like that, she turned a corner and was confronted by the looming presence of an unfamiliar portrait, its size and ornate frame far better suited for the front hall than this forgotten corridor. At first she took it for a portrait of her husband, but then her eye began to pick out the differences: the dated cut to the jacket, the cruel set to the mouth. There was a ruddy tint to his skin, as if he was a man who had spent considerable time out of doors, and the eyes were the colour of long-steeped tea instead of Barland's dark, rich brown. It gave the painting an eerie mien, the pupils following Norah no matter which way she stepped. Meeting those cracked-oil amber-brown eyes, it was perhaps the recent memory of the macabre herd of stag heads crowding the walls of the main hall that drew an odd connection in Norah's mind. From the recesses of her childhood a recollection floated to the surface: of playing in the woods at the side of Loch Katrine as a little girl. The family had rented a cottage there, and while her father spent his days fishing for brown trout Norah had been left largely to her own devices. One golden August evening she had looked up from her work—damming a burn with sticks and stones and other forest floor debris—to find her gaze locked with that of a stag. It had emerged from the treeline just across the water, far too close and impossibly large to her ten-year-old self. She could hear its breath over the babbling of the burn, could smell its musk, earthy and pungent—and beneath that, metal, for the jagged cage cresting its head was slick with blood and adorned with ribbons of shedding velvet, the freshly flayed bone glistening creamy and pristine beneath.

Its eyes were like polished chestnuts.

Norah blinked away the memory and refocused on the portrait hanging before her. This, then, was the ninth Lord Barland. The formidable resemblance, grandfather to father, father to son, made Norah wonder what else lurked behind her husband's phlegmatic facade: did he also harbour the same malign intent she could practically feel radiating from the portrait in front of her?

The groan of a floorboard made Norah spin around, and she realised she was not far from the library, down a section of corridor she had never traversed before. It was deep enough into the house that she wondered why the portrait had not been simply shoved into a cupboard or stored in the attic, but then, it was one thing not to want to face one's father and another to hide him away entirely. As she slowly turned back to face him once again and felt those umber eyes upon her, however, the urge to shroud it in a sheet rose. She would avoid coming this way, as it seemed the rest of the household already did, and hope the ninth lord rested easy in his confinement.

The house continued to creak and settle, and Norah thought she smelled the waft of earth and moss through some open passage. She checked the library, lest she had left a window ajar, but the curtains were pulled tight over firmly sealed sills. The smell ebbed as she headed back towards the front of the house, and soon the unease inspired by the unsettling portrait was replaced with a growing hunger as dinner approached. She returned to her rooms to freshen up, and then dutifully brought herself to the dining room, where an impassive Alexander Barland awaited her, as still as a painting himself at the head of the table. Gunn moved from sideboard to table, an artist arranging her tableau of sauces and meats in front of them both. If Norah had expected her pilgrimage to Thurso to be interrogated she was to be sorely disappointed, as the housekeeper merely enquired politely whether the journey had been smooth and her husband said nothing at all, as was his wont.

Keen that he should nevertheless be aware of her comings and goings, Norah recounted her observations to the room, her musings on the kirk's architecture and the minister's sermon broken only by the whisper of Gunn's skirts on the floorboards. As she neared the end of her tale Norah faltered, remembering the barbed whispers, the casual ease with which the women had gossiped and sniped, and eventually she trailed off into awkward silence, cheeks burning as the housekeeper leaned over her to refill her glass. The other woman smelled of smoke and dust, and the gaze that met Norah's eyes was knowing, as if she heard the mutterings that Norah had allowed to die on her tongue.

Even a healthy swig of wine could do little to wash the bitter taste away.

When Barland rose Norah fell into step behind him rather than stay in the empty room; by then Gunn had disappeared laden with dishes, no doubt immediately swept up in the morass of chores the house demanded. Their procession through the corridors put her in mind of nothing so much as a funeral march, sombre and shrouded in shadow. Barland said nothing, did nothing, to acknowledge that he knew she was there.

She followed him into the study and they took up stations in silence: Norah in an armchair by the fire and Barland at his desk, staring unblinkingly at the flock of papers scattered there. Perhaps it was the bromidic reading material available to her or the day's long journey that weighted Norah's eyelids and pressed her into the seat until there was nothing she could do but slip into an uneasy doze. The crackle of the fire soon became the rumble of carriage wheels on a rocky path, jolting and unceasing, throwing its passengers from side to side. A thin, reedy wail cut the air. The baby wriggled in her arms, straightening its arms and legs in her awkward embrace as though trying to lever itself free from her grasp. Isa and Peter sat opposite, staring at her. Silent tears tracked Peter's cheeks. Isa just looked angry. The carriage lurched, and somehow Norah knew without looking that the road led not to Glasgow, or even to Thurso, but straight off that scooped-out, crumbling cliff and into the roiling black, swallowed like the generations of doomed sailors who put to sea in search of sustenance, in search of a living, in search of purpose. The baby shifted in her clutches, plucking at her bosom, and Norah felt herself begin to drown.

Norah woke at the sharp sound of the door opening and blinked to resolve Gunn, her pale face a hovering spot in the gap of the door. The housekeeper held something in one hand, a compact wooden box, long and narrow, and entered the room without so much as a knock or an invitation from her master. As she approached the desk Barland shifted, raising his head to stare at her, his expression inscrutable. Norah stirred and tried to speak, her mouth dry, and let out an inelegant croak.

Immediately Gunn turned, pressing the box to her thigh. "Lady Barland. I did not see you there." Somehow it sounded like an accusation, though it was she who had come in unannounced. Norah flushed, scrambling from the chair to her feet, but before she could muster a reply the housekeeper was at the exit. "My apologies. I shall give you privacy." The door creaked as it shut, a final rebuke, and then she was gone.

Norah was left standing with rumpled skirts and wayward

hair, the fire's heat blasting her from behind while her own blush burned her cheeks from within. Embarrassment gave way to irritation—what on earth could Gunn have meant by invading her husband's sanctuary without invitation or warning? It took all her determination in that moment not to sweep out of the room after the housekeeper and press her for an explanation. She diverted her feet instead to the desk where her husband sat, his dull gaze still fixed on the door through which Gunn had beat her retreat.

"Well, I don't know what that was about." Norah's voice was high and impossibly loud, jarring her to her bones. "What are you working on?" She reached for a page, what looked to be some kind of manifest—a list of names in a dense, old-fashioned copperplate. The paper was musty and the script very faded—Norah thought she read the year '1820' before the document was wrested abruptly from her clutches. Moving with an alacrity she had never witnessed before, her husband swept the papers clumsily out of her reach and rounded on her, rising from his seat and grabbing her wrist tightly, tight enough to hurt.

"Stop that!" she said, the sound still strangled and strident to her ears. His fingers were cold, his grip like iron, and her skin burned under his touch. He didn't react, didn't give at all as she pulled against him, and as panic rose in Norah so did hot, angry bile, staining her throat until she thought she would be sick right then and there. Never in her life had a man raised a hand to her—not her father, and certainly not Peter, who dealt with confrontation with nervous laughter and reddened cheeks. Barland's touch woke an animal instinct within her to struggle, to flee, and as the seconds trickled by she felt the rabbit-beat of her heart flutter until there was nothing but the throbbing of blood in her wrist, her veins, her ears. He was strong, stronger than she could've guessed from his wan demeanour and dampened aspect, as if something outside his body gave him strength and sudden vigour.

Darkness seemed to gather in the edges of her vision, shadow branches creeping closer, and his eyes reflected nothing of the lamplight as he stared up at her, silent, unmoving.

"Let me go," she choked, wrenching against him once more, and to her great relief he did, the cold grasp of his fingers coming apart like a lock. She stepped back, nearly tripping on her skirts, and raised a hand to cradle her stinging wrist.

The words boiled up out of her, a week's worth of grief and embarrassment given voice at last. "I am your wife. You will not touch me like that ever again. If you do, I shall leave, propriety and reputation be damned. I have put up with your silences, your refusal to countenance me with even the slightest shred of interest or good favour, but I will not allow you to lay hands on me like a common mongrel." Norah heaved a breath, silence ringing in her ears. "I see now that your letters obscured more than they laid bare. What a fool I was."

Afraid of what she might say next, she spun on her heel and marched for the door before anything else could escape her lips. Behind her the floorboards creaked, as if Barland had finally wrested himself from his frozen state, but Norah did not pause long enough to glance over her shoulder. As she pushed out the door she caught something in the periphery of the dark corridor—a swirl of shadow, a flash of ivory. Gunn. Norah's temper drove her onwards in pursuit. Her husband thought he could lay hands on her without her permission. Her housekeeper thought she could come and go as she pleased, interrupting the married couple, skulking outside doors. None of it would do.

Dim and close by day, by night Corrain House was a place of extremes, a maze of light and shade. The oil lamps carved their shadows on the wood and carpet beneath Norah's feet as her wrath ate up the corridors, turning her this way and that, up that staircase, along this passageway. She paid little heed to her direction; there was no sign of Gunn after that brief, half-imagined glimpse outside the study, and so she let her gut lead the way. She stopped short in front of the ninth baron for the second time that day, his chestnut eyes flecked red in the lamplight. He towered over her, larger and taller in oil than he would have been in life. The shadows darkened above his head, warping, spreading, splitting into a network of upward tilted prongs until an enormous set of antlers crowned his head like a primal halo. The stag emerging from the woods. Norah was ten years old again, standing with soaked skirts in running water, hands numb and muddy. She spun away from the portrait and fled, off along the hallway and around a corner.

In some deep corner of her mind, in the world that existed around corners and beneath beds and behind wardrobe doors, she felt the Baron follow.

The floorboards groaned and shuddered under the weight of the stag's cloven hooves, fit to buckle as it advanced along the corridor. Norah could smell it: the earthy musk, the loam of the forest, the blood. She heard a snort. Even from around the corner out of sight its foetid breath reached her in a cloud of sickly sweet decay, of mouldering leaves and rotten meat. She pressed her back to the wall, a sigh of dust from the tapestry behind her adding its fungal aroma. She felt rather than saw its shadow stretching out before it, creeping along the floor.

It made a noise as it moved, not like an animal but like a wicker chair or a tree swing or a rowboat: the sound of timber joints creaking, of limbs bending, of a wooden ribcage heaving with each damp, laboured breath. The smell of viscera was overwhelming. In her fevered mind's eye the stag had no hide. Just a wooden shell wrapped around guts wrapped around wooden bone, a cage of roots and blood and organs fashioned into a mockery of an animal. The shadows flowed from floor to wall: it was enormous, filling the passage, now blocking the light from the lamps behind it. Its antlers were a twisted forest atop its head. She could feel the blood oozing from every gap in its carapace, hear the crepitation of its stiff, ill formed joints.

Its approach slowed, like that of a predator stalking its prey, but she was struck with a sudden and unfathomable thought: it was *glad* she was there. A sick sense of welcome, warm and rotted, spread over her like breath, and Norah gagged. She had so desperately wished to find home here, to gain acceptance between its walls, but not like this. Never like this.

The stag was almost upon her. Norah did not—could not—move. She could hear the squelching thud of its heartbeat, like boots toiling through mud. In the space between one heartbeat and the next, she ran. Through the shadows she wove, focusing only on the next turn, the next stretch of corridor. Behind her the stag keened, but she refused to look back, even as the rug bunched and slipped beneath her feet, roots and rocks tangling with her skirts, ripping at her stockings. She choked on the scent of rot and damp, and scrambled up the stairs, nearly crying out with relief when she saw the soft glow of the lamp outside her bedchamber. Biting back the sound, she threw herself at the door, slamming it shut behind her with a muffled thump.

She wanted to shout, to scream for help, but fear froze her throat. Not fear of the creature, though that still reverberated through her, dark and primal, but something more human. She was afraid that should she scream, and Gunn—or God forbid, MacCulloch—come, they would find her pressed to the door, trembling, cowering in terror from nothing at all. Frightened of shadows, of the creaks and moans of an unfamiliar house, and too flighty and frivolous to tell the figments of an overactive imagination from an actual threat. She could not, *would* not, give them that ammunition. She would have to save herself.

Forehead pressed to the wood, she waited. She listened. The floor creaked and groaned, and then settled. The smell of blood and earth faded. She was alone.

It wasn't until she was utterly convinced of her safety that Norah allowed herself to cry, deep, gasping sobs of shock escaping her, her stays fighting with her heaving ribcage as she sucked in whole lungfuls of air. She cried as she had not since arriving—not quiet, secretive little tears into her pillow but ugly, ragged howls, finally giving sound to her misery, her fear, to the marrow-deep despair that had suffused her every waking moment in the week since she'd arrived in this cursed stone prison.

She should have heeded her mother, who once she discovered their family's debt had been written off *without* the requirement for a wedding insisted that leaving Glasgow was 'folly', an unnecessary and overdramatic gesture that Norah would regret. If only she could have discussed it with Isa and Peter, but then, it was to escape their orbit that she had fled. She had listened to her conscience, to her gut, to her foolish, hopeful heart, and followed it northward, and all that had ensued since was firmly and irrevocably her failure and hers alone.

Eventually she crumpled onto the bed, not even bothering to undress or pull back the counterpane in her grief. Her sobs came in great ebbs and flows, now rushing heavily, now dwindling to foamy gasps. It was during one of these low tides that she heard a murine scratching in the corridor outside and drew herself up in alarm, but what slid under the door was not a beady-eyed intruder or nightmare beast but rather a small slip of creamy paper. Norah eyed it for a moment, pulse pounding in her throat and ears, but when nothing more came from the door or the hallway, she slid her feet to the floor and shuffled over to retrieve the note.

It was a familiar cardstock, and an even more familiar hand—ink dark, letters neat and precisely formed in that worn, scratchy dip pen.

Dearest Norah,

I have failed, and I am sorry.

I cannot hope to be forgiven for the ways I have wronged you. I neither deserve nor request it. But I do beg you for another chance. I will do better. My wretched, guilty soul may never be worthy of your affection, but I promise you: you are wanted here, more than I can say. I would have you know it.

A

A great and overwhelming wave of fatigue washed over Norah and she stumbled back to the bed, letter in hand. Slowly, wearily she pulled back the blanket and crawled beneath it, pressing her cheek to the tear-soaked pillow and crumpling the letter to her chest. It was too much to believe that this letter was indeed the herald of any real change, but she clung to that hope all the same as she slipped into a cold and dreamless sleep.

CHAPTER EIGHT

THE NEXT MORNING Norah rose early, put herself in order, and headed for the kitchen. She had been of two minds whether to join Gunn for breakfast at all, knowing it would mean broaching the topic of the housekeeper's appearance in Barland's office, but hunger and the simple desire not to be alone had won out over the potential discomfort of a confrontation. As she emerged into the grand foyer she paused to contemplate the stags peering down at her, their eyes as glassy and fixed as she imagined her own must look after the previous night's weeping. She felt barely human, and the crumpled note that had provided a spark of hope in the dead of the night this morning seemed nothing more than tinder for the hearth.

Voices drifting down the hall drew her attention, and despite her resolve she found herself tracing them to the dining room, whose door emitted a weak and watery light onto the runner. Lord Barland sat at the head of the table, and to her complete shock he looked up as she entered, and then pushed himself to his feet.

"Norah," he said, inclining his head. He swallowed. "Won't you join me for breakfast?"

She saw now—and smelled—that the spread was rather different from the overblown banquet that had greeted her in all its congealed glory that first morning. Modest platters of still-steaming sausages and scrambled eggs sat rather comically in the centre of the long dining table, and beside them—thank God—two freshly ladled bowls of porridge.

On reflex Norah glanced about herself, but Barland's conversation partner—surely Gunn—must have departed before she made her entrance, for she was nowhere to be seen now.

Rather than wait for the housekeeper to return she busied herself with the food, making up a plate for herself and then, hesitantly, for her husband. She hadn't given much thought to the fact that doing so would require her to breach the long stretch of table that normally sat between them, and as she approached, dishes in hand, she could not help but feel the weight of his gaze upon her. Her hand shook as she reached to place the plate before him, remembering the way his grip had encircled her wrist, squeezing it until the bones creaked, twinges of sympathetic pain radiating up her forearm even now. As if he could sense her thoughts, Barland kept his hands neatly folded in his lap until she stepped back, his expression a mixture of gratitude and sorrow. "My thanks," he said in that low, hoarse voice. Norah bobbed her head and scurried back to the safety of her seat. Once there, she focused her attention on the familiar porridge in front of her, its bland warmth a soothing panacea to her jangled nerves.

Neither diner spoke at first, the scrape of spoons and the clink of teacups the only accompaniment to the meal. Norah couldn't help but dart furtive glances down the table between bites, and more often than not found Barland looking back at her, though he dropped his gaze whenever their eyes met. Norah felt slightly sick; was she meant to forgive his silences, his ill treatment? Or stranger yet: had the past week all been a hideous dream?

"Gunn tells me you have set up a studio in the library." Norah swallowed past a lump in her throat and looked up once more; Barland had inclined his head as if ushering her through a conversational doorway. "Does Corrain House provide adequate inspiration?"

"It's certainly a change from what I'm familiar with." She paused, fingers clenched around the filigreed and tarnished handle of her spoon, then forced herself to continue. "Even the light is different. The shadows seem… heavier, somehow. Darker."

"It does feel that way, in the wintertime. Have you all the paints you need? If there are different hues you require, I will write for them; my factor in Edinburgh will be able to procure them, I'm sure."

"I prefer to sketch, for the most part." It had been cheaper to do so than fill canvas after expensive canvas with paints, only to set them aside when they weren't quite right. "At least for now."

Barland nodded, intent upon his conversational partner, as if she were disclosing something of great importance. "Of course. You must take all the time you need to familiarise yourself with the house, the grounds. I do hope you will grace us with your paintings soon, though. It has been some time since we have hung anything new on the walls."

That much was obvious, but it seemed rude to observe it aloud; Norah instead merely pressed her lips together and dipped her head in acknowledgement.

Their conversation continued in fits and starts as they ate, sometimes in spite of Norah's reticence. Barland didn't seem to mind, clearly going out of his way to be gracious and patient. This was such a far cry from the silent, brooding man that had pinioned the atmosphere in every room he'd entered that Norah couldn't help but reach beneath the table and pinch herself through the faille of her sleeve. It stung, but her surroundings did not waver or fade. This was real.

They were joined near the end of the meal by Gunn, who stole into the room like a shadow, clearly keen not to interrupt their dialogue. Despite her meekness Norah's eye was drawn to her; Gunn was always pale, but this morning she was a ghost painted in the same washed out colours and deep shadows as the landscape, her eyes dark ringed and her cheeks hollow. Any desire to rebuke her for the previous night's goings-on fled, and she found herself wishing she could order the woman to take a turn about the garden, or rest for a moment with a cup of tea.

She began to clear away the dishes as though nothing was amiss, as though this was normal and Norah and her attentive husband had shared breakfast every morning since her arrival. Norah was still so thrown that she didn't hear Gunn speak and the housekeeper was obliged to repeat herself to get her attention.

"Will you be wanting the fire on in the library, my lady? It's a cold day."

"I—yes, that would be pleasant," Norah said, her lips tugged into a slight frown. There was so much else she wanted to say—not least to enquire if her husband had really instigated this meal, and whether he had given the housekeeper any further instructions for their cohabitation—but she knew now was not the time or place. "Thank you, Gunn."

Barland stayed at the table until Norah had finished, then rose when she did. For a moment she panicked, thinking he intended to invite himself along to the rest of her day, but he merely offered another bow of his head. "Thank you for the pleasure of your company. I have business I must attend to, but I shall look forward to this evening when we shall reconvene." Norah's lips twitched a polite smile, though it slipped away as he departed the room, and she was left staring at the doorway, a vague sense of unease coiling around her breastbone. She had suddenly and inexplicably received exactly what she had wished for, but knew better than most that every auspicious happenstance held a rotten core.

The question remained: what rotted at the heart of Corrain House?

NORAH DRIFTED TO the library after breakfast, unmoored like a ship cut loose from its anchor. The room was homely but she found little to comfort her there; it served only to remind her of what she lacked. She was grasping the back of the wingback chair, willing herself to steady, when a faint song drifted through the open door. A music hall tune, as out of place here as Norah herself. Immediately she was back in Glasgow, her arm looped in Isa's, the smell of tobacco and greasepaint strong in her nostrils. They had argued, that night, but only after arriving home. What had it been about? Norah had spoken to someone she shouldn't have, perhaps, someone Isa was feuding with. Had she done so deliberately, or by accident? The memory was hazy and confusing. Her thoughts were so tangled and taut that she nearly jumped out of her boots when a shadow detached itself from the hearth, straightening and resolving itself into Gunn's familiar angular figure.

"Oh," Norah said, laughing a bit breathlessly at her own high-spirited reaction, "it's you."

"My apologies, my lady," Gunn dusted down her skirts— or wiped her hands on them, one of the two. "I had hoped to be done and gone by the time you arrived."

"It's just as well you're not. I wanted to speak with you." She gave herself a moment to collect herself and then continued. "Last night you came into Lord Barland's study unbidden. I am not trying to scold you," she added, holding up a hand. "I am only curious—for what purpose had you come?"

Gunn's brow furrowed and she shook her head. "That was nothing of note, my lady—I'd urge you not to be concerned with it. I'm sorry that I interrupted your evening."

"No, no, the interruption is of no importance. But you came for a reason, and I would know what it was," Norah pressed.

The housekeeper sighed. "His lordship is... a troubled man, at times, as I think you know. I have been in the habit of checking on him from time to time of an evening." Her tongue darted out briefly to wet her chapped lower lip. "I can see now that this will no longer be required, since he will have your company, which is far superior to mine."

She was lying. Norah could feel in her bones that Gunn was lying, and yet, was it not an entirely plausible explanation? After all, Barland *had* been in ill humour, and Gunn had apparently been his only company for Lord knew how long. There was no reason to doubt the story—but for the twist in her gut that told her it was a falsehood.

Gunn regarded her steadily; the mask she wore was a challenge. She had to know that Norah suspected her story and yet she offered no confession, no apology, just an impassive front that would take all of Norah's fury to breach. And as the seconds ticked by Norah found she had no fury to muster, no desire to batter against Gunn's defences, no matter how much she wished to uncover the secrets that lurked in the dark shadows and deep recesses of the house and its history.

"I'm not so sure of that," Norah said at long last, giving a rueful shake of her head. "For all we corresponded before I came here, I feel as if I have nothing to say to him now. We are strangers to one another."

"I am sure that given time he will show himself to be good company, at least," came the reply.

"Yes. Yes, I'm sure he will. I only hope I am not a disappointment." As soon as she said it Norah realised it was true; would he come to regret this choice he had made, as she did?

"Impossible, I am sure, my lady." Gunn's eyes dropped from hers, and she stooped to retrieve her basket. "I'd best leave you to your own devices."

"No, please… That's not necessary. That is… we were not able to share the table this morning. Perhaps instead you could bring tea for us both?"

"If you would like tea I'll be back with it as soon as I am able."

Norah could hear the silent refusal in the words and tried to ignore the wave of disappointment that washed over her. Of course Gunn would be glad to be rid of her, to leave her to Barland's interest and attentions. She was a fool to expect the housekeeper would have missed the quiet morning repast they had shared. "Very well. Thank you, Gunn."

The housekeeper gave an absent nod, her mind already elsewhere. She lifted a hand to tuck her hair back from her face, leaving a dark streak across the crest of one high cheekbone, a charcoal smear on pristine white paper. Norah's eyes lingered there; her thumb touched to her forefinger: a reflex, the two rubbing together as they did when preparing to smudge the shadows of a sketch.

"We're in for some fine weather this week," Gunn said. "Clear. Dry. You should get some light." She paused. "For drawing," she added. "Or painting."

Norah tore her gaze away, gave a hasty nod. "I am glad to hear it. I'm sure I will find it most diverting."

"I'm sure."

Monday passed otherwise unremarkably, save for the weather, which was (as Gunn had predicted) unseasonably fine, propelling Norah outside after lunch for a bracing walk along the cliff path. Some splashes of colour had returned to the edge of the world today, she thought—the scrubby grass a wee bit greener, the bare heather a cheery rust brown, though the northern sky still hung a white sheet over steely water.

As she traversed the cliffside she was drawn to the edge by the sound of activity; she peeked over to see small figures on the pebbly beach below. There were a half-dozen of them, most of whom were peering up at the cliff with knitted eyebrows. For a moment she felt exposed, as if they were staring straight at her, but she realised they were surveying the cliff itself, picking out the areas where wind and wave had carved away the rock. This must be the work crew then, come at her bidding—or rather, Barland's—to begin the task of shoring up the house. Norah's awkwardness and tension washed away and she could not help but wave down at them, grinning at this sign of forward progress like it was a much wished-for gift on Christmas. One of the men, a dark-haired speck, waved back and she gave a small, giddy laugh.

It would be slow work, she knew, and costly, but it was worth every hour and every penny. First the underpinning, and then a refresh of the furnishings, and before long Corrain House would begin to feel like a home. She envisioned a trip to town, picking settees and lamps from a shop catalogue, fabrics from bolts of cloth laid out before her. Had she ever had the freedom to choose, the ability to enact her vision and shape her world to her liking? Only in small, unimportant ways, but with Corrain House she would write her signature large at last.

With this discovery Norah found herself in good spirits, marred only slightly by the curious sight, on her approach to the house past the staff wing, of MacCulloch and Gunn standing close together by the side door nearest the outbuildings, deep in conversation. She was nowhere near enough to hear them and yet they both stopped talking as she passed. Norah resisted the urge to look down and away— these people were her staff and it was perfectly acceptable to survey them—but as Gunn's steady gaze met hers a shiver crept down her spine and pooled in her stomach. The housekeeper's expression was impassive, in contrast to MacCulloch, who when he turned to look her way wore a tiny but unmistakable smirk.

It could have been about anything, and yet Norah could not help but read into it, seeing fracture where she had previously imagined an undivided front. It seemed no one in the house could count an easy relationship among their effects, even those who ought to have been united by common circumstances. It was all so very lonely.

After her walk Norah returned to the library, fortifying herself with fresh tea before gathering her sketchpad and decamping into the garden—or what passed for one—in the courtyard. She had hoped that the improvement in the weather might cast it in a kinder light, and she was gratified to find this was the case. Whereas the last time she had visited it she had been left with a feeling of sinking dread and decay, today it was nothing more than a slightly overgrown, neglected space, as wild and untended as the cliffs outside. Among the pots of dried-out herbs and skeletal shrubs she found patches of growth, bits of hardy green poking through rocky soil and cracks in the brickwork. They were not the delicate flowers prized by society ladies in her mother's circle, but Norah found the sight undeniably cheering all the same.

Studiously ignoring the reaching figure at the courtyard's centre, Norah settled down on one of the ponderous stone benches, sketchpad on her knees, and began to pick out small details in black and grey. There was the climbing cling of ivy wending its way along a wall, its tendrils describing a path that was at once arbitrary and purposeful. Norah could not help but be drawn in by the spreading, glossy palms of the leaves, grasping at the stone and pulling themselves up towards the light.

Once the ivy had been committed to paper, after a fashion, Norah moved to kneel by one of the worn and pitted planters, bunching her skirts beneath her knees to cushion them. The plant within was a scrappy specimen, a long, twiggy stem with angled offshoots sprouting in every direction. It certainly didn't seem ornamental; though of course it was barren of flowers now, Norah couldn't imagine it hosting lush blooms even in spring. As she leaned in to scrutinise the shape of its leaves she caught a whiff of citrus and grass, a not-unpleasant combination that put her in mind of long summer evenings and sun. She ran her fingers over a stem and was surprised to find that it ended abruptly about six inches above the dirt, clearly having been sliced by something sharp. The severed end oozed a sticky green sap, and when she drew her fingers away the fresh scent clung to them, turning sweet and cloying in her nostrils.

She turned to a fresh sheet of paper and began to take down the plant's likeness. Botanical illustration was not her forte but she did her best to capture the leaves and stem, all the while very aware that in the absence of blooms it might be later in the year before she could begin to properly identify anything in this bedraggled little courtyard. Her drawing was a sad thing, barely more than a few scratched lines absent of colour or shade, and she shifted where she sat, trying to gain a better vantage point. She had seen pictures where the artist had evoked the very sense of being in the landscape, the sounds and scents of the surroundings, and longed to do the same. But then, had she not captured something of the courtyard with this anaemic sketch? For she could not help feeling washed out and stretched thin, as tired as this spindly growth. The light on her paper quivered; the clouds overhead thickened and blotted out the pale rays of the sun as rain began to spit into the courtyard. A chill crept across her skin. It was time to flee inside.

As she scrambled to her feet she became suddenly aware of the dark presence in her periphery, and she spun to face it, nearly stumbling. The rowan was cut in negative space before her; its shape was a crack in the world through which she could see the endless darkness beyond. It arched above her insistently—as if it knew she had been trying not to look at it or acknowledge its presence until that moment, its branches now twisting their way into the forefront of her mind.

She could feel them stretching to reach down her throat, sharp and jagged, leaving a tang of decay and blood on her tongue. She retched, once, twice, and stepped back, as if a mere pace could put her beyond its malevolent reach, but its withered, grasping fingers beckoned, curled ever closer, her toes catching on every root that had bulged through the flagstone as she fought to keep her feet beneath her. Black branches crowded the edges of her vision, blocking out the light and the memory of the light. The rowan contained all. Outwith it there was nothing.

As Norah stared up at its forking branches she began to hear whispers, sly coils of the wind whipping round her, rustling her skirts. She could not make out any words, could not parse the tongue in which it spoke, but its message was clear.

I will consume you.

ALEXANDER BARLAND WAS more subdued at dinner than he had been at breakfast, but Norah was more relieved than anything else—she wasn't sure she would have been able to make conversation, still shaken from her experience in the courtyard. Nevertheless when he rose to leave at the end of their meal, he stopped by the doorway, and inclined his head in invitation.

It took a moment on entering the study before Norah realised what was different, but as her husband moved not towards his desk but to the chairs by the fire, a glance confirmed it: the mess of old documents was gone. She couldn't help but look back at the fire with narrowed eyes before joining Barland in her usual seat. "Well," she said, picking up the nearest book, which was a singularly dry treatise on British shipbuilding, "this is... very nice."

Barland sank into the other chair, stiff-backed and tentative. The warm flames painted the planes and hollows of his face, peach light and blue shadow, like glaze on porcelain. Unbidden, a different image floated to the surface in Norah's mind—a smear of coal dust marking out the arc of a sharp cheekbone. Norah adjusted her grip on the clothbound tome in her lap as her fingers gave a twitch of recognition.

"I'm... glad you like to read." The baron's accent was not at all like either the staff's or Norah's own, she noticed now. It had taken some time to really build a picture of Alexander Barland's voice, so rarely had he spoken before today, but she could hear now the cut glass consonants and resonant vowels of an expensive education, most likely from south of the border. Norah mused that his grandfather, a self-made man from Dumfries, would likely have sounded quite different. "If there are any magazines or folios to which you'd like a subscription, please do say."

"I will, yes, thank you."

The firelight didn't reach his eyes. Those remained black, empty. He did not have a book for himself—did he plan to simply sit in silence or, worse, attempt further conversation? His right hand gripped the arm of the rather weathered wingback upon which he perched, knuckles taut. He was trying.

Norah could not help but try too. "Isa and Peter often bid me read aloud of an evening—I cannot claim any great oratory skills but they seemed to find my voice pleasing enough. Perhaps you would like me to do the same, to help you rest after a long day?"

She was perturbed to see no flash of recognition on his face at the names of her two nearest and dearest companions; though she had been guarded at first in her correspondence there came a time that she could not help but lay bare the truth of what they were to her—and she to them. Any further suspicion was interrupted as he gave a grateful nod, and Norah focused all her attention on the book in her lap rather than ponder this latest peculiarity any further.

"*The first trans-Atlantic voyage made by a Clyde ship was in 1686, when a Greenock-built vessel was employed on a special mission to carry twenty-two persons transported to Carolina for attending conventicles and 'being disaffected to Government'. American ships were most numerous on the western seas, and the East India Company had a monopoly of the eastern seas…"*

CHAPTER NINE

Monday, January 20th, 1890
Corrain House

Dearest Norah,

I can only sit in awe of the trust you have shown me in sharing what you have of your life in Glasgow. I am honoured and humbled. I should confess that—as you rightly guessed—the revelation did not come as a complete surprise to me. There has always been something in the way you have talked about Isabelle in particular that spoke to a deeper connection than that of even childhood friends. You are both fortunate to have found in Peter a life partner upon whom Isabelle could rely on to be understanding and discreet, and a true friend to you.

With that being said, I also sensed the strain you spoke of, and have privately been worried for you, though I felt I could not pry further. For a trio that sits in such a delicate balance as yours, it was perhaps inevitable that the addition of a fourth party would disrupt that equilibrium. I fear you are right that Isa's desire that her child should look upon you as a kind of second mother could be difficult to bring to fruition, not only due to the ignorance and small-mindedness of society at large but also due to the strange and unpredictable workings of the human heart. Perhaps all would be as she hopes. But if you have felt unable to be honest with her about your *own feelings on the topic of motherhood, it is hard to see a smooth path ahead.*

Is it an escape that you seek, Norah? A plausible 'out' from this Gordion knot? I would not blame you for it. But Corrain is a very long way to go merely as an exit from your current predicament.

My own feelings remain unchanged.

Yours,
A

To SAY THAT affairs had reached a state of normality was perhaps overstating, given the atmosphere that lingered over Corrain House, but certainly there had been a vast improvement upon Norah's first week. Barland joined her regularly for meals, keeping up a stream of steady, if superficial, conversation, and they spent most evenings together in his study, where Norah narrated her way through first the tome on shipbuilding, and then a volume detailing the development of the North British Railway, which was no less dry than its predecessor. She found her husband a perfectly pleasant companion, though nothing more than that—whatever rapport they had built in their letters was lacking here, and they were as two polite strangers as they dined and sat together in the firelight.

Barland never came to her bed, and while Norah couldn't help but hear the nagging voice of her mother accusing her of failing to earn her husband's attentions, she felt only relief. She had determined to bear her duty patiently if it came to it, but could not claim that the idea held any excitement or attraction in itself.

The surveying work on the cliff continued apace, and though it was not without its hiccoughs it still lent an air of progress to Norah's days. She even allowed herself to imagine inviting her friends to visit and parading them along the beach to admire the finished work, accomplished with the latest in technology and sparing no expense. Would they be impressed? Would they see her in a new light, as a woman whose will was not to be questioned but obeyed? Perhaps this was a bit much, but for the first time in her life Norah felt a small modicum of control, and it was a sweet and welcome counterpoint to the off-kilter start to her time in Corrain.

All of which was to say that she might have managed to convince herself that this life, such as it was, could well be endured, even enjoyed, if not for several other developments that followed.

First was the presence of Gunn, who grew more wan and weak as the days passed until Norah feared she had caught some kind of wasting illness. She attended to her duties as normal as far as Norah could tell, but there was a heaviness to her step that she failed to entirely hide in Norah's presence. Worry nagged at her, and she nearly spoke to her husband about it on several occasions as the mysterious ailment dragged out, but she couldn't quite bring herself to speak of Gunn to him—as though mentioning the other woman's name might give voice to more than polite concern, might crack the wax seal on a bottle kept firmly corked.

Second were Norah's own disturbed nights; nothing so severe as to cause concern, but enough to give each day a grey haze until she had her first pot of tea. She had never been prone to sleepwalking in the past, but on more than one occasion since coming to Corrain House she found herself waking in a strange room with no memory of having traversed the corridors to get there. It made sense, she supposed; her life had been upended, turned about, so it was only natural that her mind—and body—would require a period of adjustment. She grew accustomed to the feel of worn carpet beneath her bare feet and the creak of floorboards as she navigated her way back to her room in the dark and the cold. Occasionally the fragments of dreams would follow her, the deep shadows in the crevices of the hallway twisting into something sinister and reaching. Though she was inevitably exhausted when she reached her bed, sleep was slow to return.

Thirdly was a letter from her mother, which she found placed neatly on her bedside table upon waking one morning. Even a typical missive from Mrs Mackenzie would've been enough to sour the entire day in Norah's experience, but this one was especially odd, chastising Norah for her entitled complaints and chiding her for the sloppy penmanship and ragged paper of her latest letter. Norah knew better than to voice her true feelings on anything to her mother; each message home was polite but bland, enquiring into her mother's goings-on and omitting all but the barest references to Corrain House. And yet here her mother claimed to be tired of reading about the 'strangeness' and 'loneliness' of Norah's new home, briskly instructing her that all young women—or not so young, in her case—had to learn to cope with such circumstances upon entering into marriage.

> Granted, you have made quite a bed for yourself in haring off so far north, but you were quite aware of the latitude when you decided to leave. That you should find yourself isolated now is no surprise, and there is nothing to it but to put on a brave face and get on with the business of being a wife.

She read the letter several times but was none the wiser after the fourth time through than she had been the first. It was as if her mother had invented a false letter wholesale, pretending that her daughter had deposited myriad troubles at her feet in need of her motherly wisdom and experience— though it had been years since Norah had sought her advice or comfort, not since she was a naive girl. In the end she folded the letter and tucked it into a drawer, resolving to watch her words even more carefully in future. The last thing she wanted to do was to give her mother reason to doubt her choices; besides, things were improving, and soon she would be able to write with genuine pride and excitement about the life she was building for herself.

NORAH WAS ASTONISHED when she came down to breakfast on Sunday morning to find Barland dressed for public in a well-fitting if rather old-fashioned suit. He said nothing, but sure enough, as she emerged from the house into the damp, misty morning air, her husband joined her, even going so far as to open the carriage door for her. His scent twinged in her nose as she climbed past him—sharp cedarwood, sour perspiration, and a sickly, sweet-citrus fragrance that was immediately familiar and yet she struggled to place in the moment.

He was silent on the journey, as though it took everything he had within him simply to sit upright, and Norah found that instead of being pleased that he was joining her she grew more regretful and anxious with every passing mile. More than once she nearly reached to knock on the ceiling, to beg that they turn around and return to Corrain.

Thurso itself was also worse than she'd imagined. From the moment they emerged from the coach she felt like a carnival attraction. Everywhere she looked there was someone staring back at her—or quickly averting their gaze. The minister openly directed his sermon at the baron personally, as though trying to jam years of pastoral care into one service, and they departed on a wave of whispers, eyes burning into the back of Norah's neck.

Meanwhile, the whole affair obviously took a serious toll on Barland. He seemed to hold together well enough throughout the morning (for all that he did not sing a note), but by the time they arrived home he was white as a sheet, and he retired immediately for the rest of the day, not even joining her for dinner. Faced with a house apparently full of sickly inhabitants, Norah was eager to ease their burdens, but hardly knew where to begin.

"Has Alexander already eaten?" she asked as Gunn cleared her dishes after a meal of salt pork and potatoes. His Christian name felt strange on her tongue. "If not, perhaps I could take up his dinner?"

The look Gunn shot her was curious—almost hunted, somehow. "He's resting," she said.

"Yes, of course. I didn't realise the trip to Thurso would tax him so—now I see why he does not make the journey more regularly."

"He may not make the journey every week," Gunn said. She sounded almost apologetic, though Norah could not for the life of her fathom why.

"Nor would I ask him to. The gesture is enough." Norah pressed her lips together, fingers working round the hem of the napkin in her lap. "You have all tried, in your own way, to make me welcome here, and you must know I am grateful for that."

Gunn's gaze slid away from Norah's, though it was perhaps just to look to the tray of dishes in her grip. "This is your home," was all she said.

"One that I invited myself into, and, it seems, in doing so disrupted the balance that had stood for some years. I'm sorry for the work I have caused you. If it would be easier for me to stay elsewhere while his lordship recovers—"

"My lady." The words cut into her, sharp, almost a reprimand, and Norah's own voice died in her throat as Gunn lifted her head once more to meet her eyes, jaw set firm. "Please don't trouble yourself with the choices others have made. His lordship will be well. He has things in hand. He doesn't need your pity. Only your patience."

Whereas Barland's rebuke in the study had inspired her to fury, Gunn's left her speechless, all twisted up with guilt and recrimination. She dipped her head, digging her nails into the threads that hemmed the napkin and feeling them give beneath her grip. When she looked up, the other woman was already moving for the door, barely disturbing the air as she went.

She called Gunn's name and raised a hand as if to stop her, but when the housekeeper fixed her with those dark eyes all that escaped her lips was a repentant "I'm sorry." Gunn said nothing, and then she was gone.

NORAH TOOK TO walking the grounds daily after that, telling herself it was to ensure the house was quiet and undisturbed while Barland recovered from his overexertion. Whatever the reason, she soon grew familiar with the scurfy fields and jagged rocks of the coast, learning to tell where she was by this formation or that. A woman all alone in the remote wilderness should have been afraid and yet she felt no fear— at least not until she turned her steps back towards Corrain House.

Sometimes she took her boots off when she reached the beach and tucked her skirts up to protect them from the damp sand and ocean spray. It was easier to manoeuvre along the flat planes of the beach, skirting the layered limestone boulders that slumped towards the ocean. Norah rarely thought of coming there at all but often found herself padding through the sand until she was once again faced with the carcass of the beached ship, like it had drawn her there through some ineffable appeal. She would stare at it, running her fingers over the ridged, dark slats of wood and remembering the frenzied sketch she had made that day in the library. It made her feel sick but also sated, like she had managed to capture something dark and inscrutable in those strokes on the paper.

Such it was that she took her sketchbook once more to the courtyard. She had begun to avoid it in the evening, navigating interior corridors rather than cutting across, but at the height of the sun on a cool spring morning she determined to face the rowan once more. The little garden was looking slightly more alive, some shrubs perking up and even beginning to bud in the past few days. She recognised some herbs among them now, lavender and rosemary and mint, not thriving, perhaps, but surviving at least in their little stone planters. Presumably Gunn or MacCulloch must take care of them even as the rest of the courtyard grew wild.

As she opened her sketchbook she noticed a fan of jagged paper along the spine—several pages had been torn out in haste, it seemed. Frowning, Norah ran a finger over the remnants of the paper; she always removed her sketches with a fine blade, on the rare occasion when she wished to frame them or gift them. Could someone else have found her sketches and decided to tear them from the book? It seemed unlikely, for what use would Gunn or Barland have for scribbled etchings of plants and renderings of Corrain House's rooms and facade? Her mother had mentioned something about the 'untidy' pages of her last letter, but why would she have torn from her sketchbook when she had a folio of stationery in the library? And stranger still, why did she have no memory of doing so? She had the vague recollection of a lonely evening in front of the fire, perhaps a glass too many of claret... well. She had never drunk so much as to lose her memories before, but she knew it was a risk with overindulgence. She would take more care in future, at the very least to save her from any more awkward missives to her mother.

Norah flipped further through the pages, intent on finding a fresh sheet of paper to focus on, and then cast her eyes around the meagre garden for a subject to sketch. The tree was there, of course, but she pulled her gaze away almost immediately, ignoring the shiver that ran its way up her spine. There was little green or growing, save for the ever-present ivy and some bedraggled herbs, including the mystery plant she had noticed on her last visit. It looked even more spindly and haphazard in its planter today, with more freshly cut stems. She began to sketch, following the curve of its drooping shoots, leaning closer to make out the craggy edges of its leaves. The scent caught her nostrils and she had a sudden flash of connection: *this* was the acid-sweet fragrance hanging on her husband that Sunday morning by the carriage. Perhaps, then, it was used to salve newly shaven skin, to freshen clothes, or to discourage moths.

Norah sat on the bench, sketchbook forgotten in her lap as the events of that Sunday came tumbling back to her—the whispers and looks, the silent carriage rides. Barland had seemed barely aware of his surroundings at times, needing an encouraging touch from Norah to direct him to stand from his pew to sing (or rather stand in silence). He was the same in the evenings—he would carry on a conversation for a wee while, but then he would seem to absent himself: she would look his way and his dark eyes would be empty and unblinking, his mouth slack. He was like half a man. No matter how she tried to rally his interest with questions or provocative statements he could not seem to spare the energy for her; it was as if he retreated somewhere else, leaving only the shell of his body behind. In a way he put her in mind of the rowan: dark and silent, his presence an unwelcome burr in her awareness at all times.

She sighed, her gaze drifting to the trio of dead trunks that made up the warped base of the rowan tree, eyes idly tracing the path of its gnarled branches as they wove this way and that, knotting and unknotting in their doomed skyward quest.

It seemed to fill her field of vision, branches snaking across the sky; despite the morning sun the expanse was a sheer, sallow white, like an overlay of gauze across a wound. Norah's breath caught as she began to move her charcoal across the page, suddenly captivated by the shape of the tree, the way it twisted around itself, reaching ever upward.

It was trying to escape, to breach the walls of its prison. She could not help but feel a kinship then, for had she not done the very same? But unlike the rowan she had succeeded, her flight shattering not just the flagstones around her but the very foundations of the life she had been rooted in. Isa would have been happy to see her planted there forever, playacting as governess to little Alice and flaunting their relationship under the noses of unsuspecting friends and neighbours. It was a perfect solution, and yet.

And yet it had not been enough. Norah had twisted free. That doing so had landed her here, in another untenable situation, was just punishment for her crimes. She had known that the delicate balance of Isa and Peter's relationship would be rocked by her departure and yet had not even looked back as she fled. The people she had called her dearest friends, whose love and comfort had once been a solace and a boon, were now nothing but collateral damage to her selfish whims.

You take, and capture, and steal. You hunger and consume.

A snap.

A piece of charcoal fell from her grip, shattering on hard flagstone, scattering black crumbs across the ground. Norah gave a start, her pulse leaping in her throat. Her other palm was damp against the cover of the sketchbook, as though she'd been gripping it for some time, and her stomach lurched with dread, with the sudden conviction that something was very, very wrong.

Slowly, Norah dragged her eyes to her lap. Her fingers were filthy, black charcoal mixed with sweat, her skirts smudged and streaked as though she'd been wiping her hands on them. The open page of the book was filled with a mess of lines and whorls, at first just a dark chaos, but as she stared its meaning began to resolve: the rowan, its twisted form captured in dark lines so heavy the page shone like polished coal. A figure, too, human, arched back as though being lifted to heaven, but this was no rapture: it was hanging, impaled upon the bare branches of the tree like the hapless prey of a shrike.

Your stain spreads.

CHAPTER TEN

Dear Mother,

Your latest letter was received and duly heeded; you are quite right that my circumstances are not so different than many others and I ought to turn my energies to my newfound duties. It is true that my initial missives were spurred by a sense of isolation and disorientation, as you no doubt gleaned from my words, but I can assure you now that things have improved greatly. There is always a settling-in period to be had with any change, but with each passing day I grow more familiar with Corrain House and its needs—as I imagine one must do with any old house. The work I spoke of in my last letter is underway, or at least its planning is, with a great deal needing done to prepare for the structural work that is to be undertaken. The foreman was most reluctant to begin this work so early in the year—something about the unpredictability of the sea and the conditions of the cliffside—but I simply cannot wait a moment longer to press on with the improvements.

Gunn has been a great help in these moments, as well as in the planning itself. She knows everything there is to know about the house, it seems, and rarely needs consult Alexander before agreeing to this or that course of action or advising an alternative. I assume all housekeepers *must come to a similar level of knowledge about the residences they keep, for who is more concerned with their upkeep and the work it takes to maintain them? Whatever the case, I am grateful for her knowledge and for her support, especially with the foreman, who really is quite an obstinate creature. One wonders how he earns a living when he is so eager to delay or even turn down the commissions set in front of him.*

~~In my darker moments I dwell on the nightmares that break my sleep and dog my waking hours; I hear the creak of footsteps behind me when I am alone. Sometimes my mind drifts and I find myself losing minutes... hours... and I wonder if this is what going mad feels like.~~

I look forward to hearing news of the spring social. Has Mrs Mackay issued everyone with their marching orders yet? She always did like to get an early start on things. Last year it seemed her alacrity might fracture the organising committee; I do hope no such schism sunders what has til now been a well-oiled machine. Please do tell all, so that I may learn how best to comport myself when I find myself on such a committee here, as will no doubt happen soon.

With great affection,
Norah

WRITTEN CORRESPONDENCE WAS an imperfect medium; by the time your addressee received it the contents might already reference events or situations well past, or significantly changed in form. For that reason it was important to select carefully what one included, and not indulge too much in pronouncements which would only be proven wrong with the passage of time. But there was also a power in describing in words what one *hoped* to be true, for nothing looked so indisputable as those things captured in black and white.

Norah had hoped that by cheerfully committing to paper the much-improved situation at Corrain House she might solidify it in reality, but even before the missive to her mother had started its journey south, the picture she had painted of a bustling, productive period had begun to warp and fade.

In truth, Gunn's announcement that it would be she and not Lord Barland who would be Norah's collaborator on the matter of the structural work had left Norah in a state of perpetual internal conflict.

It had not slowed things down: Gunn appeared to have full oversight of the estate's budgets and logistics, and whenever something required the laird's signature it would soon be returned signed in that looping, even hand. It was Gunn who had found Norah's contractor: a Thurso man by the name of Manson, a quarryman with experience in structural work and the contacts to assemble his own team of labourers.

And so Gunn's presence was most certainly a help rather than a hindrance, but in truth that was the problem. Norah had little chance of taking on control of the household with Gunn's hands on the reins. Though the project had been hers to begin with, it felt less and less so as time passed and the housekeeper smoothly managed all obstacles and difficulties. She did so even under the strain of her illness, which seemed to have settled in to stay, sapping what colour she had and painting dark hollows on her complexion. She did not appear to be worsening but nor was she getting any better. Norah was desperate to say something—knew that this had gone on long enough now that she definitely *should*, and yet she did not.

Because as guilty as her time spent with Gunn made Norah feel, a guiltier still knowledge lurked beneath it: she was greedy for it. She would eat a quiet, companionable breakfast with her husband every morning, stoically paying no mind to the housekeeper moving back and forth, not daring to look her way until after, when she would follow her to the kitchen.

There, they would talk through the progress of Norah's plans, and while they talked, Gunn would work—cleaning dishes, sweeping, scrubbing, and Norah would watch, would drink her in until her heart was sick with it.

Gunn was beautiful: austere, yes, angular, but those dark eyes and Barland bones that rendered Alexander a dull sort of handsome were somehow intoxicating in a woman: exciting, enthralling. Gunn was graceful: in spite of her mysterious illness, she moved with a strength and surety that drew the eye with it, as though she were dancing, not doing housework. Gunn was sharp: she could not hide it behind deference now that they were working together. She knew every inch of the estate, could pull any fact or figure from her mind with a moment's thought. So Norah would watch her, would allow herself to be carried on a cloud by that melodic voice, would guard jealously the time she was allowed with her, and that, she told herself over and over, was enough. It would have to be.

THE SCAFFOLD SOMEHOW made the cliff look taller. Perhaps it was the way it marked out the layers of sediment between the sand and the base of the house, its broad wooden crossbeams measuring it out. The uprights were driven deep into the sand, the whole structure secured to the cliff itself with ropes and pitons to guard against the pull of the tide. They were constrained by nature, working whenever daylight and the tides permitted, and though it was late in the day the workmen still moved over it like ants, industrious and driven.

Norah stood on the beach, neck craned as she followed the movement of the men above her. The foreman didn't appreciate her presence, she knew, but her vigil was not in service of criticism or distrust. When she was standing there it was easier to banish her misgivings and worries, the evidence of her influence plain for all to see, calming her unsettled heart. She knew it was only her imagination that made the library floor feel as if it were shifting beneath her every step, but it still helped her tread easier seeing the underpinning taking shape against the cliffside.

She could not stare forever, though; after a time her neck grew sore and she had to turn away, one hand massaging the ache from her cold, tired muscles. The sea was quiet and glassy, slowly creeping up the beach towards them in its inevitable metre. A mere hundred yards or so offshore boats skated across the water, and it took a moment for Norah to realise they were moving far faster than the stillness around her would've predicted. She took a step towards the foam edging the sand, squinting and raising a hand to shade her eyes against the white glare of the sky. The ships' sails were swollen with wind, the vessels tossed on non-existent waves, and her stomach clenched in worry and something else—a strange, sick dread at the impossible sight before her. From this distance the men on deck were just visible, their figures rushing this way and that in agitation, and Norah could hear their panicked cries as another gust buffeted their straining sails. Surely the crafts could not take much more of this; they were no city-built vessels, sturdy against the Atlantic's unforgiving strength.

Another shout carried to her over the wind, from the direction of the cliff this time, and Norah spun around, the dread clenching her shoulders tight. Her gaze darted over the scaffolding, frantic, and then another cry drew her eye to a spot halfway up the cliff where a group of men were clustered. As she watched the frame seemed to shudder, the men throwing their arms wide to grasp at this support, that handhold, and as they scrambled a section of the cliff peeled away like it had been sliced with a knife, chunks of rock and debris tumbling down the rock face and into the sand below. Norah's gasp joined the clamour of the workmen, underscored by the dull thud of rock and timber. As the commotion settled she counted—one, three, six men—and raised a hand to press against her chest in sweet relief. No one had fallen, though the scaffolding had taken damage, several struts half-broken and skewed in the aftermath. There was another shout from above, an angry "Lady Barland" in the foreman's rough tones, and she knew that he was preparing to climb down and use this happenstance as yet more evidence of why the task was a fool's errand, as he had been insisting these past three days. She had no desire to thole yet another tirade, and so she turned away, back to the sea and the boats, but there was nothing there, only a flat, empty ocean and the endless horizon. The boats were nowhere to be seen. Norah's stomach sank.

It made no sense. She was tired, yes, and perhaps a little wrung-out, but never to the point of seeing things that simply weren't there. She had *heard* the sailors' shouts, the panic in their voices—though had it been the sailors, or the workmen on the scaffolding? Doubt flooded her, but she shored her resolve against it. She *had* seen the boats, just as she'd seen them on her first visit to Corrain. Just because no one else had, just because they were gone in the blink of an eye, that didn't mean she was wrong. It didn't mean she was losing her mind.

The crunch of footsteps behind her made her spin round, but thankfully it was not Manson but another of the workmen, a slight, dark-haired lad wearing a crooked smile. "You're all right, my lady, I'm no' here to chase you off. Mind, that is what I was sent for, but who am I to tell you your business."

"Oh, my apologies," Norah said, reaching up to scrape her hair back from her face. She tried to focus on the young man before her, putting the shouts of the sailors to the back of her mind. "I know Mr Manson would prefer I didn't come here, but it—it gives me reassurance to see the work."

"Aye you're no' the first owner to want to see the job's done right and you winnae be the last," he said, grinning. Unlike

MacCulloch there was no menace in his smile, just a good-natured amusement. Norah found herself unclenching, muscle by muscle, though she could not escape her worry completely.

"The rockslide that just happened, is everyone alright?"

"Oh aye, no harm done, just some time lost. The earth can be a tricky thing to master." Something flickered in his eyes, and Norah was desperate to ask what was lurking behind his expression, but it passed quickly and he gave her another bright smile. "We'll soon put it right."

"I've no doubt. I'm grateful for all your hard work Mister… I'm sorry, I didn't get your name."

"Just call me Davey, my lady."

Norah nodded, and considered asking him whether he'd seen the boats on the horizon. But he'd been hard at work, and so if he hadn't it would tell her nothing. Certainly it could not confirm that she was seeing things, and a fevered insistence that she was not going mad would only serve to prove the opposite. "Well, thank you, Davey," she said, taking a step back, skirts tangling around her legs. "I will leave you to it, I think. Please give my regards to your crew, your work is much appreciated. By all of us at the house," she added, the lie souring on her lips as soon as she uttered it.

"Aye, I'll tell the lads. Ca' canny, my lady—if there's been one fall today there could be another." With that he returned to the scaffolding, shouting up to the others as he began to climb. Norah couldn't make out the words, even with the stillness blanketing them, and once again wondered how the sailor's shouts had reached her.

Norah's route took her up the winding coastal trail that curved away from the village, and though the climb used to leave her winded and panting by the time she reached the top, she had now traversed it so often that today she set a steady pace up the slope, drawing deep, even lungfuls of fresh spring air as she struck out for the manor. The night was falling quickly now, a curtain drawn over the tumult of the day, and though she was not afraid Norah quickened her step up the track, her boots shedding the crust of sand she had acquired on the beach. Corrain House was a dark, squat shape in the distance, visible a fair way off on this, a clear, crisp night, and the closer she came the less she could countenance being swallowed by it.

Deferral came in the form of the wee kirk, rising out of the night as she skirted the cliffside path. She had not been back inside it since her wedding day, and though that memory brought a rush of disquiet, facing it was suddenly preferable to the prospect of stilted conversation with her now-husband over dinner. She tested the door: unlocked. Taking this as a sign, Norah pushed her way into the building. There were no lamps, of course, but a neat stack of fat white candles sat just inside. Norah lit several, casting a warm glow over the deepening gloom, and took one in hand to light her way as she moved farther inside. Though she had intended to sit in contemplation there was a restlessness suffusing the space, prodding her onward. Her feet led her past the pews towards the back of the nave, where tall, narrow windows kept watch over the barren coast.

The longer she moved through the kirk, the more her conviction grew that she wasn't alone here. The room was silent, and yet there were whispers and shufflings all around her. The air was still, and yet it stirred with the milling of bodies. The aromas reaching her nose were only that of tallow and smoke, and yet behind that there was the sour smell of perspiration and damp, unwashed clothes, of sharp brine and kelp.

The light from her candle caught on the panes of glass, illuminating the strange scratches scrawled across the glossy surface that she had noticed from outside. Norah drew nearer; here on the inside the windows were low and close enough to read. In the gleam from the candle the shapes resolved into jagged letters.

Grieg
24th May 1820

John MacAsgaill
Mary MacAsgaill
24-05-1820

Callum Bain
Matt 25:35

Stuart Guinn

Fiona MacLeod

On and on: names dates—one date, really, all that same day in May 1820.

Norah felt her skin prickle, her shoulders rising as if warding off jolts and knocks from all around her. The sensations filled her to the brim, clamoured for attention, and she did not realise that she was in fact no longer alone in a very literal sense, not until a hand gripped her elbow.

"My lady?"

Norah blinked, gave a start. Her fingers hurt: in her distraction she had pressed them against the cold pane in a tense claw, as though attempting to etch her own message with her fingernails.

"My lady."

A squeeze, and then as Norah straightened up and moved away from the window, she was released.

Gunn, when Norah turned to look at her at last, was wearing her woollen coat and a dark headscarf, which was more than Norah had managed. She was suddenly quite sure her own hair was a bird's nest and she had to resist the urge to check on it.

"Oh, Gunn. I was just…" What *was* she doing? It was as though she was only now waking up, as though she had walked in her sleep into the church, up to the window. "The words, I wanted to see what they were. These names…" She half-turned back towards the panes of glass. "Who were they?"

Gunn didn't answer immediately, and Norah could almost feel her itching to ignore the question, to instead turn the interrogation on her. Then she sighed. "Crofters, mostly. Some kelp farmers." It was a simple enough answer that told Norah next to nothing.

"But why? Why this one date, why here?" Norah tore her attention away from the glass and focused it on Gunn, willing her to break the mantle of silence that hung over the church. *Please*, her expression said. *Please.*

"This was their last night in Corrain." Gunn closed the gap between them to reach towards the pane herself, running a finger across one line of scratched words. Her hands were lean and long like the rest of her, fingernails short, knuckles slightly ruddy even in the dim light.

"The kelp kilns were done for," she went on, "and nearly every old farming family had been kicked off the runrigs to Corrain village. They were all sailors now, whether they wanted or not. But a few folk hung onto their leases in tied cottages on the estate, even though they had next to no land to farm what with it all being turned over to sheep. Barland— the laird's grandfather—he served notices, but they stayed put. So he sent in a factor."

Gunn glanced across at Norah. Her eyes glowed in the candlelight and Norah wondered that she'd ever thought they were identical to Barland's—where his were bottomless pools, hers were like the night sky.

"You'll see plenty of stone-built ruins on the estate," she said, in what seemed a total departure from the topic at hand. "Dykes and foundations and whole cottages, buckled walls, heaps of abandoned stone everywhere. We've rocks aplenty but what we don't have is trees. Timber, thatch, that's hard to come by this far north—so much so that you'd see folk build a new house and move the roof from one building to the other." She scratched idly at the markings with her thumbnail and dropped her hand back by her side.

"That's why he set fire to the thatch." Norah drew in a breath as the air in the church grew tighter, hotter, the crackle of straw and splintering wood drowning out the distant rush of the waves for a moment. It was cruel, what the factor had done, and Gunn's matter-of-fact delivery only compounded this, as if it was just a rule of nature that one man should destroy the home and livelihood of another for his own benefit. "How many died?" she asked, a fist coming to rest just below the hollow of her throat.

Gunn tipped her head to one side, eyes narrowing. "Why d'you assume anybody did? The goal was to evict, not murder." But she didn't give Norah a chance to counter, to reveal that she could almost *hear* the screams. "In the fires, only one: Úna Guinn. She refused to leave. She said she answered to nobody but the land itself."

The pronunciation of the surname was slightly different from the one Norah was used to hearing but the connection was nonetheless clear. It surely could not be a coincidence.

Without thinking Norah reached out to Gunn—she had been aiming for her hand, but the other woman twitched at the last moment, leaving Norah to awkwardly grasp the neatly hemmed cuff and the wrist bones beneath. "I'm sorry," she murmured, gaze earnest and hot. "What happened next?"

Gunn didn't react to the touch. She didn't pull away, either. Her voice grew lower, as though daring Norah to lean closer. "You'll know the story from there, or a version of it, at least— it's the same one told all over. They were told their passage was paid to Canada, and a living when they got there. I'm not sure how many took up the offer, but certainly most got on the cart to the Glasgow train the next morning. That night, though, with nowhere else to go…" Gunn inclined her head toward the windowpanes. "They spent the night here, and they left their mark behind—somebody must have packed a ring with a jewel, or a metal file. The family have really never used this kirk, so the windows have never been replaced."

All at once Norah felt the walls closing in around her, pressing in until the air was thick and hard to pull into her lungs. The circumstances could not be more different, of course, but she could not help but remark on the connection to her own situation, the claustrophobic walls of the church heralding the end of one life and the beginning of another. Where the crofters had been banished from the land she had instead been tied to it; where their homes had been destroyed, hers had been built in ash and blood.

She realised that she was gripping Gunn's wrist tightly, tight enough to turn her knuckles white, but the housekeeper betrayed no discomfort. She loosened the circlet of her fingers, then dropped them to her side, turning to face the window once again. She knew she would still see them when she shut her eyes, the candlelight running along the jagged letters like molten gold. "Nor should they be. These people ought to be remembered." The Bible reference caught her eye. *Matthew Chapter 25, Verse 35.* It was from a well-known passage, a staple for sermons about obedience and the leading of a faithful life. Norah's lips moved of their own accord, sounding it out.

"For I was an hungred, and ye gave me meat: I was thirsty, and ye gave me drink: I was a stranger, and ye took me in…"

Gunn snorted. "An ironic choice."

Norah shook her head. "A hopeful one. It's Jesus promising his disciples their final reward, their place in Heaven," Norah said. "His…" Her thoughts ran ahead of her words, and a laugh bubbled up in her throat. Once it began, she couldn't stop it, her mirth echoing around the little kirk. Gunn was staring at her in utter bemusement, perhaps even concerned for her sanity, but some moments passed before Norah could speak. "It's not that funny," she said at last. "I don't know what came over me. Only, the passage, it's the separation of the goats... from the *sheep*. So I suppose it *is* rather ironic, in the end."

At first Gunn appeared unmoved by this revelation, her gaze fixed on Norah's, her expression as unfathomable as the firmament in her dark eyes. At last, though, her lips twitched into something almost like a smile. "You are quite remarkable, aren't you," she said.

"I'm sure that's not the word Mister Manson would use," Norah replied with a chuckle. "He seems quite convinced I am a nuisance and a harridan."

"My lady—"

"Norah." The interruption was reflexive, uttered before she had fully formed the thought, but once said it could not be unsaid, and so she added. "Please. I know I am the lady of the house. But here... it's Norah."

The other woman seemed about to argue, but then something caught her eye, behind Norah, and she said instead: "Come outside."

"What? I..."

But Gunn was already turning on her heel to lead the way out of the kirk, and Norah's feet propelled her in pursuit.

Outside, it was fully dark, the sky beyond the kirk's broad doors black as pitch. The air had a bite to it, crisp and clear. Gunn did not stop, leading them around the side of the building to the cliff path that overlooked the sea. "Watch," she said, moving to stand at Norah's side, and pointing. "In the sky."

Norah frowned in confusion, but lifted her gaze to the vast expanse above the horizon. The sky was huge on rare cloudless nights like this one, growing ever larger and deeper as the stars came out. At first, that was all there was to see: the scattered pinpricks of light dusting the black. But then came the faintest of glows, and a flicker of emerald flame. Slowly the glow grew, and an undulating tendril wove its way like a fresh green shoot across the field of stars, vertical striations of light shimmering above it. It was as though a chasm had opened to another world, its unearthly light streaming through into this one.

It was foreign and unexpected enough to be eerie, and yet as she stood beneath the aurora Norah felt only awe and a strange sense of peace. The tendril grew, sprouted, began to stretch across the sky until there were bands of green radiating in all directions, washing the earth below in a benevolent glow. A liquid pulse of shimmering violet light ran across one of the edges, like pearls dropped onto a necklace, and Norah felt a mirrored thrill course through her at the sight.

Gunn seemed to radiate warmth beside her—or at any rate, her own body felt hot where their arms touched. She wasn't sure who had taken whose hand, strong, cool fingers woven tightly with hers. For a long time, neither woman spoke.

"Agnes," came the response, at last, to the unasked question. "It's Agnes."

Chapter Eleven

My dear Norah,

Please excuse my letter, which for all I know may find its way straight into the fire rather than your hands. If you do open it I beg for you to read to the end, though of course you have no reason to heed my wishes anymore, if ever you did.

It has been almost a month since you departed Glasgow and though the city marches steadily onwards towards spring it is deepest winter here at Goldsmith Terrace. I have no facility with words so I will not extend the metaphor further, but there is a distinct chill in the air which even the least poetic soul would be hard-pressed to ignore. I know it often felt as if your presence was unremarkable, just another dependable component of a well-ordered life, but if that were ever believed by the occupants of this house it has been well and truly disproven with your absence.

I fear it was your companionship that kept the balance between myself and Isa; I fear as well that alone I am unable to carry that weight. Please forgive me if this seems overwrought, but know that I am not exaggerating when I say I stand on unsteady ground now, wondering if I will ever find my way to surer footing.

Isa is a changed woman since you left. She has always been prone to fits of high emotion, as well you know, but your companionship always brought her back to herself before long. Now she swings from high to low and back again all in the space of a day, and it has become such that I do not know which woman it is that I will be sharing my table with when we sit down to dine. She is by turns angry and remonstrative, morose and stony. Poor wee Alice is either subjected to an intense battery of her mother's affection, or goes neglected for days on end. I do what I can to provide a steadier stream of parental attention, but I cannot help but worry that this treatment will impact the girl as she grows older and more conscious of her mother's vicissitudes. As a woman who herself was subject to a mother's capricious whims I do not need to tell you how damaging that may be.

I'm sorry. Oh, I'm so very sorry, Norah, to invoke such barbed pleas, but I am worried, and I am afraid. You are a married woman now, and cannot merely return to Glasgow and retake your place with us, and yet I find myself waking from dreams in which you have done just that, and those moments before I fully rouse myself are the happiest minutes of my day. I still do not understand exactly what it was that drove you from us, but I regret any part I played in the situation you saw as untenable.

Please, if nothing else write us, let us know how you are doing. Write her, *and tell her you think of her still. She may rant and shower you with scorn, but I assure you it is from a place of great sorrow and need. We need you, Norah. Please come back.*

Yours with all humility,
Peter

It was some time before Norah found the courage to frequent the library again, and it was longer still before she looked out the almanacs and botanical guides housed there. She had no intentions to revisit the pages she had sketched in the garden, but upon returning to her journal it had fallen open to the skeletal, clawed figure of the rowan tree and she had no choice but to rip it at the spine and throw the page into the crackling fire.

Ice crawled down her own vertebrae as she watched the paper blacken and curl, and she was suddenly struck by the need for distraction. Though still a reminder of that afternoon, the smudged sketches of the other plants and herbs were far less upsetting, and so she retrieved several volumes from the shelves by the window and sat down to begin her identification.

Common Vervain
Verbena officinalis

Vervain has an upright habitus and toothed, lobed leaves. Its delicate, angular sprigs grow to around eighteen inches long, holding clusters of mauve flowers. It grows in flat, moist locations.

In his Historia Naturalis, *Pliny the Elder describes it as hiera botane ('sacred plant'), citing its use to cleanse and purify altars, and its use by the Gauls to cure disease, to banish fevers, and for more esoteric purposes such as granting wishes and visions.*

The spindly plant with the acid-sweet scent was no more familiar to Norah in black and white than it had been in the courtyard—not surprising, given that according to the books it ought not to grow this far north. For such an unassuming little plant it had a long and colourful history: once she'd

identified it, every entry she found spoke of its significance—
to the Ancient Egyptians and Greeks, the Romans, the
Druids. The holy herb, the enchanter's herb, it seemed to
do everything: heal wounds, purify the body, calm turbulent
minds—even ward off evil.

No mystery, then, as to why someone might have regular
use for such a plant in Corrain House. Norah glanced across
at the library door, remembering Gunn's quiet entrance into
the study that night with Barland. What was it she had said,
that she was 'checking on him'? But she had been carrying
that box with her. And later, Norah had caught the sharp,
sickly aroma of its sap when he was near. So that was it: the
housekeeper was a believer in vervain's power to heal body
and mind, and was making some sort of salve or tincture,
which she had attended Alexander that night to administer. It
seemed an obvious explanation. Only one wrinkle remained:
why lie about it?

It was as Norah returned the botanical textbooks to their
spot that she spied something at the back of the shelf tucked
in behind the tomes of the natural history section: a small
leatherbound notebook, barely bigger than her hand. As
she pulled it out the strip that held it closed snapped along
a crease, crumbling with age, and it fell open in her palm to
reveal handwritten pages of tiny text in faded scratches of
ink interspersed with careful illustrations, some in the same
ink and some in smudged lead pencil. Flipping through,
Norah immediately recognised some of the selfsame plants
and herbs from the courtyard. The notes were in some cases
summarising much of what she had already learned from
the larger, more formal volumes, but there were also recipes
for tinctures and teas, instructions on drying and quantities.
This was somebody's personal, practical herb journal—more
than one somebody in fact, judging by the way the writing
changed partway through the book. It was not a thick volume,
and it was mostly full, the back half dominated with sketches

that looked to be more for pleasure than science. Whoever had made them had enjoyed art as well as herbalism. Norah's palms began to sweat as she flicked past birds and flowers, and sure enough, she soon found the familiar wild strokes of the rowan tree spread across the pages of the notebook. The hand was different, and it was rendered in pencil, not charcoal, but the depiction was near enough her own that it made her dizzy. Why had the owner of the notebook been compelled to drag their lead so heavily it creased the pages? Why, when all the other sketches were small and delicate, did this one take up a full two pages? Norah's stomach churned, the tea she had drunk suddenly restless and sour within.

Flustered, she stood and closed the notebook. The book had been hidden, and probably for good reason. Feeling at once very silly and inexplicably agitated, Norah replaced the book, wedging it behind the larger volumes to keep it from falling back open. She returned the other books to their former locations, and the little notebook was secreted away once more. It was as she pushed them into place that another scent wafted out to reach her; not sharp and fresh like vervain but the almost sickly sweet notes of violet and rose. Nobody in this house wore that perfume. The only person who did was hundreds of miles away, though with violets curling in her nostrils she could almost feel a presence at her side. Norah turned away but the scent seemed to follow her, even as she sank to her knees and gouged a shovelful of coal out of the bucket and into the hearth. The fire flared, ash and smoke smudging the flowery bouquet away, and Norah felt the heat prick her cheeks and forehead. She closed her eyes against the flame and the memories both.

Eventually she rose, and as she settled back in her chair by the fire, a creaking in the hallway forewarned the knock-and-entry of the housekeeper, carrying a tray. Norah gave a sigh of relief; the last thing she wanted was to be alone at that moment. Company was a welcome distraction from the unease that gnawed at her. Agnes—it gave Norah a warm little thrill to think of her as such, here and now, even though she had yet to utter the name out loud—was in her usual dark dress, head uncovered, sleeves still rolled up from her morning's work. It was the sort of thing that would have sent Norah's mother into a state of shock: a servant improperly attired above stairs, and in front of her mistress no less. In Norah it elicited only guilty appreciation at the shift of muscle beneath smooth flesh.

"I thought you'd want more tea." Agnes set the tray down on a side table without ceremony, beginning the task of swapping the fresh pot, milk jug and cup for the used vessels Norah had emptied that morning.

"Oh, oh, wait," Norah said, putting a hand out to forestall her tidying, "won't you join me?" It was another transgression, and another thrill, though she tried to keep her expression innocent as she peered up at the housekeeper.

Agnes paused, eyes flickering between Norah, and Norah's used teacup hovering above the tray in her right hand. Norah's gaze was caught by her soft inner wrist, the fine blue roots branching down into her hand, up toward the crook of her elbow. Her skin was so pale there as to be translucent and Norah was quite sure that if she looked closely enough she would be able to mark the beat of Agnes's heart at her inner wrist. Her own pulse skipped in kind.

At length, Agnes returned the cup to the side table, and poured two cups, hesitating before taking the fresh one for herself. Norah smiled and took the other, though as the seconds ticked by and Agnes remained standing she had a momentary pang of worry—would this be yet another awkward exchange over food and drink, like her dinners with Barland?

As always, she decided the only way to deal with the awkwardness was to meet it head-on. "Please, sit down, you'll give me a crick." She chuckled, and then, as Agnes slowly lowered herself into the other armchair, carried on. "I've been looking through the almanacs trying to divine the contents of the garden. I had no idea there was such an array of herbs at hand—do you use them in your cooking quite often?"

"Some of them," Agnes said, then, perhaps deciding this was an inadequate response to an honest attempt at conversation, she added, "The garden was planted by my grandmother. When she came to work at the house."

It must have been Agnes's grandmother's journal that Norah had found, perhaps continued by her mother. It reassured her, to think of these undoubtedly equally indomitable women walking the halls, tending the garden. If they too were occasionally plagued by unexplained drawing fits then perhaps her own were less worrisome than she feared. "She must have been quite talented, to nurture so many seedlings in such an inhospitable clime."

"She had a way with the earth. The women of our family always have."

"And she was at the house, then? I mean, your family has been, for some generations?" As soon as she said it Norah regretted it; if the whispers at church had been true then more than just the one side of Gunn's bloodline had been resident at Corrain House for some time.

Sure enough, her companion's dark brows twitched into a slight frown, but she did answer, at least: "My great grandfather died at sea," she said. "His wife and child had nowhere else to go, so they went into service at the house."

The house. The House. It loomed large in Norah's perception, and no more so than in her conversations with Agnes, for there was no other connection they shared but the house. She knew Agnes was literate, of course, but could not ask her what she thought of the latest Wilde or Corelli, for when would she have had time to sit and read for pleasure? Nor could she ask her opinion on music, or craft, or share a choice piece of gossip about the latest society character. No, there was only the house, and its terrible history, and its uncertain future, and balanced on top of it all, their fragile bond. She set her cup aside and folded her hands in her lap. "Tell me about them—the Guinns."

Agnes gave an exhalation of amusement—not quite a chuckle. "Ah, well, they weren't the Guinns then—I was named for my mother's line from way back. Either way though there's not much to tell. We were farmers, then crofters, then fishers, and now there's only me."

"Perhaps it's for the best." Agnes lifted her eyebrows, and Norah shook her head. "I sometimes think that the expectations placed upon us by names—by family—do more harm than good. Perhaps it's better—for both of us— to be free of those expectations. Even if it is a lonely sort of freedom."

"Not to mention remote."

"You can be as lonely in the middle of a busy city as you are in the middle of nowhere."

"Nevertheless 'freedom' is a state that tends to work best when one has opportunities to exercise it. As things stand you are free to eat porridge and walk along a clifftop." Agnes tipped her head. "What of contentment? Dare I say happiness?"

"I have always been under the impression that happiness was a thing to be made, not merely expected," Norah said, reaching for her cup.

"I never said otherwise," came the reply, a note of challenge to it.

"Then I'm glad you agree," Norah said. She took a long sip, meeting Agnes's gaze over the rim of the cup. The housekeeper's eyes were as dark as coal and as hot as embers, and Norah felt an answering heat spark inside her, licking her belly, igniting her cheeks. It was as if they had fallen into a dance, one that she had never been taught and yet whose steps were intimately known to her. She set the cup down with great care, the warmth lingering on her fingertips. "And how do you make your happiness, Agnes Gunn?"

This time it was only one eyebrow that winged upwards. "I curb my expectations."

"That hardly sounds like freedom *or* contentment to me, let alone happiness. Perhaps it's time to try exercising your opportunities." Norah leaned forward, reaching those warm fingers out to alight on Agnes's knee.

Agnes did not look down, and did not move. She did set her teacup aside.

"What opportunities would those be?" she asked. "I'm not in a position to enter into a marriage when I fancy a change of scenery."

This was beyond a challenge: it was a blow. But how could Norah chastise Agnes for overstepping her boundaries with words when she had just done precisely that with a touch? Still, the words stung, and she could not help but think of Peter's letter detailing the aftermath of her departure.

I am worried, and I am afraid.

"You make it sound like some light-hearted whim," Norah said, her voice tight. She snatched her hand back, curling it in her lap like it had been singed. "What else was I to do? Women of my station have nothing that comes without a man's name attached. No happiness, and certainly no freedom. You wouldn't understand, and nor would I expect you to."

"I'm sure you're right, my lady," Gunn said, and the epithet had never felt more punctuated than in that moment. "I should get back to work. Unless there's something else you need?"

From outside came the screech of gulls and the shout of workmen, their calls garbled, oddly filtered by the crashing waves. She was struck with the sudden reminder of how precarious everything was, perched on the crumbling cliffs, the shifting sands and unstable base for this pantomime of a life.

"No. No, there's nothing."

The housekeeper drifted from the room, the only sound to herald her movement the clink of crockery on the tray, and then Norah was alone with the gulls and the watery light through the window once more.

THEY WERE A long way from real mountains in this part of the world, but there was still some higher ground a couple of miles inland. Narrow dirt tracks wound their way up through scattered whin, blooming yolky yellow here and there as it did all year round, though it was far from as fragrant or prolific as it would be in summer.

The high ground had no name on maps, being neither steep nor distinct enough to be considered a hill. Nevertheless the hike was enough to get Norah's blood pumping, and she was out of breath by the time she reached its highest point. Once recovered, Norah struck out along the top of the rise. The map of the estate she found in the library had a little circle marked on it nearby, labelled simply *'Stones'*, and it seemed as good a place as any to aim for. She was headed directly into the low-hanging sun, and so she was almost on the landmark before she saw it: a shallow, round depression in the scrubby grass, perhaps four or five yards in diameter. Stones dotted around its edge—going by the spacings there had once been a dozen or so but there were now only nine, some standing upright, around shoulder height, and others toppled over onto their faces or sunk at an angle into the ground. At the centre of the circle was a final stone, this one large and flat, similar in footprint to a small church altar, though it only reached a bit above her knees. Perhaps it once served a similar purpose: a place of ritual, of worship.

Norah's pulse skipped as she crossed the threshold into the circle. A tiny primordial corner of her mind expected her surroundings to change—a hush to fall, the light to dim. But the sharp spring air still gusted about her, and the sickly sun still glowed above the horizon. The central stone slab was mottled with patches of pale lichen, its surface pitted and uneven. At either end was an approximately circular depression, perhaps an inch or so deep, large enough to cradle a small bowl or beaker. She traced its circumference with a finger. It was rough to the touch, and icy cold. She tried to picture it holding vessels, or burning herbs, or purifying water. What *were* the rituals of those who'd gone before?

She tore her gaze from the altar. One could see for miles from here. From where she stood the estate unfurled on every side in a rippled green-brown blanket, long depressions carved across it in parallel strips: rigs, the scars of centuries of open-field farming. Now the land was bare of anything but grass and shrubs—no waving crops, no tilled fallow earth—only meagre grazing. Here and there the rolling furrows were crawling with sheep; tiny, dirty white forms eating their slow path from field to field. An involuntary shudder snaked up Norah's spine.

There were ruins, too. Stone walls and foundations, even what looked to be most of a house in one spot—save, of course, for its roof. She remembered Agnes's story from the kirk, and the scent of burning licked at her nostrils. In which of these empty stone tombs had Úna Guinn died?

Norah blinked, and as if summoned by the mere thought of her name, a tall, dark blade of a woman seemed to slip out of a cut in Norah's peripheral vision to stand before the altar. Now the sky *did* darken, the shadows growing longer, and Norah's skin pricked as hints of frost began to lick the stone.

The woman—it seemed strange to call her Úna, though Norah knew that was who she must be—raised her hands, and something small and dirty-white materialised between them, struggling, mewling in terror. Norah tried to lurch forward but found herself fixed in place, frozen as she watched the woman—not Agnes, but so like her—lift the offering and place it on the rough stone. It bleated again and Norah was relieved to realise it was a lamb, though the reprieve only made space for a lance of sharp-edged dread as a blade flashed above the altar and then fell, swift as a heartbeat. The lamb's cry twisted, choked with blood, a puddle spreading out from its throat, rivulets creeping across the stone to pool in the basins either side. The woman—*witch*—reached to dip her hands into the hollows until the palms were slick and dark, and when she lifted them again her smile was a slashed throat, a rip in the sky.

The sheep cried again and Norah gasped, but the sound did not come from the still-writhing sacrifice between them but a more distant creature. It was only then that she remembered the weak light filtering through the clouds, the smell of damp grass, the bleating of sheep on the hillside, and when she blinked again the altar was empty and the woman was gone. Unable to help herself, Norah leaned down to press her palms to the basins, remembering the blade, and the blood. She felt a jagged dissonance, the cold rock from before overlaid with a sudden pulse of heat, and she drew her hands back with a gasp. The vision was gone, bled away into nothing, and Norah was alone. Norah had always *been* alone. Her mind had seized on Agnes's stories, desperate for answers, for connection with the house and the land, and conjured fanciful imaginings from them. It wasn't real. She was alone here, and the altar was cold.

All the same, she did not reach out to touch it again. Let it stay empty.

THE SMELL OF *soil is strong in your nostrils, the damp, flat balm of crushed green beneath it—the fields rise before you, furry hummocks that bellow in and out as the earth beneath slumbers. With a sudden great rip the pelt parts, a wound scored in the mud exposing rock that shines as cleanly as bone. Sheep pour from the tear and spread across its flanks like maggots, their flat teeth cropping, cropping, cropping at the grass as the earth beneath them writhes.*

As they do in life the maggots give way to more growth, though the creatures that grow from them are unnatural, spindly legged and strange, crowned with thorns as sharp as blades. They pick their way over the heaving earth, followed by carrion-thieves and slavering predators, their blood pooling out in great spouts when their hide is rent by iron and fire.

And all the while the land suffers, turned by a foreign hand to a purpose it does not recognise. The rocks and soil, the roots and filaments, grow bellicose and restless. The earth is old, and slow to anger, but when it does it will bring fire.

CHAPTER TWELVE

NORAH HAD SPENT weeks guiltily skirting the edge of the village on her walks. There was no obvious reason for it; she had not been forbidden to go there, and the reception she had received during her first visit had not been unfriendly so much as unmoved. Still, every time she turned her steps towards the small hamlet of Corrain she found her path drifting, imagined raindrops or approaching dinnertimes beckoning her elsewhere. The minister's most recent sermon had lingered on the importance of charity, however, in a way that had felt pointed and not a little embarrassing, and so two days later Norah forced herself to head down the long path into the village, a covered plate balanced in her shaky hands.

On her first visit the village had been near-deserted, but she was gratified to see movement between the houses and along the waterfront as she descended. Several people stopped to watch her approach, making her feel all the more awkward as she sidestepped puddles and chunks of rock littering the path.

"Hello," Norah called as she neared the first croft, where a short, compact woman sat on a weathered stone bench. The woman looked reassuringly ordinary—her straight, dark hair was parted down the middle and pulled back into a tight plait, and her woollen dress and nubby jumper looked warm and well-patched. The only piece of jewellery she wore was a plain silver chain with a cross, glinting in the low mid-morning light. "I'm Lady Barland; I've come to properly introduce myself to the people of Corrain."

"Eh, welcome, my lady." The woman nodded to her, not impolitely. "We're not used to seeing people from the house down here."

"Yes, I know. My husband, he's… not well. But I'm sure he'll be glad to know I've been down, as we hope to be good landlords to you all."

Several other villagers had drawn closer during the exchange, their eyes dark and wary; Norah glanced around and offered a hopeful smile. A young boy inched forward, clearly curious about the covered plate she held.

"Oh, yes, of course. Here, I've brought these for you." Her smile tightened as she removed the cloth to reveal a plateful of lumpy, misshapen scones. She knew they were hard as a rock, but the thought of appearing empty-handed had been worse than her embarrassment.

The boy solemnly reached out to take one; in a flash the woman on the bench stood, grabbing his wrist and dragging him back from the plate. He wriggled a little in protest but made no sound. "Did *she* bake them?" she asked, eyes narrowed.

There was only one person 'she' could be. Norah furrowed her brow. "I'm afraid these are my own handiwork." She had thought it would mean something if she had made them with her own two hands, though her baking skills were rudimentary at best.

At this the woman relaxed and released the boy's wrist, letting out a sigh. "That's very generous of you, my lady. Go on," she added to the boy, "you're alright." He reached up with spindly fingers to gather several scones to his chest and then ran off, hopefully to share with others.

"I'll make sure Gunn provides the next batch—they'll be less likely to shatter teeth that way," Norah said with a chuckle, but the other woman shook her head, one hand going to rest just below her throat, fingers brushing her necklace. Something about her manner reminded Norah of something, though the memory was foggy and hard to pinpoint.

"No need for that. The less we get from the likes of her, the better."

Norah was unsure what to say to this, knowing any defence of her housekeeper would only serve to alienate her more. She stayed long enough to be polite, attempting to speak to a few of the locals, who were mostly a taciturn bunch. All the while she chewed over the strange insinuations that swirled around Agnes, wondering what it was that set her so at odds from the people that lived not a stone's throw away. She paused on her trek back, halfway between the village and the house, casting her gaze between them. Agnes's family had hailed from Corrain, or somewhere very like it. What had caused that distance, that distrust?

She made her way to the kitchen upon returning, knowing that she'd find the woman who so occupied her thoughts there. Not for the first time she came upon Agnes knelt before the range, scrubbing away at its interior.

"I've been down to the village," she announced, moving to check the teapot sat on the worn kitchen table. It radiated a faint warmth still, and she turned to retrieve a mug. "I thought it was time to meet more of the tenants."

If she was trying to make Agnes jump with her surprise pronouncement in the way Agnes so often seemed to sneak up on her, she was to be disappointed. The woman just continued to clean, her shoulders shifting in rhythm with the circular motions of her scrubbing. "I gather you also thought it was time to do some baking."

The response was *so* disrespectful that Norah was too shocked to be angry. Even once the utterance had sunk in she found that she wasn't offended, precisely, though her pulse had picked up a little, her cheeks colouring.

"I'm afraid I haven't mastered dough yet," she breezed. "Or the range."

Agnes huffed out a breath, rising to her feet and turning to face Norah in one smooth motion. "If you could warn me next time you plan to pour half the butter in the house into the bottom of the oven I'll order extra in."

Norah's stomach gave a perversely delighted twist at this jab. She had worried that after their encounter in the library, after Norah's daring touch and Agnes's apparent rebuff, that their tentative rapport would be broken, that the housekeeper would retreat into a more appropriate register—quiet, subservient. It seemed that Agnes didn't have it in her to do anything of the sort. Indeed, as the other woman surveyed her now, she fancied there was a new glint to Agnes's eye: a new note of challenge.

She could hear her mother tutting in her ear, urging her to put this insolent servant in her place, to re-establish the boundaries between them. Norah ignored her entirely.

"Apparently they'd prefer my baking to yours, even devoid of butter," she said. "Why don't they like you, in the village?"

Agnes's eyes narrowed. She looked Norah over for a long moment, gaze travelling a leisurely path downwards and back up to meet Norah's. Then she looked away, down to her apron, dusting it off with a wry smile.

"They think I am a witch."

That was what had been niggling at her—the village woman's reticence had put her in mind of the sign of the cross made by the woman who had delivered eggs all those days ago. Norah lifted her eyebrows. "Are you?"

A sharp look. "There's no such thing."

"I might not be much of a baker but I know when a person is avoiding the straightforward answer to a simple question."

"Mm." Agnes pursed her lips, and moved past Norah to pour them both tea, the faint scent of soap and sweat disturbing the air between them.

"It's as I said before," she said, "my mother, her mother, and so on, we've always had a way with plants, with living things. At one time that would get us respect. Nowadays, what with the kirk and the poison from the Barlands and their folk… now it's fear. Suspicion. They think I'm cursed, or have cursed the estate—or both, I don't know."

Norah frowned at this—with every piece that fell into place another gap seemed to appear. "The Barlands? What reason could they have t—" She caught herself, remembering too late the biddies in Thurso. She knew the answer to this one. It had been in front of her eyes every time she saw Agnes and Alexander side-by-side.

Agnes made a face, almost a wince. "I'd gladly have a different father," she said. "But it is what it is."

Another thought struck Norah then: but for a different mother, Agnes would have stood to inherit at least part of the Barland estate. As it was she got nothing, *had* nothing, except backbreaking work and the mistrust of the entire community. "Why don't you leave?" she asked then with a frown. "This house can't hold many good memories."

"I'm needed here." Agnes did not seem minded to expand upon this explanation, and Norah fought a sudden wave of frustration.

There were moments—over porridge breakfasts and quiet cups of tea—that had an air of simple companionship so comfortable, so familiar that they made her heart ache. More than that, Agnes's little flashes of wit—what Mrs Mackenzie would have called insolence or insubordination—gave Norah a quiet thrill, spoke to a meeting of minds and a connection, instant and unspoken, that sat apart from their relationship as housekeeper and mistress.

But those moments—the little quips and ripostes, the companionable silences, the eyes met over china—were fragile. Were they to be spoken of, acknowledged in any way, they would crumble under the weight of propriety. Even a friendship was unthinkable, and so they could not think it—only *be*. And as for those longer, more appraising looks, the touches that lingered just a shade too long on a hand, or a knee… That night at the kirk, standing hand-in-hand, bathing in the aurora as its seeking tendrils wove through the velvet sky, Norah had felt sure that the growing connection she felt, Agnes felt too. The more time passed since that moment though, the less certain she was. And now, trying to catch and tease at the threads of Agnes the woman only to have Agnes the housekeeper reappear, lips pressed, secrets kept...

Norah stood. If Agnes wanted to shut herself away then Norah would not make a fool of herself trying to batter down a closed door. She was done with that, with contorting herself to win scraps of attention and regard. Let the door stay closed. She would find another way.

OVER A WATERY broth that evening Norah observed that her husband was, once again, showing signs of nerves. Far from his desolate mien when she first arrived, he was now almost *too* lively, his smile stretched a little too wide, his questions a little too keen. That being said, his answers, whenever she turned a question to *him*, were distinctly lacking.

"Mister Manson says it would be a great help should we be able to provide a copy of the architect's plans of the house. He could take a survey and draw his own, he says, but to do so would extend the timeline even further, which I'm sure you agree would be less than ideal."

"Er, quite." Barland's Adam's apple bobbed up and down in a nervous gulp. "I'm sure... such a thing can be arranged in good time... the plans, er, they are..."

"I'm sure his Lordship remembers that the architect's plans are kept with the house's title deeds with the family solicitor in Glasgow." Agnes had entered the room silently, as was her wont, two laden plates in hand. Norah inclined her head in acknowledgement, watching Barland's jerky nod. He smiled as well, seemingly cheerful, but the emotion was a shoddy facade on the angular scaffold of his face.

"Of course, yes," he said. "W—I can of course write and request a copy."

Agnes set Norah's plate before her, sweeping up the half-finished soup with practiced ease. The repast was mutton again—one of the sheep from the pasture, perhaps. Norah lifted her fork but only poked at the meat, more intrigued by the palpable tension in the room. She locked her eyes on her husband's face, watching it for every little twitch of discomfort. *Something* was scratching at the back of her mind, something she couldn't quite put her finger on that prompted her next suggestion.

"We could go together to your study this evening, if you like, and I could sit with you while you compose a letter. You seem tired; perhaps I can help."

Barland's mouth loosened to speak, his lips parting, but no words were forthcoming. He swallowed once, twice, blinking rapidly. Norah's curiosity gave way to dread. She could *feel* it suddenly, something dark and desperate within the man before her, something drawn thin and taut, ready to snap.

Agnes spoke. "My lord."

Two words, low and quiet and yet cutting through the air. It was unmistakably not a question but a warning, and it was the last straw.

Abruptly, Barland grabbed his fork, lifting it up to shoulder level in his fist, then propelling it straight down, without hesitation, into his other hand. Time slowed as the tines punctured his pale skin, tearing nearly all the way through in a single impact.

Norah's assumption would have been that such an act would have drawn gouts of blood—the skin pierced and no longer able to contain the fluid, the heart propelling a cascade of crimson in a gush that reached across the table, splashing food and face alike. So it was that her shock was further compounded when the blood slowly welled up, a dark, viscous puddle that dribbled down the sides of his hand and seeped into the snowy tablecloth beneath.

Vaguely she became aware of the activity around her: Agnes was in motion, gathering napkins, approaching Barland with a purposeful stride. Without hesitation she dislodged the fork with one concerted wrench, covering the wound with her fistful of fabric before Norah's gaze could linger any longer on the bloody site. Barland gave a keening cry, one that did not die off into silence but instead began to grow and build until it seemed to be coming from everywhere, pouring from the pitcher and the hearth and the oaken mouths of the Green Men overhead. Norah clapped her hands over her ears, watching with horror as Agnes pulled him from his seat by the elbow, her other hand still clamped over the makeshift bandage.

"Let me go!" She wasn't sure when the howl had resolved into words, but once heard, they could not be ignored. Barland begged as Agnes drew him towards the door, but Norah couldn't shake the feeling that the words were more than just a simple plea to be unhanded.

"Let me go! Please! *Just let me go!*"

Norah was still sitting in her chair when Agnes returned. She had been unable to move, eyes fixed on the dark stain of blood on the tablecloth. The housekeeper began to clear the candlesticks and platters from the table, to better bundle the soiled cloth away, and Norah rose and paced down the length of the table towards her, face pinched with worry. "What was that? What on earth is wrong with him?"

"His hand slipped." It was an obvious lie, of the sort one was meant to simply believe for politeness's sake. It put Norah in mind of her mother describing her father as 'under the weather' when he was clearly suffering the aftermath of a late night's overindulgence in port. The comparison was not endearing.

"That was no slip," Norah insisted, shifting from one foot to the other as Agnes moved from table to sideboard, sideboard to table. "I saw it as clearly as you—it was a deliberate act. Why would he do such a thing?"

"It seems you know better than me, my lady." Agnes's voice was a steel spring: hard and ratcheted tight with frustration, even anger perhaps, at Norah's persistence. Norah knew it all too well, knew she was meant to leave things be, to minimise and ignore. She would not have it.

The table now cleared, Agnes reached to gather up the blood-soaked cloth, intending to bundle it away out of sight—and Norah's questions with it no doubt—but Norah dove to intercept her, grabbing at the stiff linen just as Agnes did, and the two women found themselves elbow to elbow and shoulder to shoulder, the fabric bunched in their fists. Norah felt as well as heard Agnes's long sigh, her shoulders rising and then falling as the air left her lungs in a whoosh.

"He is not well," she said. "I will take care of him. Please, leave it be."

"He is dangerous." Norah remembered the clench of his fingers around her wrist, the dark cavern of his gaze. How long until it was someone else's blood staining the cloth? Her voice shook when she next spoke. "Agnes, he scares me."

Perhaps it was hearing her name on Norah's lips, or the trembling she must surely have been able to feel given their sides were pressed together. But Norah felt her slump a little. She released her grip on the cloth with the hand nearest Norah's, and reached across, and for a moment Norah thought that hand was about to cover her own, but then it came to rest only nearby, flattened on the table. The fingers were stained, dark red scrawling the whorls of her knuckles, inking the outlines of her short nails. "He won't touch you again," she said. How could she conceal so much and yet see right to the heart of Norah in turn? "I promise."

It was all Norah could do not to turn and shelter against her strength, drawing reassurance from her unwavering physical presence as well as her words. The candles flickered behind them, their light barely reaching the middle of the room. The blood on the tablecloth looked nearly black now. "Perhaps he should be sent away. There are hospitals, in Glasgow, where he could receive care, they could—"

"They can't help him." Agnes's interruption was too abrupt and a little too loud, ringing like a glass bell in the long, high room. She straightened, easing the tablecloth from Norah's grip to wrap it up. "I assure you, if he's committed to a sanatorium, he will never leave it, and your position here will become plagued with suspicion and doubt. I assume that is not what you would want. I have taken care of him for many years. Please trust me to know what he needs." She turned at last towards Norah. "Please, trust me," she said again.

Norah nearly laughed; what trust could they have between them, with Agnes obscuring and obfuscating at every turn? But she could not look into the woman's dark eyes without thinking of Barland's, and the resemblance between them. *I have taken care of him for many years.* How long had it been Agnes and Alexander, stuck together in this dark and decaying house— brother and sister, master and servant, afflicted and carer? Who was she to think she knew better, newly come and clearly as likely to make things worse as improve them?

With a shaky sigh she relented, nodding her head. "Of course. He is your… charge. I shall not interfere."

Agnes inclined her head in acknowledgement, or perhaps satisfaction. "Having you here has taken a toll on his composure," she said. "But he will settle, given time."

Perhaps that was what they all needed: time and the chance to acclimatise to the new stresses upon them. Norah swallowed and stepped back, her gaze caught on the crumpled bundle of linen in Agnes's arms. Would it wash out, she wondered, or was it stained forever?

"I will leave you to your work, then. Goodnight, Gunn."

If Agnes was hurt by Norah's retreat to her surname, she did not betray it.

CHAPTER THIRTEEN

YOU ARE ENROBED *by the wind.*

It urges you forward, a steady hand at the small of your back. You reach the edge, and curl your toes over it. You no longer feel the cold. Before you and beneath you only the coal-black sea, the inky starless sky. Is it air or water that fills your lungs with each tidal breath? Are you suspended above the waves, or beneath them? The ground falls away, the air rushes to meet you. The black spindle mast of the shipwreck rises like a fresh spring shoot, and your heart opens to welcome it.

WHEN NORAH GASPED awake her heart was thumping so hard that it took a moment for her to realise that in fact the banging sound was external—heavy footsteps battering along hallways and up stairs. As soon as she could move she was out of bed, pulling on a robe, half-trotting, half-hobbling on sleep-stiff legs to throw open the door of her room just in time to see a heel disappear around the corner. Without hesitation she set off in pursuit, climbing higher in the house than she ever had before, reaching a narrow, cold hallway very much like the one beneath it.

It was MacCulloch ahead of her, his heavy outdoor boots she'd heard echoing like an alarm, and in some corner of her mind she noted footsteps behind her too, but she didn't stop to see. At the end of the corridor, the corner of the house, was a heavy vaulted wooden door, studded, hanging open to reveal the stone spiral staircase beyond: the north-west turret. She could already feel the cold as she climbed, the narrow apertures unglazed and open to the elements. Nevertheless it hit her like a blast as she emerged onto the roof, the air still and yet bitter, cutting right to her marrow.

It was hard to see at first. Even under clear skies and a waxing moon it took a while for the eyes to adjust. Once she did, she could see that there were in fact two figures on the roof. One was MacCulloch, just ahead of her, strangely crouched, creeping.

The other was her husband.

Alexander Barland was dressed as he had been at dinner, though he'd shed his jacket. He was standing not on the narrow walkway that skirted the inside circumference of the roof around the courtyard, but atop the low stone parapet that represented the only barrier between that walkway and the overgrown flagstones below.

Suddenly her feet were ice, rooting her to the cold stone, a statue who could do nothing but watch as MacCulloch inched closer, arms raised for balance. Barland barely seemed to notice he was not alone; his gaze was fixed on the rocky horizon, more alert and alive than Norah had ever seen him. There was fire burning in his eyes, the sheen of madness and hot iron, and Norah's chest clenched in fear and, if she were to admit to it, the slightest hint of anticipation, of elation.

Behind her someone pushed past: Agnes, her dark dress and hair a blot against the steel of the night sky. She stopped on the walkway just ahead of Norah, holding out a hand, palm facing toward her, and Norah felt a minor twinge of affrontery at the clear gesture for her to stay back. Who was Agnes to tell her what to do in such a situation? Fighting past the almost physical weight in her chest, Norah stepped forward.

"Alexander!" The name bubbled up from her throat, still tasting strange and unfamiliar on her tongue, and for a moment he looked as stunned as she felt, turning away from the steep drop to fix that coal-bright gaze on her. It was as if he had run a poker straight through her. His attention caught, Norah tried, "Come away from there. Come back inside with me!"

In front of her, Agnes shuffled forward, and Norah's pulse skipped with renewed anxiety not just for her husband but for the woman now skirting perilously close to the edge in her approach.

"You shouldn't be here," Barland said, his scratchy voice cutting through the cool, calm air right to Norah's ear. And then, lest she miss his meaning. "You should never have come. It's wrong; we were wrong to do this. None of us should be here."

He wasn't even looking at Norah now but at Agnes, who had stopped edging towards him and straightened up. Barland's shirt clung to his rail-thin frame with sweat, his hair wild. He was panting, though his breath barely seemed to disturb the air—unlike Norah's billowing in clouds before her.

"*Enough,*" Agnes said. "*That's enough. Stop this.*" She did not even pretend to couch the instruction in deferential terms, and something in her tone vibrated in Norah's ribcage, as if Agnes's voice was being doubled by a cello or bassoon. In that moment there was no question who answered to whom, and Norah's confusion deepened even as she panicked for the safety of the people before her.

"It needs to end!" He didn't shout—he barely seemed capable—but the words were hoarse and strained. "I see that so clearly now. Can't you? Agnes, please, can't you see that?" He lurched like a pine in a breeze, stretching his arms out to either side like Christ on the cross—he even had the punctured hand, his bandage stained dark where it had soaked through. Norah found that her feet had unfrozen themselves and she started forward, though she could not easily get past Agnes and was obliged to stop at her side.

"Alexander, whatever mistakes you believe you have made, I beg you to come down from there. Come inside with me and… and we'll talk. About all of this."

Something about this seemed to give Alexander a moment of pause. He looked at Norah, seemed to see her there for the first time. "You're so kind," he said, almost too quietly to hear even on this calm night. And then, "I am so sorry." With that he rocked onto his back foot, clearly poised to launch from the parapet.

MacCulloch took this as a signal, making his move. He sprang forward suddenly, closing the gap to wrap his arms around his master before throwing his whole weight backwards. Both men landed on the roof in a tangle. Barland struggled, even landing a punch on MacCulloch's broad jaw, but there was no question of him breaking free.

Agnes was at his side in a moment, helping MacCulloch haul the laird to his feet, half guiding, half dragging him back towards the turret door. Norah was obliged to step out of the way as the trio shuffled past, though as she made to follow along Agnes broke away and caught her arm—cupped her elbow as though helping her just as she had on the rocky, knotted path that first night.

"You should go back to bed," she said. "I'll warm a brandy and bring it up. Just need to lock up here."

Her tone was matter-of-fact, as if the commotion had been nothing more than a loose shutter needing secured, and Norah stared at her, desperate to believe it was nothing more than a misunderstanding. Agnes tugged her inside, gently but without brooking any resistance, and as she listened to the sounds of struggle echoing up the stairwell the spell was broken. The cold seeped into Norah's bones until she felt shot through with ice. She paused as they reached the bottom of the staircase, watching as MacCulloch marched Barland down the long hallway into the shadows.

"Go on," Agnes said, not unkindly. "It's late. I'll go with

him." Norah nodded dutifully and shuffled off towards her own room, descending stairs and corridors that twisted and swirled around her like smoke. By the time she reached her room she felt heavy with fatigue, and she barely paused to shrug off her shawl before crawling back between the sheets. There was little residual warmth left, and she shivered, pulling the blankets more closely around her in an attempt to banish the chill that had crept through her. When she closed her eyes she could still see dim figures lurching before her, hear the croak of her husband's desperate words as sleep rolled over her like a storm.

"You shouldn't be here. You should never have come."

THERE WAS NO cold mug of brandy on the nightstand when Norah awoke—if Agnes had come by she had clearly deigned not to disturb her mistress's fitful slumber. There was instead merely a slip of paper, so small that Norah nearly overlooked it as she sat up and rubbed the crusted sleep from her eyes. It fluttered to the floor as she threw the blankets back and she had to stoop to retrieve it, wincing as her calves protested the movement, and the cold floor beneath her feet. At first Norah took it for a blank scrap, but upon looking closer she saw it bore only three words.

I am sorry.

Three words, and one initial. A sharp, precise 'A.' was inked at the bottom, and as Norah stared at it something came unclasped in her brain, still fuzzy and malleable from sleep.

Ignoring the further aches and protests of her body she leapt to her feet, pulling on stockings and girdle and layers of fabric until she was, more or less, properly attired. With rapid steps she hurried, not to the kitchen, or the dining room, nor to plead at her husband's door, but to the study. Upon opening the door she could not help but gasp; the previously-tidy room had once again been transformed into a state of chaos, with papers strewn over every available surface as if the wind had crept in and blown them about. It made her task that much more difficult, but she set about sorting through them, ignoring the seventy-year-old passenger manifests that had once seemed so mysterious, rifling through the newer documents until she found what she was looking for: a tenancy agreement dated eight years ago, written out by the factor but signed, as she had hoped, by Barland.

The script was quite different, the press of the pen much heavier, and the 'A' in Alexander was elaborately drawn—a far cry from the spartan letter that had adorned the paper in her room.

Norah felt as if the air had been driven from her lungs all at once. Now that it was here before her in stark black ink there was no denying the difference. She reached out to trace the letter, feeling the furrow it had left in the paper, listening to her ears ringing a tinny, high-pitched peal. She had been a fool. The hand that had written the apology, the earlier note in her bedroom, the letters she'd received in Glasgow—was not her husband's.

There was only one person it *could* belong to.

Norah pushed to her feet, knees shaking, and grasped for the back of the nearest chair. She gulped in a breath and let the document flutter to the floor. She did not need proof: the dull pain in her stomach, the ringing in her ears, the prickling heat in her cheeks all served as testaments, her mind at last catching up to a truth her heart had long suspected. Nevertheless, proof she would have, for she knew exactly where to find it.

THE DINING ROOM was empty. Norah was only passing by on her way back downstairs, but she noted as she did that the table was bare of either the performative banquet of her early days at Corrain or the more functional breakfasts she had begun to share with her husband—himself also absent though that came as no surprise. The room had the appearance now almost of an empty stage, a set undressed of its painted flats and furniture and props. It fitted her mood.

That she was drawn towards the kitchen was no surprise; in the house it remained the one chamber absent of strange happenings and nightmarish images. It made the impending confrontation all the more regrettable, as Norah realised that soon she might have no place to escape to, no safe harbour from the rest of her life, but it could not be avoided. She would rather become unmoored than allow herself to be lied to a moment more.

The housekeeper was there, standing at the bunker, sharpening a long knife on a whetstone. The rhythmic scraping rang in Norah's ears and set her heart hammering. She swallowed past the lump in her throat, aware that she blocked the doorway as she stood there working up the courage to speak.

"It's Agnes—the A. It's always been you."

At first, Agnes appeared not to have heard her at all. Metal sang over stone beneath her long, lean fingers, her eyes on her work.

"I don't know what you mean."

"I've seen his writing. But more than that, I've spoken with him, spent time with him. Do you really expect me to believe that man is the same one I corresponded with—the same one with whom I shared intimate details of my life?" Norah's voice was sharp, as keen as the knife in Agnes's grasp. "Do you really take me for such a fool?"

At length, Agnes's hands stilled, and she lifted her gaze to Norah's. Her eyes were dark-rimmed and bloodshot, but steady all the same, still and deep. "What can I do for you, my lady?" It was a carefully modulated version of the question, but Norah parsed it all the same: *What do you want from this? What do you hope to gain here?*

159

"You can tell me the truth! No more deflections, Agnes Gunn: the truth. I deserve that much!"

Agnes's lips twitched at this, twisted into a tiny, mirthless smile. "It is not a question of what you deserve, my lady, but what you will want to hear. What you can bear to know."

"Stop deciding for me what I can and cannot endure." Norah's cheeks were hot, her fingers curled, nails pressed into the soft leather cover of the notebook she clutched. "This house—this *life*—has been nothing but ordeal after ordeal, and yet I am still here, still standing."

"No indeed, no matter what the ordeal you seem determined to endure. If you wish to leave, nobody will prevent you."

If you wish to leave. If only it were that simple. Even in the absence of the threat of scandal, of ruin, of humiliation if Norah returned home—not to mention how her mother would react—there was now the question of the wheels Norah had put into motion here, the home she had begun to build. She had come too far to admit defeat now. Crossing the threshold of the doorway and entering the room, Norah was at Agnes's side in a few short steps, slamming her hand down on the counter, her evidence pinned beneath it, pressed open at the offending pages. No drawings here, the neat botanical illustrations gnarled, feverish sketching safely out of view. Only a series of lists: Latin nomenclature with common names at the side, cooking and steeping times, ingredients with quantities converted for scale, or volume for weight, all in a neat, oh-so-familiar hand, with a cheap dip pen that often split on the downstroke.

"I could not leave Corrain House now even if I wished to," Norah said, and she was surprised to find she was shaking— not with fear, nor cold, but with hot, righteous anger. "But nor can I stay without knowing the truth of the letters that led me here. Will you deny the evidence?"

Agnes's bone-white fingers wound around the knife, and she looked away. She said nothing, moving to the long row of cupboards and opening its appointed drawer. More scraping—soles on flagstone, wood against wood, the sounds of friction, resistance. Norah let out an involuntary gasp of frustration, releasing the book, which immediately flipped back to the page with the rowan tree sketch, as though it had been held open there so often that this was how it naturally laid. This reminder of the twisted rotting heart of Corrain House did nothing to assuage her anger, and she rounded once more on the housekeeper even as Agnes refused to turn her way, staring down into the open knife drawer. "Did he even see the first letter?" Norah pressed. "Did you take dictation before you took it upon yourself to seduce me? *When did the lie begin?*"

Agnes flinched at this—at last, a reaction. "There was no lie in the sentiments expressed," she said quietly. "Nor in the reassurances given. Nor in the warnings. You were told that Alexander Barland was a troubled man. You were begged not to throw in your lot with him as an escape."

"And yet he said he admired me. Looked forward to my missives. Did he even read them?"

The drawer growled and snapped shut. "What do you think?"

"How could you?" Norah longed to grab one of the skillets that hung just out of reach and clatter it against the table, the floor, anything to drive home the depths of her ire. "How *could* you? You made me believe I was wanted here, that I could find a home!"

Agnes spread her hands on the counter in front of her, shoulders slightly hunched as though bracing for a whip. "I tried to warn you. It could have been just letters. It was never meant to be anything more than letters."

"Whatever your intentions, I am here now!" Another step and Norah stood behind Agnes, close enough to drag her fingertips down the rough wool of her dress. "You brought me here, to this house." The rhythm of her heartbeat was a drum, anger mixed with something headier to flush her cheeks and catch her breath.

"I am sorry." Agnes turned, suddenly far too close. Norah felt her breath on her cheek—oats, milk, tea. She went on in a murmur, looking anywhere but directly at Norah. "We can find a way for you to return home without scandal. A story. An illness, perhaps." Her tone was at once entirely flat and utterly wretched. Now Norah did reach for her, curling her fingers into the waistband of her apron, hooking to her like burdock.

"You say you are sorry, but I don't want your apology," she said, her eyes only on Agnes. "I am not ill, and I will not go. But I cannot—will not—stay in this house alone."

She felt as well as heard Agnes's chest fill and empty with a shaky lungful of air. Finally, she met Norah's gaze. Her eyes were a sky full of stars. "I fear I misunderstand you, my lady." It could have been a warning, or even a rebuke, were it not for the gentle touch of fingertips on Norah's arm, the tiniest catch to her voice, usually a song and now barely above a whisper.

Suddenly Norah's anger was gone, replaced with a great yawning need that only Agnes could abate. She had convinced herself that her affections were one-sided, but the tremble in the other woman's touch spoke of repressed reciprocation, and more—a mirrored urgency, a twinned hunger. Norah kissed her then, pressed close, desperate to forget the betrayal, the late-night panic, the isolation—desperate to fill her senses with nothing but Agnes.

It was an awkward thing, at first, a moment of colliding noses and teeth, but with the tip of a head, a cupped jaw, they found their fit. Agnes kissed like she was drowning, deeply, open mouthed, drawing back only to suck in a fresh supply of air. Norah could barely countenance even that much distance between them, shifting her lips in those moments to press against Agnes's angular jaw and the hollow of her throat.

Strong, cool fingers combed through her hair, raked across the nape of her neck, clutched for purchase at her waistline, at length anchoring there to push them apart.

Agnes surveyed her from beneath dark, furrowed brows as a cornered animal might its hunter: wary, intent. She said nothing. Norah opened her mouth to speak, but found no words ready for the moment. What she had to convey to Agnes was greater than any statement, more urgent than any vow. Before she could gather her wits Agnes released her grip on Norah's hips, and slid out from where she was pinned against the rough wooden bench. She fled through the kitchen's back door to the pantries and storage rooms, where Norah dared not follow.

Chapter Fourteen

That was the day of the first accident.

Progress on the underpinning was painfully slow. Sometimes whole days were lost to high winds, the tides, or repairing the damage to the scaffold from said elements. The day after what Norah could only bear to think of as 'the roof' was deathly still, and Manson had assembled his whole crew that morning in the hopes of making some proper headway. Desperately in need of distraction, Norah walked out to see the work, wrapped tight against the chill air and still burning with unspent ardour.

It was gratifying to see the full cohort at work, and a reminder of the true strength of human ingenuity and industry. Together the sweat-lashed men heaved and secured the enormous timber props to support the corner of the foundations while they were excavated for reinforcement, a cavity slowly opening up on the cliffside as they removed earth and loose rock, to be replaced with cut stone and mortar. It was no easy work—each prop was at least twice the size of a man, and much heavier besides—but with the clever use of ramps and pulleys the heavy beams were swung into place. There was a growing pile of rubble on the beach itself, and a few men toiled at whisking it away in handcarts, labouring twice as hard in the shifting sand.

One of the men spotted her and paused in his efforts to wave a hand at her; Norah smiled and lifted a palm in his direction. It must be Davey, happy to see her even if Manson was not. He turned back to his work, and Norah felt a fleeting regret that he would not come down to speak with her. But then, even though his time was hers, in effect, it was better spent at these tasks than reassuring her about their progress.

Though she had intended this as a diversion, even the industrious endeavours of the crew could not keep Norah's thoughts from drifting to Agnes Gunn. She had never before seen the woman looking anything other than poised and composed, and so the memory of her from that morning—desperate, tousled, her pale cheeks stained with heat—could not be escaped.

Shaking herself from her reverie, Norah returned to the house, settling herself in the library secure in the knowledge that the work occurring directly beneath her would soon yield its rewards. The harrowing events of the night before, the electrifying yet confusing encounter with Agnes in the kitchen that morning, all floated at the back of her consciousness, overlaid and muffled by the heartfelt belief that Things Would Be Alright. She had the power to fix what was broken—first, the house itself, and before long, the people within it.

The longer she sat, however, the more the echoes drifted up to haunt her: Barland's desolate cries on the parapet of the house, Agnes's cold and seeking fingers across her scalp. She could not concentrate on her books; the library began to feel close, the fire roaring merrily until the air itself licked her skin with its heat. Norah began to perspire, the droplets plastering her hair to her forehead in sticky strings and dampening the fabric beneath her arms. She felt like she had just run full-pelt up the hill from the beach instead of sitting staidly in her armchair; her pulse was quick and panicked.

Desperate to banish this sudden flush, Norah lurched from her chair over to the window, all but covered by the heavy curtains. She jerked them back and dug her fingers into the frame, leaning all her weight into it as she struggled to push it upwards. For a moment it resisted and she fretted that the frame may have swollen fast, but then it inched open, slowly at first, and then all at once, the panes rattling as they shot up. Norah nearly fell against it, and half-arrested the movement until she was hanging out the window, the cold air instantly chilling her sweat-soaked skin. She could hear the cries of the gulls that wheeled overhead whenever the men were at work, eager to pick off any worms they unearthed, and the occasional banging or shouted instruction from the workers themselves.

The sounds of life were almost comforting until the scream came: a sudden howl of pain that cut through the wind and the bird cries straight to Norah's very marrow.

She clutched the sill with both hands, frozen, listening as the cliff below blossomed with shouts and further cries of agony to mingle with the gullsound. It was impossible to know what was happening, but one thing was certain: something was very wrong.

When she could take no more Norah peeled herself away from the window, hurrying towards the library door, pursued by the inarticulate screams of the men and gulls. She had reached the large stair that led down to the main hall when Agnes headed her off, coming up the stairs as she descended. She met Norah headlong, catching her upper arms to still her.

"My lady."

"Did you—"

"I heard—MacCulloch has gone to find out what's happened."

"We ought to send him for the doctor," Norah said, peering wildly over Agnes's shoulder as if the catastrophe might manifest right there on the stairs. "The sound, it wasn't—they need help!"

"We'll find out what happened first." Agnes lifted on tiptoes to bring herself closer to eye level with Norah from her lower step. She frowned. "Let's get you some tea," she said, giving Norah's arms a little squeeze. Norah managed a nod, allowing the housekeeper to guide her towards the kitchen as she continued to strain for any sound from outside. The thick walls of the house wrapped around them until all she could hear was the muffled sound of their footsteps on the rug. Indeed everything felt muted, suddenly, numb, as though the scream had stilled the whole world.

By the time the tea was brewed and poured, MacCulloch had returned, with Davey. Norah's momentarily lifted spirits at a familiar, friendly face were soon quashed by the worry etched on the young man's face.

"One of the lads—Fraser Stevenson—he caught his leg on something, ended up hanging," Davey said, a set to his mouth that suggested he'd witnessed the moment in question. "It's broken for sure. We've splinted it, but he'll need to see a doctor."

"Of course," Norah said, standing so abruptly that her tea sloshed over the side of her cup. It was hot enough that her skin began to smart immediately, but she pushed aside the sensation to focus on the workman's ruddy face. She felt guilty relief that the injured man wasn't Davey himself—selfishly she could not stomach the idea of the one friendly face in her day twisted in pain. "MacCulloch will drive him to Thurso, we'll get the carriage ready right away. Is he—is there more? It sounded... I've never heard a sound like that."

Davey hesitated before stepping a little closer, and for a moment it seemed like he might have a response to this, but then he glanced around, his attention diverted by the arrival in the kitchen of Manson, the foreman, looking grim and sweaty. "No need for any excursions to Thurso," he said—apparently he had heard Norah's last words through the open door. "The boy's from Reay. We'll take him home and the doctor will come to him there. I'll take him myself—we're done for the day anyway. Tide's coming in."

Norah became vaguely aware of a background murmur. Over by the stoves at the other end of the kitchen, MacCulloch was talking to Agnes. He loomed close, head bowed, and as

Norah watched he took hold of Agnes's arm. She shrugged it off immediately, but it was enough to send a bolt of visceral anger through Norah. How *dare* he touch her uninvited? Cheeks burning, she dragged her attention back to Manson, who was now speaking with uncharacteristic fervour.

"—be doing this, it's a fool's errand to fight against the elements like this. You'd be better off moving the house back from the cliff, stone by stone, than going from beneath."

"I'm sorry for the harm that's come to Mister Stevenson, sir, but you must know what a preposterous suggestion that is," Norah said, her irritation at MacCulloch creeping into her voice.

Manson seemed unsure what to say to this response to what had obviously been a jest on his part. His mouth flattened to a line. "Well, that's us down three men now," he said. "I'll do my best to replace them."

"Three, why three?" Norah was vaguely aware that MacCulloch and Agnes had stopped talking and were now watching her conversation, but she refused to let herself look their way, instead looking between Manson and Davey, who would not quite meet her eyes but at least did not look displeased with her.

"John Black and Graham MacInnes won't come back. They saw the accident, claim there's… something under the house."

"Surely they knew the conditions would be difficult when they signed onto the job."

The foreman's greying brows drew together into a confused frown. "Aye, they did at that," he said. "Nevertheless, they're not coming back."

"Well then you must hire more," Norah said, and ignored the fact that she sounded like a petulant child. "Or if you cannot find any locals willing, I will have the laird write to his factor in Glasgow and we will bring men to us. Surely it cannot be difficult to locate a few young, fit men for a few weeks' work!"

"I said I'll do my best, my lady," Manson replied, glancing to one side and then the other, clearly looking for an exit to the conversation. Norah huffed out a sigh and tried to arrange her features into a more sympathetic expression.

"Please, go attend to your man. Give him my best wishes for a quick recovery—MacCulloch will help you with his transport."

"Oh, before you go," Agnes cut in, and she moved over to one of the kitchen drawers. Norah caught a flash of a series of bags and tins and a slim wooden box within before she withdrew a tiny brown glass bottle, which she handed to Manson. "It'll help," she said, "with the pain. 'Til you can get the doctor to him."

Davey glanced back at Norah one last time, shooting her an apologetic smile before following Manson out.

It felt to Norah as though MacCulloch dragged his feet exiting the kitchen to leave Norah once more alone with Agnes. It was the housekeeper who broke the silence that followed.

"Would you like anything to eat with your tea?"

Norah shook her head, sinking back onto the bench and reaching for her cup. She couldn't quite banish the memory of Davey's face, the trepidation that had contorted it as he had reported the incident. "What do you think he meant, that there was something under the house?" she said, looking up at Agnes.

The other woman pulled her thin lower lip between her teeth to chew it for a moment, surveying Norah through narrowed eyes. Then she sat down also, across the table from Norah. "MacCulloch said the lad—Stevenson—claims a root moved and caught him, says that's how his leg was trapped. I imagine the others heard him."

"A root? But that's imp—" Norah swallowed the word, tasting damp and bark. The sudden, looming figure of the rowan tree overlaid her vision until it dimmed the merry glow of the hearth. But that tree couldn't have roots that deep or reaching.

Agnes lifted one shoulder in an almost-shrug. "Probably his foot caught on one of the beams or a bit of rock, and he panicked. They're all spooked—folk are superstitious up here. The tide, the height, the weather… they'll be telling themselves all sorts of stories."

Norah nodded mutely, her tongue still tangled and heavy. Stories, only stories. She lifted her cup in the hopes that tea would loosen the snarl, a familiar citrus tang slipping down her throat. She forced herself to breathe deeply between sips, until the rowan was not a looming spectre but merely a tree, crooked and dying.

"This has all been quite taxing. I think I'll go to my room, to rest."

Agnes tipped her head to one side. "Would you like your food brought to you there?"

"Perhaps… yes," Norah said, with a half-hearted nod. "Yes, just for today."

It was some time later that Norah felt well enough to leave her room; what light was left outside was rapidly fading, sending her rooms into shadow. Rather than fuss with candles and hearths she gathered herself and made her way downstairs, hoping she might find Agnes and a measure of comfort—or distraction.

Unfortunately, the first person she encountered was the last one she wanted to see: MacCulloch, who she had last seen muttering to Agnes in a vaguely threatening manner. Norah spotted a small stack of papers in his hand, and on a hunch, cleared her throat, causing him to pause on his way down the corridor, presumably heading for the office.

"Is that the post?"

MacCulloch lifted his broad chin in confirmation. Never one to stand on ceremony with servants, Norah was nonetheless irked by his manner. Still, she tamped it down. "I'll take it," she said, holding out a hand, but the groundskeeper made no move to hand it over.

"There's nothing for you the day."

Another wave of irritation. "MacCulloch, when I ask for something as simple as the household correspondence, I don't expect an argument. My husband is not well, as you know, and not to be disturbed. If there's something he needs to see urgently I'll ensure he gets it."

The man's sandy eyebrows winged upwards, but he gave a shrug, and handed Norah the handful of letters. "You'll find there's trouble getting any more men on the crew, after this," he said, taking a step closer, the lamps casting his shadow long across her path.

"After the collapse? Surely these accidents happen all the time," she replied. "We're paying a fair rate, besides."

"It taks more than the promise of a bit of cash to make a man go where he's not wanted," MacCulloch said portentously. "The stories'll spread now—by the end of the week half the coastline'll have heard, and they'll be thinking it's not the first time something strange has happened up at Corrain House."

Norah frowned, shuffling the letters in her hands as if she could tidy her thoughts just as easily. "You've clearly heard these stories, and you're still here."

"Aye, well. I'm not easy to frighten." The look he gave her was unreadable, but it made Norah shiver just the same. "Not when the reward for staying is so high."

"Mm. I'm glad you agree our wages are fair. Thank you for these," she added, waving the letters between them. "I'll let you be on your way." With that she turned and headed back to her rooms, ignoring the feeling of his gaze on her back.

The hearth was banked when Norah entered, and her first act was to kneel down before it and stoke it to a merry flicker. Slowly the heat began to spread, taking the edge off the chill in the room. She retrieved that day's mail from the side table she had set it on, opening and checking each without ceremony. She tamped down the slight twinge of guilt at each broken seal: after all, it would not be the first time letters had been intercepted in this house, and she was only trying to help. One letter, though addressed to her husband like the rest, was in fact pertaining to the works on the cliff— an invoice for the erection of the scaffold, the cost of which made Norah gasp aloud. Another two missives were receipts for bills paid for food and wine, which Norah barely looked at—in particular she had little interest in seeing how much wine she had consumed more or less singlehandedly in recent weeks.

The fourth and final letter was from a man named Evander Fenwick, who Norah recalled from her search of the study to be the factor for the Corrain estate, responsible for managing what little activity took place on the land beyond maintaining the house itself. Fenwick painted a dry and rather dire picture of the estate's accounts: as Norah had suspected, it ran at a considerable loss, requiring a steady supplement from the Barland fortune. Though the situation sounded sustainable enough in practice, it clearly ate at Fenwick in principle, and he wrote—not for the first time by the sounds of it—to urge Barland to grant permission to secure new contracts with sheep farmers.

Though sheep are admittedly not as profitable as they once were, there is a well-established Borders shepherd of my acquaintance who is still going strong and who has several times expressed to me his interest in securing a fresh tract of grazing land. I would be very glad to negotiate a good rent on your behalf. Further to that, I urge you to reconsider your decision to allow the leases from the farmers currently using the Corrain pastures to run their course without renewal. In the absence of good terrain for deer stalking, it's my belief sheep are the only potential enterprise that can rejuvenate the estate's finances and allow you to break even—particularly given your recent decision to pour funds into the structural work on the house.

Norah frowned down at the letter. Why would Barland be so determined to allow the Corrain estate to ail in this way? All assuming, of course, it was *Barland* with whom Fenwick was corresponding... Once the thought occurred, it was impossible to shake. Agnes had been the only person Norah had seen dealing with accounts relating to the work crew. Agnes obviously had access to the Barland letterhead and seal.

And Norah had *watched* Alexander defer to Agnes on matters of the estate.

So that was it. Not only had Agnes written to Norah masquerading as the baron, she was running the estate accounts foreby—and apparently running it into the ground. In spite of herself, she stole a glance behind her at her own strewn correspondence from Corrain House, and a wild temper rose in her throat, pulled her to her feet, propelled her to the dresser. It was the work of a moment to grab a handful of paper and return to the fire with it, but as she stood over the flames, the random selection of pages crumpled in her first, the heat seemed to sap the anger back out of her, to replace it with something decidedly more complicated. One of those tell-tale 'A's caught her eye and she sank to her knees right there on the hearth rug, smoothing the missive out on the floor. It was the very last letter—a short one.

Corrain House
Tuesday, February 4th, 1890

Dearest Norah,
By the time you read this you will be packing to leave—if indeed you even receive it in time. I hope you and your mother are both in good health and spirits.

The house is readied for your arrival. It is a rather bleak outlook in winter, I regret to say, though once in a while there are crisp, fresh days with clear skies as blue as you've ever seen that make the endless grey easier to bear. I am both eager to see you in flesh for the first time and, I must confess, trepidatious. More than once I have wanted to write urging you to call this off, all of it, and yet I have not the courage to do so myself, my better judgement defeated again and again by my selfish need to have you here with me. I fear you will one day look back on these letters and wish I had been braver. But there it is.

Please know that whatever you may think of the man you meet in the coming days, no matter how quiet and reserved he may appear at first, you are very much desired.

Ever yours,
A

These past weeks that final epistle had gnawed at Norah. Why had she not heard the alarm bells in its every line? Why had she not heeded the warning, taken this final chance to call everything off? Reading it again now, something else began to work upon her.

There was no lie in the sentiments expressed.

Whatever you may think of the man you meet… you are very much desired.

A

She closed her eyes tightly against a sudden rush of sense memory—strong fingers digging into her hips, cool lips pressed hard against hers.

She did not burn the letters.

CHAPTER FIFTEEN

THERE WAS NO wind, and yet somehow the scent of smouldering wood floated in the air.

The night air was calm and yet cold enough to bite, the flagstone walkway searing her bare feet. The sea rushed in her ears, her chapped lips sticky with salt even up here. Alexander's plaintive, desperate howling echoed in her ears, even though she was alone on the roof, standing not on the edge but near it, looking down.

The rowan was some way below and yet she could see every crack, every shadowed groove writhing on its bark. It was a grasping mass of tentacles. It was a twisted nest of dead branches. Its darkness defied perspective, denied the eye any sense for distance, its snaking black tendrils at once far and near, as distant as the stars and yet close enough to pierce her flesh.

The smell of woodsmoke filled her nostrils now, her every sense overwhelmed: the burning, the salt, the rushing tide, the black, black tree. There was shouting, too, far off, her name, over and over.

"*Norah*."

Agnes's grip was firm on her arms, shaking her to her senses, and yet as she woke Norah found that the dream would not shift: no warmth seeped back into her chilled extremities; no lamplight mellowed the silver glow.

"Agnes?"

"What in *Hell's name* are you doing here?" Agnes was dragging her now, stumbling, away from the edge, one arm around her beneath her armpits as though supporting a drunkard to stand. "How did you even get up here? I locked it last night!"

"I…" Norah trailed off, distracted by Agnes's presence, the cold seeping into the soles of her feet, the acrid bite of woodsmoke in the back of her throat. How *had* she come to be here? She unfurled her fingers but there was no key gripped there, only the pale lines of her palm and the reddish half-moons left there by her nails. She raised her gaze to Agnes's face, the housekeeper's harsh expression split with concern. "I don't know," Norah muttered, swaying on her feet. "I don't remember. I was dreaming, and then I was here."

Agnes's eyes flitted back and forth across Norah's features as though she could discern some extra information from them, but soon pulled back and took Norah's hand. "Let's get you back to bed."

By the time they reached her bedroom Norah felt more grounded, though that only meant the strange sensations that lingered in her memory felt all the more twisted and disturbing. Dream bled into reality, and detachment became agitation. She shivered as Agnes led her to her bed, and as the other woman pulled down the coverlet she shook her head. "No, not yet. I need… I need…" She began to pace the room, arms wrapped tight round her middle. What she needed was answers, but was Agnes able—or willing—to provide them? "This house," she tried again, "that tree. There must be more to them. Something to explain the dreams."

"It's been a strange day," Agnes said, heading Norah off as she went for another turn of the room, reaching to ease her arms loose. "Get some rest. I'll bring you some tea."

"No, I don't want to rest, I want to understand what is going on!" Norah flailed ineffectually, her hands coming to clutch at Agnes's dress front. "Please, Agnes… is it going to happen to me?"

Agnes frowned. "I don't know what you mean."

"The… malady that has afflicted Alexander, that drove him to the roof—what if it's affecting me too?" Norah's throat clenched, as if now that she had voiced the fear she could speak nothing else.

"That will not happen."

"Then tell me! Tell me what's lurking under the house, the tree… you've been here for so long, you must know what's down there…"

"My lady, no, it's late—you have everything confused—"

"Don't you dare 'my lady' me, Agnes, *talk* to me, I need—"

Agnes cut her off then not with words but with a kiss, sudden and yet so sure, so definitive that it brooked no argument. She tasted sleep-sour at first and a tiny, blurry corner of Norah's mind wondered: how *had* Agnes known to come find her on the roof? How had she even known she had left her own bed? But as much as she wanted to pull away and demand an answer—answers to everything—the kiss sparked an outpouring of heat that banished Norah's chill in the way no pan-warmed sheets could, of need that filled every part of her, pushing back even the questions that had seemed urgent seconds before. Agnes kissed her, and kissed her, and Norah kissed her back, and they did not stop.

IN THE MINUTES where Norah's mind navigated that narrow, winding path from sleep into waking it was difficult to say *which* of the events of the night before had actually happened, if any. The bite of cold stone on bare feet, the yawning, bottomless darkness of the rowan tree. And then, after, warm lips on hers, the delicious rake of short nails down her smooth spine, calloused palms over soft thighs. She was alone now, of course, but that slight unmistakable ache, the scent that clung to the sheets, the fact she was clad in nothing at all beneath the covers, spoke to the fact that at least the second half of the night's memories were very real indeed.

She chose to focus on that, pushing her misgivings aside in favour of luxuriating in the feeling of—if not being loved, at least being *wanted*, and quite desperately, if Agnes's seeking lips and desperate touches were to be believed. They had not spoken any further that night, and Agnes had departed before Norah woke, but she still felt the other woman's presence there now, in the careful drape of the blanket over her body, the way her nightgown had been folded neatly after being strewn across the floor in hungry abandon.

Eventually she rose and readied herself for the day; to tame her hair took some doing, and her cheeks shone with high colour that would have had her mother tutting in disapproval. Were the roses in her cheeks from remembrances of the night before, or ruddy evidence of her excursion on the roof? No—no. Dreams did not bring on fevers.

Today was a new day, and Norah had a new mission. She had seen neither hide nor hair of her husband since the roof two nights before. If Agnes was to be believed, he would be sedated in his room, for his own good, as well as that of the household. Though Norah flirted with the idea of divorcing herself from any responsibility for her husband and his wellbeing, she could not in good conscience allow herself to ignore him completely. She was the mistress of this house, and she would carry out her duties accordingly.

She knew approximately where his bedchambers were: further into the bowels of the house, down a dark corridor flanked with dark paintings and dark wallpaper. Despite her newfound resolve it took a concerted effort to force herself down the hallway, every fibre of her being rebelling against the feeling of being swallowed by the seemingly endless passage.

When she reached the door she found it ajar, and upon pushing it open was surprised to find the room far less oppressive than she feared. It was large—larger than her own, though that was not unexpected—and had the benefit of several tall windows, each of which had been uncovered enough to let slices of watery light filter in. The faint smell of musty linens and sleep mingled with the fresh scent of herbs and carbolic soap, a stale but not wholly unpleasant perfume.

A figure sat by the unlit fire: Barland, dressed, albeit in his shirtsleeves. A cup sat unattended at his elbow. He did not react to her entrance; indeed Norah wasn't entirely certain he'd even seen her. His entire mien was cadaverous, dark shadows pooling under his eyes and in the hollows of his cheeks.

She hesitated; she could still turn away, depart to the library and pretend she had never come. She was clearly excused from any wifely duties, after all, and doubted her presence would make much difference at all to his near-somnolent state. Indeed, if his last chilling words were to be believed, he would prefer she had never come to Corrain House at all.

And yet. Putting aside the obligations of a married woman, forgetting what was polite and proper, how could she countenance leaving him here alone in the dust and silence? He had been party to her deception, yes, and his behaviour had swung erratically from disinterested to manic, but even a man as unwell as Lord Barland deserved compassion. Perhaps especially him. Norah ran her hands down her front and straightened her spine.

"Well," she said, assuming he would not register the distinctly forced nature of her cheerfulness, "here's where you've been hiding away. I hope you'll forgive the intrusion." He said nothing, eyes fixed on a spot several centimetres from the mantelshelf, and maintained his dead-eyed gaze even as she moved closer and then knelt close to his feet. An apron would have been a boon just then, but she managed to shovel the coal into the hearth and coax a small fire from it without soiling her skirts too badly.

There was little else in the room to provide distraction, but she was pleased—and relieved—to find a well-thumbed Thomas Hardy novel tucked away on a shelf after some searching. There was only one armchair in the room, but she dragged the padded bench from the foot of the bed closer to the fire and settled herself on it quite comfortably. "I'll start from the beginning, shall I?"

There was no answer, and so she began to read.

Never before had the sound of her own voice seemed so loud and intrusive. She was used to the sounds of life dampening her own contributions: the clink of crockery, the settling of furniture, the flutter of a fan. Aside from the low crackle of the fire and the occasional flick of pages, there was nothing in this room that moved, nothing that broke the silence. Norah found herself growing louder and louder, as if trying to fill the space with noise, but it only bounced off the walls and came back to her warped and off-putting, until she had no choice but to drop into a murmur. Barland didn't remark either way. Eventually she stopped reading aloud altogether, sitting in what she hoped was a companionable silence while her eyes skimmed the page. Every so often she would sneak a glance at her husband, who continued to occupy his chair with a quiescence the envy of any statue.

It wasn't just his stillness that gave him the air of a marble simulacrum; his skin was washed out, pale, and Norah couldn't help but remember the portrait of the Ninth Baron with its ruddy cheeks and keen amber eyes. There was a man who no doubt had walked every inch of his land, assessing its potential, planning how best to make use of the acreage afforded to him. Had Alexander ever cast an eye over the land of Corrain? Or had he turned those duties over to Agnes early, preferring to sit inside, hiding from the stark but arresting landscape around them?

A rasping near the doorway tore the silence and snagged Norah's attention, though when she looked over there was nothing to see. Though it had almost sounded like the dragging of heavy footsteps, the only person it might be was Agnes, and Norah knew the housekeeper's step was so light as to be almost undetectable at times. Not only that, but it had sounded as if it had come from inside the room, though the door was still pulled to, just as she had left it after entering. Had it been the wind, or the shifting of an old house? Surely that, and nothing more. If only she could convince her body of this certainty. She looked back to the book in her lap, the back of her neck prickling with the sensation that they were no longer alone. Worse still, Barland seemed disquieted, his dark eyes darting about the room as if searching for—for what?

"What is it?" Norah murmured, setting the book aside and turning to take in his agitated demeanour. Though it should have reassured her that he had heard it too—that she was not going mad—she was anything but. Barland looked to her, and his thin lips trembled, halfway between a plea and a grimace. "Don't worry," Norah said then, reaching over to take his hand, feeling the rustle of the bandage beneath her palm. She kept her eyes on his face. She would not allow her gaze to be drawn to the deepening shadows spreading around his head, the dark antlers of the stag. "I'm here."

The rasping continued, quieter now, and the scent of pine and loam crept through the room. At first it was almost pleasant, but then a darker aroma took hold, a rotten note like meat left too long untouched. She held onto his hand tightly, her other hand going to cover her nose, and to her surprise he turned his palm upward to squeeze back. Something unclenched within Norah, and she gave him a tight smile before slipping her hand from his and rising to her feet.

"Well. Perhaps it is a bit stuffy in here, don't you agree?" She began to stride about the room, pulling the curtains open and then muscling the sashes upwards until there was a whiff of fresh air circulating. It was cold, too cold, really, but it smelled fresh, of salt and the sea, and banished the stench of dirt and decay that had saturated the room. Norah didn't stop there, but opened the door wide as well to encourage the breeze through, and then retrieved a blanket from the end of the bed, draping it across Barland's knees and tucking it tightly. He cast a look up at her, and though she still found him difficult to read, she thought he looked grateful. After stoking the fire hotter with a fresh application of coals, she seated herself again and took a deep breath. Nothing but fresh sea air met her nostrils, and the faint cry of gulls reached her ears.

Agnes, generally able to affect an impassive demeanour in the face of most occurrences, could not hide her surprise when she entered the room with a tray at around midday to find Norah there by the fire with her husband, the room alive with a biting sea breeze.

"My lady. I assumed perhaps you were out walking," Agnes said, moving to shut the windows and the curtains without a rebuke. "You haven't eaten."

It wasn't a question, but Norah shook her head anyway. She hadn't, and as the words were spoken her empty stomach floated suddenly to the front of her awareness. She glanced at Gunn's tray: A bowl of porridge and a glass of water. Apparently Barland had spartan tastes indeed.

"I can bring something up to you here? Unless you'd like to accompany me back?"

"I'll come with you," Norah said, setting the book aside. She was content that the presence, whatever it had been, was gone. "Goodbye, Alexander," she said, rising from the bench. "I will see you on the morrow, if you are amenable." He nodded once, and it felt like the closest thing to a connection they had shared yet.

"There's more porridge," Agnes said as they neared the kitchen, "or there's a broth and some fresh bread." She had not looked Norah's way once as they made their way across the house, as though she was Orpheus and Norah her

Eurydice. Norah longed for a glance, a touch, but knew it was a foolish hope; even in a house as empty as this there were still rules to be followed, propriety to observe.

Norah would have been surprised to be met with the same open affection she had received from Isa; she could not imagine Agnes folding the soft curls of Norah's mousy hair around her cold fingers, or giggling whispers of adoration as they traversed from one room to another in search of entertainment, but this taciturn neglect was like a slap to the face. Had the *entire* night been a dream—not just the roof but what had felt so very real, so very *true* between them?

She murmured a request for the broth and bread, and was served a bowl at the kitchen table. The sweet, mealy aroma of the bread banished the twist in her stomach, and she fell upon the meal without hesitation.

Agnes took a seat opposite her with her own bowl, and the two ate in what felt to Norah like a tense, strained quiet. It was only when she dared to look up from her bowl to find Agnes watching her, eyes dark with something akin to possession, that she knew the silence was not borne of indifference.

Suddenly Norah was thrown back to the night before: Agnes's lips on hers, Agnes bearing her down to the bed, Agnes's nimble fingers picking apart her corset and chemise until her bare flesh puckered in the cold of the room. And then there was heat, and release, and it hadn't been tender, but it had been exactly what Norah had needed. Agnes's eyes stoked that same need in her now, and it was all Norah could do to finish her broth, the sound of the spoon along the bottom of the bowl a rough scrape across her senses.

"Will you be in the library this afternoon? I haven't lit the fire yet."

"I thought I'd walk down to see the work; I'm sure it will be warm by the time I return."

Norah recalled MacCulloch's condescension when she'd told him she was headed along the beach that day in Corrain, and braced herself to be warned about the tides. But Agnes only nodded. "It's just Manson and two others today," she said. "I think he gave the other lads a day to pull themselves together."

"I hope it won't delay progress too much," Norah said, frowning. As with every time she contemplated the restoration project's failure, her pulse began to hammer in her throat. "We can't afford to waste time."

Agnes tipped her head to the side. "Why such urgency? The props should hold strong for as long as it takes."

Norah swallowed, her throat suddenly dry as ash. "The cost… we cannot afford to pay for all this labour indefinitely," she croaked.

A raised eyebrow. "Perhaps—though a few weeks are neither here nor there."

Norah bridled; she needed no reminder that Agnes knew the accounts of the house inside and out. How long had she been managing them? How long had it been her hand on the pen, controlling the fate of Corrain House and the people tied to it? In that moment Norah took a decision she'd been mulling in the back of her mind ever since she'd read the letter from the factor.

"Evander Fenwick wrote to Alexander a few days ago," she said, "urging him to lease out more pasture, and to renew the contracts we have."

A second eyebrow lifted to join the first, though Agnes's face was otherwise impassive. "Did he, aye? First I've heard of it."

"I intercepted Alexander's mail since he is indisposed. Since I'm his wife." There was really no answer to this, and Agnes did not offer one. Norah continued. "I've decided that Alexander is going to write to him with permission to do as he sees fit."

This got a reaction. Agnes's mouth flattened to a line. "Norah, that's not a good course of action."

"Can you tell me *why?*" Norah was aware of the topsy-turvy nature of their situation; as mistress of the house she had no need of a servant's opinion, and yet she was hungry for it, desperate to understand the unvoiced warning in her words.

Agnes said nothing. Apparently she could not. Norah stood, rather abruptly, and a flicker from across the room caught her eye. The polished copper pots hanging against the wall shone in the light from the ranges, reflecting a distorted image of the room back at her. She could make out her figure, dark and solid in her woollen dress, and the twisted shadows behind her, framing her head, reaching with pointed fingers towards the low ceiling. For a moment she smelled mud and iron, thick and heavy, and felt a flair of triumph. Once more she had found a way to bend the situation to her will. "Then that's decided. I shall write to him today."

Chapter Sixteen

And so Norah's days took on a new shape; her mornings were spent with Barland in his room, reading or embroidering as he sat in his chair, mute and still. Occasionally she would speak to him, expecting no response and receiving what she expected. It would have been relaxing save for the infrequent moments where he would rouse just enough to take notice of her, to turn those fathomless, empty eyes her way. In those moments she would excuse herself, pretending it was her choice to vacate the room and not an inescapable response to his muttering and agitation.

Leave, go, you should not be here.

After lunch she would walk out on the grounds, often visiting the worksite at the base of the cliff to gauge the crew's progress. She took to making a headcount daily and noted a slow but steady dwindling of the workforce, occasionally bolstered when Manson carted in another handful from the surrounding areas. Standing on the beach and watching them work she could see no reason why they would find it more objectionable than any other job, but clearly there was something in the conditions that drove them away. Davey remained, thankfully, and would occasionally sneak time away from the job to pass the time of day with Norah, his sunny smile a salve for Manson's glowering looks.

Meanwhile, Fenwick had apparently acted immediately on receiving 'Barland's' assent to his plea: within days he wrote confirming that there would presently be a fresh flock arriving at the Corrain pastures.

Leave, go, you should never have come.

Her evenings she spent in the library, composing letters and sketching until her fingers were stained with charcoal. At some point she would retire to her bed for nights haunted by cold stone and dark branches, salt and woodsmoke. Somehow Agnes was always there, soothing her, pulling her back from one edge or coaxing her over another, whispering her back to sleep. She never undressed. She would strip Norah bare, peeling off her nightgown to better access every inch of her, but the gesture was never returned, and though she received Norah's ministrations eagerly, Norah was obliged to delve beneath starched layers of skirt and petticoat to deliver them. This was disappointing to Norah, who longed to feel Agnes's body pressed to her own, but she did not push the matter: there were any number of reasons Agnes dared not risk such a thing, each more sensible than the last. They never spoke of it in the cold light of day, sharing only fleeting, hungry glances over meals or when the housekeeper came to stoke the fire.

Leave, go, you cannot stay.

And then there were the moments in between: waking, sleeping, or neither at all. Sometimes the evenings found her wandering the long corridors, drawn by eerie squalls that sounded like nothing so much as an abandoned infant, left cold and hungry in some forgotten wing of the house. Norah's bare feet mapped the creaking floorboards and worn carpets, her limbs growing heavy and cold. Each time she neared the source of the sound her steps would speed up until she was practically running, only to skid into a cold, empty shadow of a room. She would hurry to the window, throwing back the curtain and pressing her cheek to the cold glass to listen for the howling wind—but without fail the night outside was silent and still.

NORAH'S SKETCHES THUS far had been concentrated on the garden and the landscape around the house, but it was perhaps unsurprising that people began to creep onto the pages. While the portraits she had attempted in Glasgow had always fallen short of her ambitions, something about the inhabitants of Corrain House meant she could not help but sketch face after face in the margins of her pad. Both Barland and Agnes had countenances born to be captured in charcoal; their gaunt cheeks and dark eyes stood out on the paper, shaded in grey and sable. Though she soon grew tired of putting Alexander's profile to the page she grew only more enamoured with Agnes's likeness, sketching it from all angles, even daring to capture on paper the memory of the other woman's face crested above her, head thrown back, eyes shut tightly, thin lips slightly parted, unbuttoned at the neck just far enough to expose the perfect hollow where her collarbones met. Though normally she kept her sketches to herself, she was so ensconced in a full-page portrait of Agnes, regal and severe, that she didn't notice the housekeeper's entrance late one evening.

"I brought some t—what is that?"

Norah jerked away from the sketchbook, her cheeks warming at the sight of the other woman. "Oh, just a wee portrait; I grew tired of the same plants over and over."

Agnes put down the tea tray and held out a hand and Norah surrendered her pad without a second thought. Her sketches were imperfect but serviceable and she was not ashamed of them—indeed her drawings of Agnes captured their subject in a way that few of her previous portraits had. The housekeeper leafed through the past few pages of drawings—Norah thought she saw her note the study from beneath with a slight lift of the eyebrows. Then, in a single gesture, she wrapped her fingers around several pages, ripped them clean from the pad, and threw them on the fire.

"Excuse me!" Norah was on her feet on an instant, reaching towards the hearth as if she might be able to rescue the pages from the crackling flames. "You have no right to burn my things!"

"My likeness is not your possession," Agnes countered sharply.

"I didn't… They're only *drawings*. No one but you would ever lay eyes on it!"

"I can't afford to take that risk." Agnes turned to Norah, bringing them face to face. "No likeness of me exists, nor can it. I know you must know that—MacCulloch told me what those wifeys were saying in Thurso."

"Surely their gossip makes no difference here nor there! No one listens, and if they did, 'Lord Barland' certainly has enough sway that he could put pen to paper and take them to task for it."

"That is not how this works. And in any event I will not have those flames fanned by the existence of portraiture."

"So you'll stay in this house unseen and unremarked, for— what? Propriety?" Norah took a step closer, eyes fixed on Agnes's pale face. "Do you truly care about what they say?"

"I don't. But you should." Perhaps realising that her reaction had been galling in its extremism, Agnes reached for Norah's hands, gripping them to command her full attention. "Make no mistake, Thurso may be no metropolis, but those women are part of social circles and gossip rings crossing over with Aberdeen, Dundee, and all the way to Glasgow. I know that there's not a lot of love lost between you and your mother, but I don't think you want her hearing fourth-hand about this family's scandals. Particularly not when these stories tend to grow in the telling. Who knows the state it would be in by the time it reached Glasgow."

Norah could feel the cage of 'decorum' and 'respectability' begin to close around her, tightened by the distant but still pernicious influence of her mother—and those like her. She had come all this way to escape scandal, but it seemed to follow her like flies on a carcass. Only Agnes's grip on her hands kept her from descending into impotent despair, and it was this that allowed her mind to return to a phrase that had niggled at her as soon as it had been uttered.

"You said MacCulloch shared the gossip with you—was that what he was speaking of, that day in the kitchen?" Norah frowned, trying to remember exactly how long it had been: a few days? A week? Had it been longer, or had it only just happened? "I saw him take your arm, I should have known he would try to impose himself on you over it. He should be disciplined, I'll not have him treating you that way."

"In the kitchen?" Agnes frowned in thought. "Oh, on the day of the accident? No, no, he was just telling me what Manson told you, more or less. Leave it be; there's nothing you can do about that."

"He looked as though he was threatening you."

"MacCulloch is no threat to me." Norah got the distinct sense that Agnes was trying to will this to be true by saying it aloud, but it rang hollow; they both knew that a man, any man, could be a threat if he so desired. She felt the iron grip of Barland's hand around her wrist again and withdrew her hands quickly from Agnes's grasp in reflexive alarm.

"All the same," she said, rubbing at her wrist and the phantom shackle encircling it, "you will tell me if he acts inappropriately to you again? I would protect you as best I can, with what little power is afforded to me."

Agnes nodded, but it was clear in her expression that they both knew how little power that really was.

NORAH HAD NOT returned to St Peter's in Thurso in the weeks since her visit with Alexander. Even now, her soul adrift on an ocean of secrets and despair, she could not bring herself to face that particular segment of society. She did not think she'd be able to look those women in the eye again without telling them exactly what she thought of them. Whatever lingering irritation she had felt at Agnes's destruction of her work had now been replaced with anger at the gossiping biddies who'd made such a thing feel necessary. No, she could not go back to church services, choosing instead to sit in contemplation in the wee family kirk down the cliff path, in communion with the displaced crofters who'd etched their names on the windows—the MacAsgaills and the Griegs, Callum Bain and Fiona MacLeod and oh, the Guinns: Stuart, who had left, and Úna, indomitable Úna, who had stayed behind to burn, who flickered in Norah's periphery ever since that day at the stone circle, whose fierce spirit burned on in her descendant. But she did need to escape Corrain House, properly, at least for a few hours. And so it was on a Tuesday that Norah went in search of MacCulloch—as for myriad reasons she couldn't quite bring herself to send an instruction with Agnes.

From Norah's observations the groundskeeper tended to run errands and do any work further afield in the mornings, arrive back around lunchtime, then stick close to the house in the afternoons tending to the horses, taking care of running repairs on the house, and tidying the rather miserable gardens. So it was today, when she found him working in the low-walled vegetable plot to the rear of the kitchen. He was using a foot plough of the type she'd first seen down in Corrain, turning neat furrows of sandy soil in preparation for planting. She knew he had sensed her presence in his periphery, for though he did not stop his digging, he did begin to smirk.

Tamping down the irritation that his expression dredged up, Norah waited until he finished a row and turned back for another before speaking. "I'm going to Thurso tomorrow. I'll need the carriage ready first thing."

"Of course, miss." MacCulloch didn't pause in his task, his light eyes flicking only briefly to Norah before focusing back on the dirt. "Whatever you say."

"My lady." Norah didn't recognise her own voice at first; it was steely and terse.

"Eh?" Now he did slow, then stopped, his smirk only growing as he leaned a forearm on the cas-chrom.

"I am the lady of the house. You will refer to me as such."

"Aye, of course." Norah could almost hear his thoughts, for they so mirrored her own: what authority could she truly command? She had precious few staff and no society, no replacement should she lose him, no punishment she could exact. She had no dominion, no sway, nothing except Agnes's pity and cooperation. And MacCulloch knew it. "As you say, *my lady*."

Nostrils flaring, Norah bit back a further reprimand and nodded before turning on her heel to depart. She could feel MacCulloch's stare on the back of her neck as she approached the house, prickling the hairs as well as her ire. Memories of his interaction with Agnes flooded back, the easy entitlement with which he grabbed her arm, the anger on his face. Suddenly the drive into Thurso seemed interminable, and she prayed for clear weather and quiet roads.

Friday dawned wet and windy, but MacCulloch at least followed her instructions to the letter, and after a somewhat awkward porridge breakfast with an Agnes who still would not meet her eyes, Norah emerged from the house to find the carriage already awaiting her. The wind battered the coach as it ploughed along dirt roads and through deep puddles, but the road was fairly flat and straight and they arrived safely, albeit shaken about and rather later than planned.

Compared to Glasgow, Thurso's High Street was a pale and diminutive imitation, but after the isolation of Corrain House it felt like a bustling metropolis. Norah stood on the corner beneath her umbrella and drank in the sights for a good few minutes, eyes roaming over the colourful, bustled dresses and well-shone shoes of the passers-by. Even the mud and drizzle could not dim the spectacle that was blessed civilisation, and it was with some reluctance that Norah pulled herself away to seek out the local post office. Nestled between a fishmonger and a cobbler on the main street, it was a small but well-appointed establishment, a deep, narrow shop lined with shelves replete with stationery.

She could not help but stop to admire the stacks of paper tucked into their cubbies—octavos and billets above, commercial notes below, and all in a thick weight and creamy colour that spoke to Norah of fine quality. She had been glad when the fashion for embellishments and gilt borders had passed; it seemed to her that they only served to distract from the words their pages bore. In some cases, such finishes seemed to be used precisely *for* this effect, diverting attention from poor penmanship or subpar substance and allowing lazy correspondence. She had no need to purchase paper now, of course; the familiar stock with the Barland family crest was hers to use as freely as she wished, though she had continued to use the remainder of her personal supply to write to her mother.

She fingered the envelopes, sealing wax and stamps, though there was a small supply of gummed envelopes as well, for those in a particular haste. Black-edged stationery sat in its own receptacle, as if allowing it to mingle with the rest would somehow pollute them with its mournful purpose. Her mother's envelopes still bore a thick black edge, though Norah suspected that this was because her mother could not bear to waste what had been purchased rather than any lingering sentimentality over her father's passing.

When she came to the notebooks Norah's perusal turned more pointed; she selected several and flipped through them briskly, testing their weight, the stiffness of their paper, their dimensions. Eventually she settled on one that would be adequate as a sketchbook as well as a place to keep her notes about the library and garden, and moved on to the final cabinet deep in the bowels of the shop. Being mostly supplied with epistolary paraphernalia rather than art supplies there was a scant variety of charcoals to be found, but Norah stocked up with what she could in the way of sketching materials and ink, and with her selections she made her way to the little desk at the back of the shop to pay. Though she had brought some paper notes with her the rather wizened old woman behind the register fixed her for a moment with a beady eye and the first words from her mouth were, "The Barland account?"

"Ah—yes, I suppose so," Norah replied. The idea that her identity had been so easy to ascertain by this complete stranger did little to soothe her nerves, and Agnes's caution once again echoed in her thoughts. "I don't suppose there's any mail for the estate?"

The woman cocked her head in thought, then nodded. "Aye," she said. "It usually goes on to Reay and your man picks it up from there."

Norah knew this, of course, and took a small pleasure in the fact she was disturbing the ever-smirking Jamie MacCulloch's routine. "I'll take it with me."

The postmistress clearly didn't much like this change to convention, but apparently couldn't think of a reason to object, for she rose and shuffled through the door behind her, leaving Norah alone in the shop. Her eye was drawn to a little display case on the desk: a fountain pen, with a smooth black barrel and polished nib that spoke of elegant lettering. It was undecorated save for a tiny red gem inset at the tip of its cap: a garnet. The case was not locked, and Norah dared to retrieve the pen for examination, hefting it in her grip, letting it rest in her palm until it warmed from the heat of her body. She felt her cheeks flush at this and hurriedly set it back on its cushion as the postmistress reappeared with a small stack of letters.

"Is this your only fountain pen?" Norah asked, gesturing.

At the old woman's nod she felt a twinge of disappointment— now that the idea had struck her she had hoped for a selection from which she could choose the perfect specimen. Nevertheless, she had it boxed and added it to the rest of her assembled purchases to be parcelled up.

She did not look at the letters until she was safely ensconced back in the carriage. Two were for her husband, one large and thick and presumably containing some kind of work-related documentation. The third had the address lettered in Mrs John Mackenzie's large, looping hand, and Norah's heart sank. She had hoped for something pleasant to read, not her mother's sour opinions and irrelevant gossip from back home.

By the time they arrived back at Corrain House Norah was thoroughly wretched; between the increasingly heavy rain and her mother's missive the ride back had not been a pleasant one. She muttered her acknowledgement to MacCulloch and trudged into the house, letters and purchases wrapped in her arms. She was thoroughly soaked by the trip from coach to house, and perhaps Agnes anticipated this, for she emerged from the direction of the kitchen only moments after Norah pushed the great front door to a close, a steaming bucket in each hand. "I've made the fire up in your room," she said. "And drawn a bath. Nearly." She lifted the buckets.

Discomfort somersaulted in Norah's stomach; in truth, she wanted nothing more than a soak in the copper tub, but was immediately filled with guilt at the effort such an endeavour involved for her solitary member of staff. Agnes raised her eyebrows expectantly, and Norah could not help but remark in the straightness of her back, the lift of her chin, the ease with which she hefted the vessels she carried. The mysterious ailment that had afflicted her seemed to have passed, and she once again looked, if not hale and hearty, then at least as indomitable as she had seemed upon Norah's arrival. "Thank you. That is most welcome."

Norah felt strangely vulnerable, stripping off her wet clothes while Agnes filled and fussed with the bath, fetching soap and towels before disappearing with a promise of tea. Though by this point she had been unclothed in Agnes's sight on more than one occasion it felt different in daylight, no red wine or dark dreams to blunt her propriety. Once in the water she felt safer, somehow, the old-fashioned copper tub a protective cocoon. When Agnes returned she was carrying just a small cup, no tray, and accompanied by a sweet, spicy aroma that prickled at Norah's nostrils, almost astringent.

"I thought perhaps a hot toddy instead of tea."

Norah aimed a grateful, drowsy smile over the rim of the tub. "Careful, or I might grow so fond of such treatment that it'll have me running outside at the merest hint of rain."

"Well, you may do as you please, of course," Agnes said, in a tone that Norah could not quite place as either dry or fond. Perhaps, as was so often the case with Agnes, it was somewhere in between the two.

The toddy was bracing and pleasingly tart, with only the faintest hint of honey to counteract the sour lemon. She soon set the cup aside and sank beneath the surface of the bath, listening to the muted liquid sloshes and the creak of floorboards through the strange medium of the water itself. She had taken a deep breath before submerging, and she was free to bask in the feeling of the hot water stinging her skin as the seconds ticked by. The noises around her began to distort and twist the longer she stayed under, slowly warping into the groaning of a ship in distress, the slap of waves sharp against its sides. There were shouts, too, low, panicked voices rough with salt and fatigue. She couldn't make out the words, but the sentiment was clear: defeat. Terror. Regret. What had once been water not long from the kettle cooled, bit by bit, until she felt her limbs start to grow numb and heavy, chilled by the embrace of the deep. An eerie wail reverberated in the metal casket, and it was not her but it was, the remaining air rushing from her as a heavy weight settled on her chest. She clawed her fingers towards the surface, now metres above her, and kicked as hard as she could against the weight of the water.

Norah surfaced with a splash, gasping as her hands found the sides of the tub. She had already found purchase by the time Agnes reached her, leaning over with a frown. "Did you fall asleep?"

Norah shook her head, but the words that tumbled out of her mouth were a nervous, "I must have. How silly of me."

Agnes lifted an eyebrow. Did Norah imagine her gaze flickering briefly downwards? "Try not to drown, eh?"

"I certainly will." As Agnes turned away Norah reached out for her, damp fingers sliding across the back of her hand. "There's letters on the dresser—I retrieved them while in Thurso. You'll want to have a look. And something else I picked up while I was there," she added, as casually as she could manage.

"Something else? Wh—" Agnes cut off. Norah had not wrapped the gift or removed it from its plain brown box, only written on the little paper cuff that held it closed: *For A.* With it, she'd placed a small jar of ink.

Norah almost reassured her that she needn't open it there and then, but she didn't have to, for Agnes scooped up both letters and the fountain pen and ink, still in their boxes, and made for the door.

They did not speak again that day. Norah finished her bath, dressed, and ate dinner in with her silent husband. That night there were no bad dreams, for Agnes appeared shortly after she retired, helping her undress and then bearing her down onto the bed without a word.

When Norah woke the next morning there was a note on her pillow.

You are wanted here. I would have you know it.

Its lines were crisp and smooth and even, in rich indigo. It was not signed.

CHAPTER SEVENTEEN

THE KELP BOOM in Scotland was comparatively short-lived. As the Highlands and Islands creaked under the strain of their population and struggled for income, kelp had been a brief saviour. During the Napoleonic wars and the trade wars that accompanied them, Scottish kelp farmers—or their lairds, at any rate—had profited hand over fist from the kelp ash used to make soap and glass. But it was a precarious state of affairs, and when the wars ended the whole industry imploded in the space of a few years, a footnote in the story of the land. Its remnants, like the runrigs, were carved in furrows in the earth, the overgrown pits and drystane ricks and the broken stacks of the kelp kilns.

Norah wrapped her arms around herself and turned away from the ruins to look down over the little row of houses on the seafront below. It was the first day of the year that was almost warm, or at least mild enough to be pleasant. Even a touch of sunshine and blue skies couldn't make the village of Corrain look anything other than miserable.

"There's no grass for laying out, and not enough sand to dig firepits. So they had to load it in barrows and haul it up the hill to dry and burn it."

Agnes had surprised her with the suggestion that they walk along the high road that afternoon. She came to stand beside Norah now, shoulder to shoulder.

"There was never much kelp to be had here, not like Orkney or the Hebrides. The shore's not right; it drops away too steeply."

Wrong for kelp. Wrong for sheep. Wrong for deer. No wonder this was one of the few estates that had held out against the unstoppable march of the Sutherland behemoth buying up every inch of land around it. It simply wasn't worth it.

"I don't think I ever truly appreciated the luxury of idleness until I came here," Norah murmured, eyes travelling the slope of the hill, measuring its angle. She had made that trek almost daily and her calves were banded with muscle beneath soft flesh, but it still made her ache to think of traversing it with a laden cart, hour after hour after hour. "To think, some of us waste our days tittering over tea, never knowing how fortunate we are."

"Little point dwelling on that. It is what it is."

"You may say that, but I'm sure there's some that will resent us for it. And rightly so. Especially when their struggle against the immutable elements is rewarded with upheaval and banishment."

Agnes only sighed, folding her arms and turning her gaze upward, out to sea. It was shimmering in the sunlight today, though Norah still hardly dared look at it lest she once more see those phantom boats on the horizon.

"It's the Vernal Equinox today," Agnes said. "Twelve hours of light and twelve of dark. It's a crossing."

Something unfurled in Norah, a seed of hope, a buoyancy that lifted her shoulders and lightened her mood. She turned to Agnes with a shy smile, reaching out to brush her fingers against the back of the other woman's hand. "I can't lie and say I don't welcome the light." Agnes released her grip on her own arm to capture Norah's hand, turning in toward her, leaning down to touch their foreheads. In that moment Norah could almost forget what had gone before, who and where they were, and emboldened by this sense of being out of place, outside of time itself in a borderland between dark and light, she stepped back from the ridge, tugging Agnes with her.

The pit from the old makeshift kiln had filled out over the decades since its last use into a shallow depression, grown over with grass and overlooked by the short, half-crumbled ricks and hollowed stacks. It served well enough as a shelter from both the wind and any prying eyes, and as the sun sank and day faded into gloaming, Norah burned anew.

"We used to holiday together when I was a child—Isa's family and mine." When Norah spoke, Agnes shifted next to her in mild surprise at the broken silence. They had never spoken after, not in bed. Here Norah felt more clear-headed somehow, less delirious. "Her family had a cottage on the Isle of Arran, in Sannox. There's a beach there called the Fallen Rocks with these enormous yellow sandstone boulders, and Isa and I would run off and climb among them where nobody could see or follow us. We'd find a wee hidey hole there, and…" She chuckled, reaching down to tug at her skirts, smoothing them from their rucked tangle around her legs. "At least there's no sand here." Her laughter died away as soon as it had come; those memories were sour now, overshadowed by her desertion and guilt.

Agnes didn't reply. Norah pushed up onto her elbow to look at her properly, to gauge her mood, when a familiar scent crept into her awareness: woodsmoke.

Her stomach knotted. It was unlikely in this waning light that Agnes noted the grimace that stole over her features. Norah closed her eyes and took another breath. The smoke remained, curling into her nostrils and down her throat like whisky.

The land burns. You press your torch against brush and branch, you cut peat, you dig coal. All around you, smoke rises.

"It's happening again," she said, voice thick with fear. "Even now, wide awake, I smell it—the smoke." Agnes stirred now, her attention piqued, and Norah reached for her, clinging to her like a buoy in a roiling sea.

"You're all right…"

"No, you don't understand, that smell, it *haunts* me, the thatch—"

"*Norah*." Agnes sat up, pulling Norah with her, grabbing her hands to still them where they plucked at her dress. "Listen to me. You are not imagining anything. I smell it too."

The air had a catch to it now, cooler and damper as the dark encroached and a haar rolled in, but they could just make out the plume of smoke rising from the shore. Down the hill at the end of the row, right outside the tiny box of a kirk, was a gathering of what must be every soul in Corrain. They were nearly all women and children, a few older men, numbering perhaps forty in all. The villagers milled and watched three figures—they looked like boys just shy of working age—who were hard at work with some manner of contraption. Through a sheen of sea mist Norah could just make out a vertical section of timber, supported by one of the boys, while the other pair held a rope that they sawed back and forth as if engaged in a tug of war.

"What are they doing?"

"They're lighting the needfire."

Norah had never heard the words spoken together before and yet they kindled something primal within her, like her bones and blood knew them.

"The boys are using a sort of bow drill—the cord wrapped around the wooden pole turns it. The smoke is from friction. Look at the windows in the village—what do you see?"

Norah frowned. "Nothing."

It was true—the village was dark, the squat, square buildings lit only by the waxing moon, which rose from the sea eagerly, as if it too wished to witness the needfire's arrival. Night was close, no longer held at bay by lanterns at the window, and all around them was a hush, the birds and insects barely stirring in the twilight.

"Every flame in the town has been stopped—every fireplace doused, every candle snuffed. They'll all be relit from the needfire. It's an old, old ritual."

Norah found herself holding her breath too, eyes fixed on that point where the smoke eddied and curled. They were balanced there together—all of them—on the precipice of darkness and light, and it was only through sheer force of will that their fate would be decided.

"Why do they do it?" she murmured, tearing her gaze away to find Agnes's pale face. "Why this? Why now?"

"It wards off evil. Ill winds, disease, blight. Curses. They do it now because it's a turning of the year. A time for protections and spells. Don't be fooled by that kirk. Some traditions die hard. We've never forgotten where we come from."

Folk are superstitious up here.

Yet this wasn't merely a knock on wood, or the sign of the cross, or a pinch of salt over the shoulder. This was a deep and ancient magic harking to the earliest days of humanity, conjuring that which had set humans apart from animals. Norah watched on, transfixed, as the tiniest glow flickered into being at the point where the tip of the pole rested on the hearth board. Somebody threw something over it—tinder, presumably, dried grass, then kindling, and slowly, carefully, a campfire was built over the virgin flame. The fire grew as the moon climbed high overhead, the smell of woodsmoke was replaced by the scent of burning peat, earthy and slightly sour, and one by one, the villagers took their turn lighting their lamps and brands from the needfire. Someone began a song— call-and-response, Norah thought she heard the seeds of a psalm tune in it, though she couldn't make out the lyrics, the consonants lost to the night breeze. To every questioning call, the answer was a cacophony of voices, every singer weaving in and out of tune as they meandered on their own path to the end of the line. Then at last the people of Corrain scattered apart, twinkling dots scurrying back to their crofts to relight fires and bedsides with the pure new flames they held.

"We should get back," Agnes said. "It's getting late."

Norah watched as the last doors closed against the night. The needfire burned on, unattended, its purpose served. Beyond it, the beach disappeared into the haar.

"Do they do this often?" Norah asked then. "Every equinox? Every solstice?"

Agnes took a shade too long to answer, and Norah knew what she was going to say.

"Only when something's not right."

"What's wrong?" Norah turned to Agnes, reached for her hand. Agnes's fingers were ice-cold, her grip like iron. "Agnes, what's not right?"

Agnes blinked, and a muscle tightened in her jaw. "I don't know," she said.

YOU ARE AFRAID of the border places.

You are afraid of that strand of silver that divides the land from the sea. It promises only uncertainty, change. You cross it quickly, never linger. You put out to open water and you never ever look back lest you see something there you could not stand to lose.

You are afraid of the dawn and of the gloaming. Not day nor night, the light that can conceal—or illuminate— too much. The time when the sky beckons you to look too deeply, to see the places that hide at the corner of your eye, fairie castles and summerlands.

You are afraid of priests, of maidens on their wedding day, of unchristened babies and the dying. You are afraid of all those with one foot in this world and one in the next—as if the next world cares.

You are afraid of thresholds—you carry your brides across them, and your dead out through the wall lest they know the way back. You bury the sinful and unbaptised beneath the perimeters of your kirks.

You are afraid of the courtyard. Enclosed on all sides and yet open to the sky, that cursed tree grasping for the light. Growing things where nothing should grow.

You are afraid of the moments between not knowing and knowing. That limbo between the path not taken and the consequences of actions.

You are afraid of the fork in the road.

CHAPTER EIGHTEEN

SPRING'S ARRIVAL AT Corrain House should have been a joyous occasion. Even here, this far north where plants and people alike had to brace against the wind and weather, the new season brought with it a hint of warmth, the start of a long thaw and the slow growth of new life. Everywhere Norah looked there was change; tender shoots of grass poking up through last year's silage, the chirp and flutter of juvenile whinchats with their mottled breasts. The vegetable garden that MacCulloch tended daily began to issue forth seedlings, curling their heads up towards the querulous sun, and the herbs in the courtyard garden were flush with sap and new vegetation.

The land was stirring.

Norah felt renewed as well, as if there was a liquor in her veins wakened by the change in seasons—or perhaps it was Agnes who quickened her. Every touch, every look from the dark-haired woman was a flame to her kindling, igniting her without even a word. They maintained what boundaries they could, playacting at propriety in front of Barland despite his incapacity and coming together only in the dark, secret places kept for women.

Her bedroom was one such haven; no one ever stepped foot over its threshold but them. When Norah woke one morning with the dull ache of cramps radiating through her middle she was especially glad of this; Agnes arrived a little later at her bedside, clearly having missed her at breakfast, to find her curled into a ball under her blankets, eyes shut resolutely to block out the world, though she was not tired enough to go back to sleep. Agnes seemed to know this, for she didn't attempt to wake her but rather spoke without preamble.

"I brought you tea," she said. Then after a pause. "And some napkins." There was the sound of pot and cup alighting at the bedside, of liquid being poured, and the aroma of mint and chamomile wafted Norah's way. She cracked an eye open.

"How did you know?"

"Not much gets past me. I thought you knew that by now."

Norah pushed into a sitting position and reached for Agnes's hand to stop her as she made for a chair. "Here, with me."

"I've just made the fires."

"I don't care." Norah shifted over as Agnes kicked off her shoes and climbed up beside her. She smelled of perspiration and soot. She reached for the tea immediately, pressing the warm china into Norah's palm.

"Drink. It'll help."

Norah obeyed, closing her eyes and sinking against the other woman as she sipped the brew. "Thank you," she murmured, feeling something unclench inside her. "I'm no layabout—I'll be out of bed soon enough. I merely couldn't face the day quite yet."

Agnes said nothing in response, but she did reach into her apron pocket. "You have a letter," she said. Norah recognised Isa's hand before even seeing the Goldsmith Terrace return address, and her stomach gave a twist completely unconnected to her monthly misery.

"How are the Sinclairs?" It was a confused moment before Norah remembered that, of course, Agnes knew well of her old companions from the letters she and 'A' had exchanged. The pain of that betrayal was so dull now—there, still, but blunted with every day that passed where Agnes showed her, with deed if not with word, that those letters had held at least one truth: she was wanted here, very much. Just not by her husband. In light of this the enquiry after the Sinclairs felt almost like a dig, mixing with her guilty heart and cramping belly into a sour soup. She scowled, and set the letter aside.

"I'll read it later," she said. Wrapping both hands around her teacup, she instead let a different memory catch her.

"Isa used to bring me tea, sometimes," she said. "Just the usual, nothing medicinal—though I think she always fancied I was putting it on for attention. She never seemed to suffer much from her pains, and I always wondered how she had been so fortunate."

"Not all women are the same," Agnes said. "She would have done well to recognise that."

"Perhaps." Norah glanced across at the letter. "Certainly, she failed to appreciate that my lack of interest in the ordinary life of a woman went far beyond my disinterest in the companionship of men." Isa had loved Norah—loved her still, if Peter was to be believed. But she also loved married life, loved parties and shopping and church on a Sunday, wanted a tidy, well-appointed home, and children to share it with. She cast her eyes sidelong at Agnes. "You never wanted one? A child? You could have married…"

Norah felt her chest shift with an amused little huff. "Even if that idea had appealed, what would I do with a child?"

"You could have passed on everything you know about the land, about herbs—your grandmother's recipes. Your family legacy."

Strong brows knit together. "Some legacies are better forgotten," Agnes said. "It's been a long time since my family has known anything other than pain. The fire, the drowning, my mother…" Her eyes narrowed, and Norah caught a momentary flash of something dark and hot there, a rage buried but ever burning, a coal seam fire deep beneath the earth. "I'm happy to see an end of it." Then she gave Norah a little nudge, and carried on in a lighter, chiding tone. "You're prevaricating. Read your letter, come on. Get it over with."

"I cannot face it, not today." She pressed her lips together, exhaling a sigh through her nose. She put her teacup aside, placing it very deliberately not on its little saucer, but on the letter, as if to weigh it down, to keep it from springing open where it lay. "She has supposedly been driven to melancholy by my absence, my silence. Peter wrote to beg me to write to her, and now she writes to beg the same, or for me to go to them, or to go to hell, more likely."

Agnes's arm stiffened a little where it lay across Norah's shoulders, though her tone was light enough as she spoke. "You could. Write, or visit."

"I won't." She almost spat the words, irritation sending its questing roots out through the regret and nostalgia. "She treated me like a doll to be taken out and played with as she pleased. They all did. To Mother I was a constant disappointment, never thin or pretty or genteel enough. To Peter, a playmate for his wife, an amusing diversion that barely interfered with their lives—he never saw what we had as having anywhere near the same weight their marriage did. I thought that Isa felt differently but in the end she was just the same. She wanted me neatly tidied away into my own little room, the live-in nanny, just another piece of her perfect, ordinary family." And so she had escaped. The arrangement with Barland—with A—had fallen into place while Isa was still confined to her bed and Peter too distracted to notice her absence. At the time it had seemed like fate.

Agnes drew her arm back a little to turn and look more fully at her, head tipped to one side. "Would it have been so bad? You spoke of being trapped, but there you would have been invisible. Largely free to do as you pleased, all under the same roof. You've spoken of freedom from the responsibilities of your position in society before. It sounds as though that was just what you were offered."

"To the world I would have been a servant."

"I see."

Too late, Norah realised her mistake, and her whole body went cold—and not only because Agnes had now entirely withdrawn from their embrace. She reached to catch the housekeeper's arm before she could get up from the bed. "It's not the same," she said. "Whatever you're thinking, you mustn't. You must understand, Isa and I grew up together, we holidayed together, our families were friends—"

"Whereas I have always been your servant."

"No! No, that's not… you run this estate, and your father…" Norah stuttered, clutching at Agnes, who did not flinch away, but did not relent either.

"I don't have a father. You make much of the supposed freedoms afforded to me by my relative unimportance. You turned down those exact freedoms." Agnes leaned a little closer. "Admit that you did not want to lower yourself. Admit that you believe you're my better."

Norah's cheeks felt hot, her eyes burning. Her heart thrummed in her ears, muffling her own voice as she protested. "I don't. I don't believe that. Truly, whatever foolish ideas I've held, whatever I've said, you must know I don't believe that. It wasn't only that, with Isa—it was that whole life: the baby, the walks in the park, church on a Sunday, I just couldn't imagine playacting like that. Pretending to be normal. I couldn't face it."

You welcome it: the barren coast, the house on the cliff, the impossible garden with its impossible tree, this strange, frightening woman and even your strange, ill husband. You welcome the ghosts and the shadows, the weight of history, the phantom scents of brine and smoke and iron. You could rule this broken domain.

For a moment she could feel the stag in the room, smell the loam and guts, hear the laboured breath and creaking wooden ribcage. Perhaps Agnes saw something of this in her eyes, because she reached out, grabbing Norah by the wrist, anchoring her back in the moment.

"This place is a very long way from normal," she warned. She was close enough now that her breath cooled Norah's burning cheek. "You may have run too far."

Norah didn't dare speak: she did not know what to say to calm the waters. Instead, she closed the gap between them and pressed her mouth to Agnes's, desperate for this moment of division to be over and resorting to the one way she knew to convey how she truly felt, *willing* Agnes to hear her, to answer. At first, Agnes did not respond, but then she gave a tiny, muffled groan, the grip on her wrist tightened before releasing altogether, arm snaking once more around her. Always more at ease with physical rather than verbal displays of emotion she matched Norah's kisses with surety and insistence, reaching to cup her jaw, her shoulder, her breast, apparently unheeding of any tenderness, though in her growing ardour Norah's pain was mostly forgotten. Agnes bore her down onto the bed, and it was only as she began to push Norah's nightdress up her thighs that it occurred to her to stay her hand.

"There's blood."

Norah's stomach twisted with perverse satisfaction when Agnes gave a dismissive snort in reply.

"I know," she said, her lips brushing Norah's as she spoke, her touch questing onward undaunted.

Agnes knew. Beyond the tensions, the inequities, the lingering doubts, Agnes knew her. She knew Norah bled, and cried, and *wanted*—she saw *her* as nobody else ever had. As Agnes's fingers slid home within her the breath Norah drew felt brand new, felt like surfacing for air, felt as though she'd never breathed before.

Saturday, March 22nd, 1890
Goldsmith Terrace

Dear Mrs Barland. No, that sounds wrong even now, and I cannot think of you as anything other than:
    My beloved Norah, and—
    My terrible Judas,

I should have known you were lost to me the last time I saw you: your demeanour was distracted, your gaze already elsewhere. At the time I had thought it was only awkwardness at holding my darling Alice when your arms had never cradled anything so small and so precious before. What a fool I was, when all along you were already gone, lost to the rich laird in his big house. If only I had taken heed when you first mentioned his name and his gracious forbearance in light of your father's embarrassment. But how was I to know your head could be so easily turned, when Peter and I were extending everything we could to you: a home, independence from your terrible mother, and the truest parts of our hearts.

It makes me wonder now if that love was not enough. If perhaps love is never enough, or at least that which I can offer. I look at Peter, at Alice, and question whether I can give them what they need, or if I will prove inadequate in their eyes, too. If they are bound to leave me as you did, and then I will be alone. Sometimes I welcome this feeling, and sometimes I cannot stop crying for fear of it.

Oh Norah, how could you? I do not want you to return; I shall spit in your face if I should see you again, but I do wish you would tell me what lack there was in our loving home, what need went unfulfilled. If not for my sake, then think of Alice. Whatever I am due, she deserves only the best.

Alas no longer yours in friendship,
Isabelle

Norah crumpled the fine paper in her fist and let it fall. It danced across the rocky ground, caught in a sea breeze's eddy, and then was borne over the high cliff on the same breath of air. She felt nothing but a dull ache as it disappeared, a pain more remembered than real.

In the end she could not bring herself to read Isa's letter while in the house, and so she had taken the high path to Corrain—not the one down past the kirk, but the longer, flatter route taken by the cart as far as the ruined kilns before it turned sharply down to the village. Only once she had followed the path out of sight of the house had she stopped to open it, her body buffeted by the wind as she navigated Isa's elaborate and looping script. There had been no surprises in those lines, except perhaps the lack of invective and anger, of which Norah knew the other woman was well capable. Perhaps the months had allowed her temper to burn itself out, leaving only this melancholic acrimony. It seemed a shame, in a way, that it should end like this: Norah, alone on a rocky outlook, Isa, alone in her loving family.

Had there been a way to salvage what they had lost? If so, Norah could not see it from here. She had felt guilt for her actions, yes, and regret, but she could not countenance choosing any other path for herself once Isa had declared her intentions. The person she was, the life she desired, would not fit neatly into anyone else's expectations. She cast her gaze down on the village, movement from below reminding her of other lives, other people. The wood from the needfire had been removed the day after the ceremony—whatever remnants of timber remained would not be wasted—but the evidence was still there in a blackened patch of ground. Now that spring was in full swing the little plots around the crofts were a site of constant activity, everyone old—or young—enough to work putting their backs into turning earth and planting. It was a harsh and bitter life, with little time for rest or frivolity. Though it had seemed foreign and strange at first, Norah knew now that she belonged there, with Agnes. The scoured landscape and crumbling house were part of her now, wormed beneath her skin until she could not escape them. She had come home.

SHE ALMOST STARTED down towards the beach, but in truth even if she hadn't been warned off by Manson, the tides were so ferocious at the moment that she didn't quite dare—the workers were now accessing the scaffold exclusively from the topside. And so instead she hiked—almost scrambled really—back up the steep path to the high road. From there she struck inland, paying little attention to her route. It was nigh impossible to get lost—Corrain House was always there, a dark stitch on the fabric of the land pinching everything towards it.

As she turned her feet toward the scrubby, undulating fields she realised that the world had gone quiet; there were still the waves, of course, unceasingly beating against the shore, but the cries of the gulls had ceased, and she could hear nothing from the village behind her, though a moment before it had rung out with the chop of spades in earth and the grunts of the men and women wielding them. All was still.

The longer she stood the more the silence built around her, until she could hear the harsh rasp of her own breath and the rhythmic beat of her pulse in her ears.

Unnerved, she nearly turned back for the house there and then, but in the end stubborn determination won out, and Norah kept to her course inland, trekking across damp, spongy earth toward the little rise with the stone circle. The whin was blooming properly now, and in recent days she had begun to hear bees humming among their deep yellow blooms, but not today.

It was so hushed that Norah began to wonder if there was any life at all to be had, or if some fiat of God had snuffed it out entirely, leaving her the only denizen of the silent landscape.

And then a scream split the stillness.

Her heart leapt in her chest, a wave of nausea sweeping over her. The sound seemed to have come from the direction of the house; she threw herself into motion, stumbling over the scruffy tufts of earth and wheeling her arms for balance. Her gasps for breath filled the cavernous silence, and then she heard the scream again, guttural and piercing all at once. Blindly she followed it, a prayer caught on her lips that it should not be Agnes, or even Alexander, roused from his stupor into another violent episode.

Norah wasn't sure how far she had run when she heard the wail again, not far from where she was, now taking form as a moan that slid off into a deep, stomach-clenching groan. She swung her gaze wildly, an echoing keen in her own throat. It had sounded so human, so real, that she nearly didn't stop when she stumbled upon the prone figure of a ewe sprawled in the grass, its sides heaving wildly.

Upon seeing her the animal flailed, one dark eye rolling back until she could see the ring of white that haloed its strange rectangular slit of a pupil. It wailed again, straining, and she was suddenly struck by the iron tang of blood and saw the crimson smear across the grass. Had nature herself laid this tableau, or had something more sinister put it out for her to find? Norah dropped to her knees and gulped breath, watching as the sheep arched its back and pushed, pushed, the smell of blood and shit stronger now, almost gagging her. She reached to help, finding the knobble of legs in the wetness, but her fingers slipped from them once, twice, until she thought to yank her cuffs over the smooth of her palms.

The sun wheeled overhead. Wind ruffled the grass almost playfully, while Norah leaned back on her heels and pulled.

You bend the land to your will. It bleeds for you.

The sheep screamed again, and then was still.

At Norah's knees lay a figure, twisted and slick, a morass of organs and skin and bone. The lamb twitched and let out a mewling cry, the sound a dagger in Norah's heart. It could not live, could never have lived, and as she watched, it took one final, feeble breath, and then there was nothing.

IN YOUR ARMS *it is a warm, soft weight, at first limp, as though boneless. Then it twitches, undulates, and a tiny pink appendage snakes out to grasp at the air. A wet burbling gasp, a hiccough that turns into a cry, high pitched: not overloud, and yet you feel it piercing your eardrum, needling its way into your brain.*

The baby opens its eyes, pale, crystal blue like its mother's, gazes not at you but straight through you as though you aren't even there. Its scrunched-up face is a picture of indignance, resentment, mirroring your own feelings in this moment as you stare down at the object of your inevitable undoing, the end of everything.

She wants you to love it. To take one look down at this creature she grew inside her body, and to see… what? A part of her? A perfect, tiny replica? You note its father's dark hair—it even has a little bald patch just like his, and you feel… not jealous—some deep down part of you knows you would not want this even if you could have it. Rather, you feel hollow. Wretched. Guilty. Try as you might, you can't muster up even a shred of love for this tiny, wriggling larva.

This was a test you were destined to fail.

CHAPTER NINETEEN

THOUGH THE SUN'S journey grew longer day by day, it did not seem to penetrate the shadows of Corrain House. The house's dark wood and dated wallpaper seemed to rebuff all attempts at illumination, to swallow any light that hit it. It was a house built of shadow.

The work crew were hammering in fresh props, rendering the library too loud for art or reading or contemplation. Norah could not keep her mind on anything these past few days, and she had already spent as much time in the presence of her catatonic husband as she could thole that morning, so she gathered her new notebook and charcoals and made for the study on the other side of the house. She was beginning to know the house, to recognise the creak of this floorboard or the slightest tilt of that painting, this peeling paint, that frayed hanging. Familiarity did not breed fondness.

She half expected she might run into Agnes on her travels—the other woman tended to be finished with the bedrooms, by now—beds turned down, fires made—and on to the rooms that would come into use in the evening. What she did not expect was to turn onto the corridor where the study lay to hear voices raised behind its door, which hung slightly ajar. One of the voices was Agnes, sounding her usual measured self. The other was MacCulloch.

"—the ideal time, with this blasted cliff affair. A few pounds here or there will be noticed by no one—nobody is going to crosscheck with Manson, not when the records are coming from the man himself."

"It's out of the question." Agnes spoke with the tone of someone deliberately only giving half their attention. Norah had taken that same tone with her mother.

"It's simple. Even I could do it and I'm not a numbers man."

"Oh, I *can* do it. I won't."

A long pause. When MacCulloch spoke again his voice had lowered, taken on a serrated edge.

"Careful, Agnes. Remember it's not just your reputation at stake here. Not now we know about your wee sojourns with her ladyship. A word in the right ear and she'll be 'the Lady Gunn' to half of Glasgow by Easter." A loud creak. This Norah recognised: her preferred fireside wingback was on a board that protested when moved, and a perverse anger flickered alive in her at the idea of that man making himself comfortable in her chair.

"You think about it," MacCulloch said now, his voice growing louder by the moment. Norah wasn't sure whether or not she wanted to confront the groundskeeper but she knew she did not want to do it in that moment, face burning and eyes bright with both humiliation and fury, so she ducked quickly back round the corner. His heavy tread halted right at the door, close enough that Norah heard a quiet little chuckle before his parting remark.

"Nice pen. Payment for services rendered?"

A pause.

"Go to hell." Agnes's voice was low and steady, every syllable injected with a restrained rage, a fire that twinned with Norah's own and stoked it higher, and it was all she could do not to charge MacCulloch as he emerged, turning the other way down the corridor—presumably to the main hall and exit.

When his footsteps had faded entirely Norah pushed herself off the wall and hurried towards the study, still aflame with indignation. If Agnes was surprised at her entrance she didn't show it, barely looking up as Norah stamped into the room. She was seated at the desk—Barland's desk—and Norah's ire was tempered slightly to see the sleek new fountain pen in her hand. Where Norah would have been in high colour at MacCulloch's insolent tone, Agnes looked pale and composed, her dark hair pulled back into a smooth, tight knot.

"I heard him. MacCulloch." Norah did not dance around the subject; Agnes did not appreciate prevarication, and she was too incensed to pretend politeness. "Is he *extorting* you?"

Agnes pursed her lips down at the ledger in front of her. "It's nothing to be concerned about." The desk was scrupulously clean: she had tidied away all Barland's old papers once more while he kept entirely to his bedchamber.

"How can you expect me to disregard the fact that my groundskeeper is expecting you to perform financial malfeasance in order to pay him off—and he is threatening *us* if you continue to put him off?" Norah's voice dropped at this last clause; not because she suspected anybody might overhear her, but because to even speak the fact aloud somehow seemed to loose its power into the world.

Agnes laid the pen down carefully. "This estate keeps MacCulloch very comfortable and will continue to do so. He knows on which side his bread is buttered. He'll simmer down." Agnes looked Norah over, her sharp gaze scanning up and down the length of her as though checking she was entirely present and correct. "How are you feeling?"

"Fine, I'm—fine." The longer Agnes's gaze rested on her the more Norah fidgeted; she *was* fine, wasn't she? Upset, angry at MacCulloch, perhaps, but that was all.

At length, Agnes nodded. "Just take care of yourself," she said. "Don't worry about MacCulloch."

This sudden concern on Agnes's part felt at once touching and patronising and Norah lifted her chin, jaw set in a tight clench. What of it that the sounds of lambing out in the fields now made her flinch; that the smell of any red meat, no matter how well cooked, made her stomach turn? She was only tired, her sleep disturbed by dreams and somnambulation, and despite that was perfectly capable of managing her household.

"Is there anything else I should know?" she asked then, flattening her hands against her skirts.

"Nothing that comes to mind, my lady," came the smooth reply.

Norah wished nothing more than to be able to believe that, but Agnes seemed to live in a world of shadows and concealment. What was to say she wasn't lying now, thinking it was in Norah's best interest to remain in the dark? Perhaps once she would have been naive enough to believe she deserved such treatment, but no more. She would uncover the truth and set things to rights with or without Agnes's cooperation.

She could not stay in the office where the housekeeper would undoubtedly keep watch over her like a sickly child, and so she retreated to her rooms, settling down to sketch hazy scenes of springtime. They were unsatisfactory, both in execution and in the catharsis they offered, and eventually Norah drifted over to the window to stare out at the surrounding landscape. Even with the new carpet of green spreading around the house the land felt fallow and unchanging. It wasn't just the view, either: the curtains, the wallpaper, the upholstery—everything about Corrain House was caught in time. How was it that in her fleeting moments with Agnes she felt so alive, so vital, and yet at other times felt as if she were trapped in amber, the slow, sticky smut encasing her until it was hard to remember anything else?

A figure outside the window caught her eye, and she pulled herself out of her melancholic funk just in time to register it as MacCulloch, shovel in hand, making his way purposefully towards one of the outbuildings. Before she could stop herself Norah was trotting for the door, rekindling the fire that had ignited in her as she'd overheard his threats.

The stable was only just large enough for their two horses, both now safely stabled while MacCulloch shovelled dung into a rather dilapidated-looking wheelbarrow. He was sweating through his shirt, though the day was fresh enough that her breath misted the air in front of her. He had not seen her, but perhaps he was used to being sneaked up on by the ever-silent Agnes, for he did not jump when she said his name, only straightened and turned, shovel still gripped in his beefy hands.

"My lady," he said with a deferential tip of his head that could not have been anything other than sarcastic.

Channelling the self-righteousness of Mrs John Mackenzie, Norah drew herself up. "It has come to my attention that you have been making insinuations about another member of staff." As soon as she said it she felt stupid; the house only had two servants in total. "I have come to tell you that this must stop immediately; I will not brook such behaviour from anyone in my employ."

MacCulloch's face was blank for a moment as he processed this. Then his lips twitched, quirked upward at one corner. "Don't know what you mean, my lady. I've never said a word about what goes on within these walls to the folk beyond them."

"No, though that doesn't mean you won't in future if you don't get what you want, does it? What a sad man you must be, how low your moral fibre, to think that threats and coercion will not say more about you than the lies you spread."

MacCulloch's smile grew, and he took a step closer, tossing the shovel idly from hand to hand. "I can't see as you've any call to be talking about moral fibre, my lady."

For the first time since she had heard the exchange in the study Norah felt fear, though she fought not to show it. Was it fear of exposure, of scandal? Or something more base than that—the fear of a sharp weapon with a strong arm behind it? "You shall not speak to me that way," she said. "Or I will have you thrown out on your ear, with no reference to fall back on."

The man's eyes narrowed. "That wouldn't be very wise, would it?" he said. "Given what I know. It's all very well to say

it's my word against yours, to say nobody would believe me…
but are you sure?"

Because there was no smoke without fire. And because, of
course, it wouldn't be the first time such rumours had spread.
And then there was the matter of Agnes running the estate's
books. Was that something that could be verified? Might it
prompt investigation from external parties? Tears pricked at
Norah's eyes, but they were borne of anger, not despair. How
was it that this man could hold so much power over her—this
boorish, greedy man whose only thoughts were of himself
and his own advancement? Perhaps it was better to take that
risk than to let him wield such authority over her thoughts
and actions—but then, it wasn't just her reputation at stake.
Agnes, too, would be brought low by his stories, and unlike
Norah she had no standing to shield her. There would be no
future for them if she were to follow through; no hope that
they might weather that storm.

"You horrible man," she spat, and his sly smile grew as he
loomed over her. "I'll see you punished for this, I swear it.
When Alexander is better, or when I'm more settled here and
have a handle on the accounts myself, there'll come a time
when these threats don't work."

MacCulloch lifted his eyebrows. Then he laughed—a big,
full-chested sound that rang around the tiny stable and made
the horses shuffle in surprise.

"You think you know what's going on here," he said. "You
think you're in control, but you've barely scraped the surface.
That witch has you wrapped around her finger." He was
closer now and Norah could smell him, sour breath and stale
perspiration mingling with the grassy tang of horse dung.
Her back hit cold brick: the wall. She hadn't even realised
she'd been backing away.

"Don't you dare talk about her—"

"It's not her who should be afraid," MacCulloch said. He
leaned over her, hand pressed to the wall behind her. "I can

226

protect you, if you want," he said. "I know what's going on here. What her and those women before her have done to these men. But not to me. I'm in control here. I can tak care of you."

Norah heard the offer—or the threat—loud and clear, and her reserve snapped: she brought both hands up to his chest and shoved, hard and suddenly, sending him staggering backwards and off-balance. For good measure, she surged forward and lashed out with a savage slap, so hard it stung her hand.

He swore, and rose back to his full height, bringing his hand up to return the blow in kind, and in that moment it was as though everything slowed, the next few moments passing at a languid crawl.

"*Stop.*"

The voice was Agnes... and yet not Agnes. For this voice had something else to it, some indefinable quality, a timbre that went wider and deeper than any human voice could, that filled her whole head. She remembered once attending a grouse shoot with her father, back when he'd still allowed his little daughter to do boyish things, and hearing a shotgun blast up close. Agnes said only one word, and that word sounded like the shotgun, like that sudden deep boom that penetrated her ears and shook her brain in its skull.

MacCulloch seemed no less impacted. He pulled his arm away immediately, using it instead as a shield, as though he could somehow defend himself from Agnes's impossible voice and definitive, insuperable demand.

Norah whirled to see Agnes in the stable doorway, her tall, thin frame appearing in that moment to fill the entire entrance. Lit from behind by the late-day sun, she was a shadow, a looming silhouette, a spectre. Norah should have been relieved, but she could not feel anything but the thrashing of her own heart.

"*Get out.*"

MacCulloch froze momentarily. Then he fled. The spade hit the ground with a thump, forgotten, as he stumbled out past Agnes and off into the mist. Norah nearly followed, compelled by something she didn't quite understand, but was arrested by Agnes's hand on her arm.

"What…" Norah blinked, the throbbing of her hand calling her back to what had just happened. "He was going to—Agnes, we must send him away!"

"We can't. He's right—he knows too much. But he'll leave you be, I promise."

"How can you know that? You saw him just there! How much are we paying him for his silence, his obedience?" Norah took a shuddering breath, every fibre of her being taut, ready to snap at the barest provocation. "We're neither of us safe with him around."

"I know it, because I will make it so," Agnes said. She tugged Norah closer. "Listen to me: I can and will keep you safe. I will deal with MacCulloch. Just trust me. Please."

Norah folded herself against the other woman, taking solace in her strength, her certainty, even as MacCulloch's words shivered down her spine.

"That witch has you wrapped around her finger. It's not her who should be afraid."

And Norah was afraid, but not of the woman whose grip was as much a vice as an embrace around her. But even iron could shatter in the cold, and as they stood there, pressed together in the draughty barn, Norah felt ice thread through her veins at the thought of losing what she had only just found.

You grasp tighter and tighter, but it slips through your fingers like water. You begin to fall.

CHAPTER TWENTY

AS SPRING ADVANCED and the weather grew incrementally warmer, the courtyard was revealing yet more of its secrets. Day by day, shoot by shoot, bud by bud. Norah sketched them one by one, pressing some between the pages of her sketchbooks until it seemed as though everything she touched had an herbal, leafy scent to it. At first she was reluctant to revisit the little notebook she had found, and instead identified them in the writings of Pliny, Turner, Blackwell. *Levisticum officinale, Viburnum opulus, Vinca major*—many plants she knew by appearance or common name, all growing together in this impossible little pocket of life. But so many were considered to have medicinal qualities, used in elixirs and salves and poultices, and Norah could not resist returning to the corner of the library where she'd re-hidden the journal. It was inevitable, really—why else had she secreted it back on a shelf after that day in the kitchen? Reading it over now the connections were plain: this was the journal of generations of wise women. *We've always had a way with plants, with living things*. Of course, if the villagers of Corrain were to be believed, it went beyond that. *They think I am a witch*.

Norah flipped through to the end of the book where the sketches were, stopping when she reached the two-page image of the rowan. Going by its position in the book and the relative freshness of its lines this sketch must have been made by Agnes's own mother. Knowing now what she had only suspected before regarding Agnes's parentage, it was hard not to view the sketches in a new light, to try to put herself into the mind of the woman who had rendered them. What had Agnes's mother felt, gazing up at those grasping branches? Had the tree wormed its roots into her mind as it had into Norah's?

Norah studied the wild sketch for some time, shaken from her reverie when a fat droplet landed on the page. Wiping her eyes, she snapped the book shut once more and stuffed it back in its hiding place. She had assumed that Agnes hid the notebook lest Norah find it and see her handwriting, all a part of the grand deception of the letters from 'A'. It occurred to Norah only now that she had more likely buried this evidence of her mother's troubled thoughts out of sight for her own peace of mind, months or even years before—that it quite possibly had nothing whatever to do with Norah. She recalled her righteous anger that day with an uncomfortable twist in her stomach.

THOUGH SHE TRIED to maintain a presence in the library she was driven from it regularly enough by the sound—and sensation—of the construction beneath her feet that she eventually decided to decamp for good. With Agnes now using the study openly Norah found she quite fancied returning there herself, imagining evenings spent in companionable silence in front of the fire. She gathered up the most-thumbed books of reference and her art supplies and began to ferry them across the house one afternoon as sounds of hammering seemed to reverberate through the very bricks of the hearth.

It was as she was stacking her growing pile of sketch books for transport that they escaped her grasp, sliding across the table and onto the floor. One sheaf of loose leaves slid from within their leather case as it fell, scattering across the polished wood. Norah sank to her knees to gather them together, but as she lifted the first piece her heart leapt into her throat.

She had never seen this picture before.

It was a broad pebbled beach at low tide, rendered roughly in charcoal. The sea beyond was a tangled scrawl, a wild flourish. The focus of the piece was the carcasses of three wrecks, half-submerged in the sands, their masts rising like crucifixes from the blackened ribcage of their hulls, casting long smears of shadow upon the shore behind them.

There was no question that the work was her own: she recognised her usual issues with perspective and proportion. But she had no memory of its creation.

Frowning, she stared at the sketch a moment longer and then set it aside, reaching for the next. Again undeniably her work: a study of the garden from one of the interior rooms, dominated by the dark, heavy figure of the rowan tree—but she could not recall standing there to plan the drawing, nor the act of creating it. She traced her fingers over the dark lines, willing herself to remember its conception, but the longer she looked at it the more she was convinced the memories could not be dredged from the depths of her mind.

Over and over she repeated this—there were warped depictions of the Green Man, mouth gaping, leaves spilling forth; dancing flames rendered in frenzied detail; even one hollow-eyed, sunken-chested lamb that she had to put away from herself as soon as she had turned it up. But the worst was the bottom of the pile of papers: rendering after rendering of Corrain House on the cliff, a dark, jagged crack running up through the rock and into the bowels of the house itself.

She pulled the loose sheets back together with shaking hands, at a loss as to what to do with them. Had there been a fire in the hearth she might have burned them there and then, but as it was, she could only stuff them roughly back in their leather slip and secure it tightly. She shoved the case to the bottom of her pile of books and portfolios, hoping to banish the disturbing images from her thoughts.

Agnes was not in the study when Norah entered, and Norah was relieved. She did not think she would have been able to look at her without blurting out what she had found. Agnes already seemed concerned enough about Norah lately, often checking in with her throughout the day, bringing her tea, asking after her. She tried to pass it off as casual interest, but Norah could tell that the housekeeper was keeping an eye on her.

With the discovery of these sketches, Norah could no longer pretend that the worry was not warranted. Though she had tried in vain to retain some modicum of control over the situation her mind was slipping loose from its mooring more often now, whether sending her out onto the roof in the middle of the night or bidding her hand create these nightmarish images. Her earlier attempts to broach the topic with Agnes had fallen on deaf ears—the housekeeper had always told her that she was well, that there was no risk of her following her husband's descent—and yet she now had concrete evidence that these assurances were false. Whatever she would admit, Agnes knew as well as she did that a darkness was encroaching. How soon until it was something neither of them could brush away with fevered kisses and hollow promises?

She was determined that she would address the issue with Agnes when next she saw her, that very evening, if possible, and demand to learn everything Agnes knew about this place—of its history, of Barland's ailment and of the possible connection between the two. Whatever she was concealing, no matter her intentions, it had to be aired, before Norah was caught in the same spiral that had rendered her husband a hollowed shell of a human being. She took a seat at the fireside, tamping down a visceral shudder as she remembered MacCulloch's 'visit' to Agnes here, pictured him lounging in this very spot to casually extort the estate. She settled herself deeper into the chair, banishing his presence and reclaiming the space for herself, for the small, safe bastion that it was against all of it—everything else. Flipping to a new page in her sketchbook, she began to outline the jagged outline of Corrain village, glad of the distraction and the chance to start afresh.

She hadn't spent a great deal of time in the village itself after her visit with the scones, reluctant to puncture the privacy of the folk eking out their existence there, but she had often stood on the rise by the kilns and stared down at the wee settlement, counting the houses with their little plots, mapping the coastline at low tide and high, and she felt she had it committed almost entirely to memory now. The equinox, the night of the needfire, for all that it was a ceremony to which she was not invited and most certainly would not have been welcomed, felt almost like a moment of connection now: syzygy, where the seasons, the people of Corrain, and Norah herself were aligned at a turning point.

Norah's gaze was drawn to the flames leaping and writhing in the fireplace. In her mind's eye, she stood with the people of Corrain, lighting a brand from their needfire, carrying it up the hill to renew the lamps and fires of Corrain House. Could it drive out the illness that had seeped into the bones of the place, and in turn into its inhabitants?

"Shall I make us some tea?"

Norah gave a start. When had Agnes entered? Had she fallen asleep? Certainly her eyes ached. She shifted, twisting in her chair to see the housekeeper stationed behind the desk, pen in hand, though she placed it down now and pushed to her feet.

"Yes, always," Norah said, pressing her knuckles into her eyes until stars wheeled in the blackness behind them. "Or perhaps something stronger—it's late enough, isn't it?"

"If you fancy some brandy there's a bottle in the cabinet."

Norah did indeed fancy some brandy, and urged Agnes to join her. Though the housekeeper refused the beverage she did join Norah in the second chair by the fire. Every emotion on Agnes's part tended to be rather muted, but Norah thought she was beginning to get the measure of her, and at that moment she seemed ill at ease, not quite relaxing in the chair. Under her watchful eyes, Norah sipped her brandy. It was old, but not quite spoiled. It would do.

Eventually Norah felt restored enough to speak, though she found herself suddenly self-conscious and shy under Agnes's close scrutiny. Lord knew Norah had spent her early days at Corrain House a bumbling interloper; that Agnes had not dismissed her as a fool unworthy of her attention was a miracle, and one Norah resolved never to test again. She had intended to show Agnes the sketches she had found, to ask for her help in understanding their mysterious appearance, but as she was warmed by the brandy—and by Agnes's gaze—the desire to expose this newfound frailty waned away. "I thought I might spend my afternoons here now—the building works are quite cacophonous, and I can barely hear myself think in the library. If my presence is amenable to you, of course."

"Of course," Agnes said. Then added, "This is your house, my lady. You may go anywhere you please in it." Words that would once have sounded polite to the point of hostility, Norah sensed a little humour to them today. Agnes was teasing.

The knowledge warmed Norah more than any tipple. "My mother would never enter my father's study," she said then, tipping her head to rest against the back cushion of the chair. "Not because he forbade her—I don't think he spared much thought in the matter—but because it wasn't a place for ladies. She used to tut any time she would see me emerging from it when I was a child. But it was the most interesting room in the house: so many books and trinkets to look through, papers to draw on. And," she added, dropping her voice, though there was no one there to overhear and be offended, "the fact that Mother never ventured there may have been part of the attraction."

Agnes's lips twitched into an amused smile. "Is she well? Your mother. I saw a couple of letters arrive with your return address."

"Well enough—at least as well as she ever is. I gather her physical health has improved after many visits from Dr Campbell, though I know from experience he'll have done no more than take her pulse and nod sympathetically at her list of woes before prescribing sugar pills for her supposed 'ailments'." Norah shook her head; her mother's antics were much easier to stomach from several hundred miles away, but even here she could not escape the litany of complaints the woman had on all manner of subjects. "I shall not bore you with the rest of the contents; suffice it to say that it seems my absence has had very little effect on her general wellbeing and contentment."

"And what of your wellbeing, and the absence of your mother? D'you not miss her, in spite of her foibles?"

"Oh, of course—perhaps because of them. You cannot spend thirty-odd years with someone and not grow fond of them, despite their best efforts to the contrary."

Agnes nodded slowly. "Perhaps you might want to spend the summer in the city after all," she said.

"You've tired of me already?" Norah tried to keep her tone light, but her hurt must've shown, for Agnes left her seat and moved to kneel before her, reaching for her hands.

"There is nothing I want more than to have you here, in this house," she said. Her grip on Norah's fingers was cool and tight; her voice was low. "Everything I have done... it was borne of my selfish desire to have you here. I hope you can forgive me for it."

At that moment Norah would have forgiven her anything, if she could have summoned the ability to speak. All she could offer was a shaky nod, clutching Agnes's hands as if she could convey the depth of her feeling through that alone. They had both been so isolated before: Agnes in the looming house on the hill, Norah in the tumult of Glasgow. Had it been fate or happenstance that had brought them together, that had touched spark to kindling?

Norah had never had a love that was all her own, nor one based on her true self. Her father had doled out a portion of his affection, but reserved most of it for his business and the gentleman's club where he would spend his evenings. Her mother's love was given on sufferance, with the knowledge that it would increase if only Norah could be thinner, quieter, more obedient. And though her connection with Isa had been genuine, and deep, it had always been split, first with Peter and then even further with the arrival of their child. Norah's place in their lives grew smaller and smaller until she could no longer contort herself well enough to fit. Here, there was only Agnes, and there was only Norah, and Agnes, against all reason, seemed to want her exactly as she was, to delight in her body with its unfashionable curves, to enjoy her sharp tongue and her defiance and even her rawest most exposed emotions. Agnes saw her—all of her, even the parts she might prefer to keep hidden—and wanted her. Wanted her badly enough to deceive her, to risk discovery and disdain should Norah not return her feelings.

"Then I shall summer here," she managed at length, her smile small but genuine. Agnes, eyes shining in the pulsing light from the hearth, pulled at Norah's hands, and she needed no further invitation to slide off the chair and kneel before her on the rug. Their kisses were laced with salt.

CHAPTER TWENTY–ONE

The day dawned bright and clear over Corrain House. As usual Norah woke alone, but even an empty bed could not sour her mood after the previous evening. Something had shifted between she and Agnes last night; before there had been no doubt of the pull that drew them together, like the moon and the sea, but now they had fully charted the tides of their desire.

It wasn't just the way their bodies fit together, though Norah had never known such heights as when Agnes would press her against the coverlet, teeth grazing her breast, her stomach, her thigh. It was the moments before, when she would catch the hint of a smile on her lips, and after, Norah's soft frame pillowed against Agnes's strength, their breath rising, falling in unison. It was knowing that Agnes wanted her there, had always wanted her there, and that whatever might come she would not have to face it alone.

The house felt, for once, like it might be a home.

A pot of tea and several thick potato scones sat on a plate at the bedside. A glance out the window confirmed the cart was gone—Agnes was off to Reay, then, and Norah was on her own for breakfast. She poured herself a cup of tea and nestled back down into the warmth of the blankets, nibbling at a scone as she tested her gently aching muscles. What they had begun in the study had finished here, in the four-poster bed, and the fire had burned away to embers by the time sleep found them.

After a leisurely breakfasting she rose and dressed and checked on Barland, who had already been dressed and helped to his chair by the fire. Rather than linger there she returned to the study to tidy away the glasses and cushions that had been overturned in their passion, and then knelt to build the fire in the hearth. Suddenly despite the pleasantness of the day Norah found herself longing for the night, when they could once again return to filling the house with memories of their own creation.

Eager to pass the time, Norah sat down at the fire to read, skimming absently through the book she had left on the side table the day before. She could not swear to have absorbed it all, but it did at least help the minutes to pass more or less painlessly. When she next stood and peered out the window she was pleased to see the cart was back in its usual place; her stomach curled at Agnes's return. Setting aside the book and carefully checking her hair and dress, she hurried towards the stairs, knowing the housekeeper might well be unpacking her acquisitions at that very minute.

The kitchen was empty but for a lingering scent of infusing herbs, the kettle on the stovetop still warm to the touch. There was the evidence of Agnes's shopping trip—some fresh eggs in the basket, a cloth-covered bowl near the stove that might hold proving dough. Feeling daring, Norah moved past the ranges and peeked through the door to the back scullery, a place she'd never before so much as seen inside.

The astringent smell from the kitchen gave way to the sweet, tarry aroma of carbolic soap as she took in her surroundings, a narrow stone-floored room with whitewashed stone walls and various containers and cleaning paraphernalia. There was a copper bath, smaller and older than the one she'd used herself, and two large wooden washtubs next to a well-used mangle.

A splash of colour caught her eye: one of her own dresses laid over one of the tubs, hanging half inside it. It should not have been a strange sight—after all, Norah had been here for some time and several of her dresses had been laundered, and yet something about the sight of it conjured a sick feeling in her stomach, and she had to force herself forward into the room.

The tub was half-full of water, its surface filmed with a foamy scum. It smelled of vinegar rather than soap, and the water itself had an orange-pink tint to it. She could see now that the dress was caked in dry mud down its skirts, but the sleeves and bodice had obviously been deemed a more urgent matter, soaked as they were with what could only be blood.

Norah's heart leapt into her throat, her palms suddenly slick and hot. In an instant she was transported to the field, knelt in the iron-streaked muck, warm, slippery flesh of the newborn lamb in her hands. She had gathered its limp, dripping form up into her arms—she knew it was dead, and yet she could not simply leave it there to rot alone. What then? What then? Her mind raced, the memory resisting her attempts to surface it, stuck like an anchor in a muddy seabed.

She stumbled back, turning away from the scullery in horror and disgust. The kitchen, once a warm and welcoming place, now seemed to press in around her, and she remembered now— she had stumbled here, half-numb, half-panicked, the body clutched to her breast, insensible with grief. What had Agnes done? She must have coaxed it away from Norah somehow, led her to a chair, helped her shed the blood-stiffened dress. Norah remembered a warm bath, Agnes's hands in her hair, a mug of hot cocoa after she had been wrapped up tightly by the fire. The lamb gone, but not forgotten—or not yet, at least.

Had Agnes burned it? Buried it? Whatever the case, she had taken it away, and washed the traces of blood from Norah's hands and face, and then she had said nothing more.

Memories of Agnes's concern surfaced now, at the time so innocuous, almost warming. Checking in on her while she sketched, bringing her tea, peeking a head through the door as Norah readied herself for bed. She had told herself that it was kindness, affection, but now she saw it for what it truly was. Agnes had been watching her, charting her descent into madness even as she denied it to Norah's face.

She clawed her way blindly to the sink, running the tap and splashing water over her face, holding her hands beneath the stream as though it could wash away the memory of the blood and mucus. In search of a towel, she found instead an apron, hanging on the peg by the door. It was already soiled: a dark smear led down into its large front pocket, heavy with a flat, square object.

In her mind's eye, a sketchbook tumbled from Norah's hands to the floor in front of the fire, and was retrieved by a sure pair of hands, secreted away out of sight. Norah heard a quiet moan, felt it reverberate in her throat.

An involuntary tremble rippled along her arms as she now turned over the pad. Corrain village was there, drawn as if from a boat in the bay, each little home picked out along its shore. Every house was engulfed with flames, curling up into the sky, smoke gathering above in a cloud that dominated the whole top third of the page, black in places, coaldust sitting proud on its surface.

Like the rowan tree, like the crumbling cliffside, this was her handiwork. She had sent Corrain up in flames, scoring the paper with deep furrows of her charcoal stick as she described the smoke that hung over the houses like a dark miasma.

Agnes had seen this. Agnes had known. Agnes had said nothing.

Norah set the sketchpad aside with shaking hands. The scent of herbs was strong, and strongest among them was the sharp, sweet tang of vervain.

How many times had she accepted tea with that same aroma, drinking it down without a qualm? And Barland, whose very pores seemed to exude it at times, insensate and docile. She gagged, and ran for the door.

The dark hallways seemed to bow and swell as she traversed them, corridor to stairwell to corridor, blindly following her feet on their well-worn path through the house. She went by instinct rather than intent to her husband's chamber, her gut feeling what she had not the presence of mind to decipher: where else would the fresh-made tea be bound? The heavy door announced her entrance with a mournful creak as she burst in, not knowing what she would find, knowing only with an inexplicable certainty that it would break her heart.

The cloying scent of the vervain mingled with that of juniper and peat smoke. Alexander Barland sat in his chair where she'd left him, but beside him, perched on a stool, sat Agnes. On the floor in front of them sat a vaguely familiar slim, narrow box, open to reveal contents both glass and metal, though Norah's stare was immediately drawn not by that but by the figures by the fire. Both Alexander and Agnes had their left arms bared, sleeves rolled to above the elbow, upper arms strapped with belts. Agnes wielded what Norah vaguely recognised as a large metal syringe, currently inserted at the crook of Barland's arm, and was slowly depressing the plunger. Blood was trickling freely from a puncture in the same spot of her own arm, but she seemed heedless of either that or Norah's entrance, her focus entirely on the procedure at hand.

At first Norah could not speak, could not move, could only watch as the plunger made its slow downward journey, glinting oddly in the firelight. "Stop," she croaked at last, faint from the sight of blood or the wicked needle or the dawning horror of her lover's betrayal. "Stop that, unhand him!"

Agnes did not stop. She did not speak. The plunger hit its mark, and she carefully withdrew the thick needle from Barland's arm. Only then did she look up at Norah.

"It's done," she said simply.

"Alexander? Alexander!" Her husband did not react, not even as Gunn began to wind a strip of bandage over the site. If anything he seemed more benumbed than before, his gaze dull and flat.

"What did you do to him? *What have you done?*" Norah's

241

voice broke, foretelling the flood that threatened to drown her entirely. "MacCulloch, those women, the things they said... I thought..." What had she thought? At the time she had thought, she supposed, that they sensed what she had, that Agnes was like her, not... whatever *this* was. She remembered the villagers from Corrain, crossing themselves. At the time she'd assumed it was something about the house that frightened them, but now... "What *are* you?" Norah began to back towards the door one hesitant step at a time.

Agnes looked up sharply at this, eyes narrowing a shade. "Whatever it is you are thinking, Norah, you are mistaken," she said.

Norah ached to believe these words, but the evidence was too irrefutable to ignore. Blood and herbs, secrets and lies: the tools of a witch wielded against those closest to her. No wonder Norah had been losing memories, losing time—they had been stolen from her, just as Barland's very essence had been sapped away, leaving him a senseless husk. Norah's eyes flicked to her husband, but there was no recognition there, no aid from that quarter.

She needed help.

MacCulloch had seen through Agnes's facade. Loathe though she was to invoke his particular brand of violence and coercion, she had no choice.

Norah turned and fled.

Faces and antlers bracketed the corridors, an endless gallery of death presiding over her flight. Each step was a danger, and she stumbled over threadbare rugs and uneven floorboards as though tripping over roots in a forest, only blind panic keeping her upright and advancing. She flew down the stairs and out the front door, heedless of the cold drizzle of rain that immediately began to soak through her collar and sleeves. MacCulloch was nowhere to be seen and Norah let out a sob, her chest tight with fear. Onward she ran, away from the house and down the cliff path towards Corrain village.

She could not erase the sight of Agnes and Barland, a dribble of blood in the crook of their elbows, crimson on bone. They had never looked more like brother and sister in that moment, twins with one soul between them, one still, one animate. How long had she been subsuming his will, acting on his behalf? Long before Norah had arrived, that much was clear. What power Agnes wielded; what evil she embraced.

Those dark eyes had been Norah's undoing, the hunger in them captivating, the fire a welcome peril. She had wanted so much to burn that she had forgotten that she would be engulfed; body and spirit, mind and memory.

The day had turned overcast, the haar obscuring all but a few feet in front of her, but Norah plunged on through regardless, down the hill and past the kirk to the shore. Her feet trod a familiar route of their own accord and soon her shoes were sinking into the soft sands along the base of the cliff towards the wreck. The sea roared in her ears, and though she was beneath the cloud line here everything was rendered grey by its cover, rock fading into sand into sea into sky. It was wet and cold, and she tasted salt but wasn't sure whether it was sea spray whipped into her face or her own uncontrollable weeping as she cursed her utter naivety. How could she have been so foolish?

You are wanted here.

But wanted for what? A question Norah had never asked in her giddy hope that she had finally found a soulmate, someone who could love her and her only. The rowan's black shadow arched over her, its grasping fingers wrapping around hers.

Whatever dark purpose Agnes had in doing what she did to Alexander Barland, surely she planned the same for Norah. Perhaps it had already begun—the 'calming' teas, the porridge and meat and wine with which she'd been plied these past weeks: every one of them could have been laced with whatever poison had rendered her husband insensible.

I will consume you.

Norah had seen flashes of Agnes Gunn's anger, her bitterness. Always cold, always tamped down. But how long had it smouldered? Was it revenge that motivated her, a desire to see the Barlands suffer for what they had done to her family, to the folk in their care? Norah could almost have understood that, but why then had she been drawn in?

Norah's skirts were growing heavy with seawater, the tide lapping around her calves, the grey sands sucking at her feet as she toiled along the shore toward the wreck. The wind was at her back, and she fancied she heard voices on it, calling her name, pleading with her to turn around, to come back, and on she waded.

A black mast rose from the water ahead, the skeletal prow of the fishing boat reaching out towards her. The curve of its hull was a palm of invitation, of friendship, the tide rushing in and out of its interior. Norah's skirts fanned out around her in the water like the fins of an ornamental fish, the cold water bringing a welcome numbness. She could see figures moving on the battered boat, now, fishermen thrown back and forth by the unforgiving waves.

Why had she come here? She had meant to stop in the village, pound on every door, claim sanctuary in the kirk. Perhaps she knew she was tainted, as the villagers surely knew, and that she would find no safety or rest there, for she had reached it and turned away, double-backed along the shore. She pressed onwards, the water up to her waist now, sucking at her every step. If she could only reach the ship she would be safe; she knew this as surely as she knew that the love she felt was no mere ensorcellment but her truest undoing.

A wave buoyed her up, tugging her feet from the sandbank beneath, and Norah gasped and flailed her arms in a desperate attempt to keep her head above the surf. Her limbs were heavy and cold, her dress a lead weight, and it was all she could do to roll her head back and suck a gulp of air before the next wave crested over her. Again and again she fought against the current, kicking towards the black spar, and again and again she was ducked beneath the waves, salt water filling her mouth, her nose, until every breath was a heaving cough. Around her was nothing but grey—the waves, the haar, the cliffs—and so she barely noticed as her vision began to dim, creeping in from the edges until there was nothing but a pinpoint of black ahead of her. She reached for it, desperate, choking, and the last thing she felt before darkness overtook her was the touch of fingers on her wrist.

YOU HAVE SOUGHT *to conquer the sea as you have the earth, put out on your rafts, your barques, your steam ships, bent on making your mark on every corner of the map, determined to empty the oceans as you have the forests, to hunt, to farm. You chart lines from point to point, and where you cannot go you dig and build new channels, you bend the water to your will—viaducts and canals, bridges and dams.*

And yet here beneath the surface lies another world. Your body is at once a stone, an anchor, and weightless, suspended. Your hair and clothing flow around you, unfettered, your body unburdened by gravity but rather at the mercy of the inexorable push and pull of the moon.

Your senses are of little use here: smell gone, touch numbed, eyes and ears dimmed. From the second you dip beneath the surface you are dying moment by moment, counting down your heartbeats to their last.

You will never have dominion here.

CHAPTER TWENTY–TWO

THE ROOM WAS close, and far too warm. Norah feebly pushed back against the blankets mounded over her, wrinkling her nose at the smell of seawater and peat smoke. She was sore, her limbs and chest aching, her throat raw, but she was alive. Whole. *Safe*.

A figure stirred at the edge of her vision, rising and swimming into view. "Will you let me help you drink some water?" Practical. Matter-of-fact. Unhesitating. Norah's treacherous heart warmed at the familiar manner even as her stomach seized with dread.

"Get away." Her voice was barely a whisper, but she put the full weight of her betrayal and disgust into it. "I will not have you near me."

"Very well." Agnes stepped back, moved to the little fireplace and reached for a poker. "There's a cup by the bedside."

"I'll drink nothing you give me."

"It's just water."

Agnes prodded at the burning turf, still shimmering in and out of view as Norah's eyes struggled to retain focus in her half-awake stupor. Where were they? Norah had never been in this plain white-walled room before, or in this hard, narrow bed.

Norah reached for the cup with trembling fingers, steeling herself as she raised it to her lips. She would not show weakness here—at least, no more than she could help, prone and entirely at the other woman's mercy in this strange room.

Gulping down the water, she immediately began to retch as it threatened to come back up. Eyes watering, she pushed herself more fully upright, waiting until the coughing had subsided before setting the cup aside. "Where am I?"

"My room. By the time we got this far I didn't much fancy the stairs."

There was wry amusement in Agnes's voice and Norah wanted to scream at her. She could see now that Agnes had her hair loose and hanging down her back in wet tendrils, and was clad in what looked for all the world like a man's nightshirt, her long legs bare beneath it. Norah herself, she realised now, was naked beneath the thick mound of blankets. She swallowed heavily and pulled the blankets back around herself, as if cotton and feather could provide any protection against the forces Agnes wielded.

"What do you mean? You—you found me?"

"Found you?" Was she amused or incredulous? Her tone was so even, so calm, that it was hard to tell. She spoke with the grim surety of the condemned. "No, I didn't find you. I was after you from the moment you left the house."

Of course she had been. Agnes wouldn't have wanted to lose the laird's wife, not after working so hard to secure her. "I wish you had let me drown," Norah said, closing her eyes against the glow of the fire.

"Don't be ridiculous."

Norah's eyes flew open. "Ridiculous? That's what you call it, when I am destined to become no more than a living corpse in this mausoleum of a house? *Ridiculous*?"

Agnes replaced the poker on its stand, and turned back to Norah. The room contained only one chair, and it was right by the bed. Agnes instead moved to lean against the wall beside the fireplace, arms hanging by her sides, palms pressed to the rough whitewashed plaster behind her. "I know you're not going to believe me right now, but I am doing everything I can to try to protect you from exactly that."

Norah's laugh was a bitter bell. Agnes was correct; there was no way Norah could believe her, but every fibre of her being longed to do just that. Who was more deluded—Norah, or the witch who had captured her? "I've seen how you protect people. I want none of it."

"You don't know what you saw."

"I know exactly what I saw," Norah said, though her voice betrayed her uncertainty.

"Tell me, then. Tell me what you've seen—not just today, but these past weeks. Tell me what I have done. To him. To you."

"You've controlled us! Manipulated us!"

Agnes merely quirked an eyebrow at Norah's outburst, and it was so infuriatingly calm that she carried on hotly. "You've used the vervain to keep us docile—I looked it up, you know. The Enchanter's Herb? No doubt it helps you to work your magic on us. You've lied, you've hidden things… I found the dress, the drawing. You *knew* I was going mad and you told me I was well, keeping all evidence swept away so I could not even trust my own memories!"

"The dress." Agnes drew a long breath in through her nose. "Do you… have you remembered what happened, then?" She had grown a little tense, Norah saw, her fingers steepled against the wall where she'd rested them.

"I—" Even now Norah's mind rebelled against recalling that afternoon, a chill sweeping over her and causing her to burrow into the blankets as her skin pricked with goose pimples. "There was a sheep. And a… lamb. It was born not right."

"You were in pieces when you arrived at the house with it gathered up in your arms like a bairn. It took a wee while to convince you to hand it over." Agnes's voice was thin, stretched tight. Norah realised that as calm and even as she sounded, it was taking some effort to remain so. "Norah, I did not do this to you. There's something else at work here. I have been trying to *help* you, not control you."

Norah balled her fists in the rough blankets, fighting the urge to fall for Agnes's deception. "And Alexander? Was that helping, what you were doing? Is it helping to rob him of his vitality, his faculties?"

Agnes exhaled slowly—it was not quite an irritable sigh, but Norah could feel impatience nipping at the edges of it. "Think on what you saw in that room. It was not something I would have wished for you to see, but you must realise: I was not robbing him of anything. I was giving it."

Norah cast her mind back: the slow depression of the plunger in perfect detail, how it seemed to inch downward in the space between her heartbeats. Her grip on the sheets loosened, shoulders slumping. It felt true.

"Giving what?" she murmured, feeling as if she was approaching the edge of a precipice—though of understanding or delusion she wasn't sure.

"That's a difficult question to answer. No two people believe the same thing about what makes us who we are. Whether we have a soul, an… essence. Vitality. Whatever you want to call it, Alexander's must be replenished, or he fades away to nothing at all."

That much was not hard to believe, but something niggled at Norah. "There was a point, not long after I arrived, where he seemed almost normal."

Agnes hesitated. "You seemed so lonely. I thought maybe, if I gave more, helped him come back to himself…"

"You mean…" With a sudden dawning horror Norah remembered Agnes's own fading health during that period, her drawn face and stooped shoulders. Norah had fretted for her, worried that her duties were too draining, but if her story was to be believed it was something even more elemental that had caused her decline. "This can't be possible."

"Maybe not. Nevertheless it is where we find ourselves. But Norah, as much as I wish we could ease you gently into this understanding, I don't think we have the time."

Agnes pushed away from the wall and stepped towards Norah, began to reach out before she caught herself.

"Alexander was always melancholic; even as a boy he was plagued by darkness. I thought that this force that worked on him, that it was something he succumbed to only because it was in his nature to do so, because the guilt ran in his blood, because loneliness came so naturally to him. I thought you, with all your strength of will, your natural honesty, your *life*, would be safe. I would never have allowed you to come here if I thought you would be vulnerable in the same way. It seems clear I was wrong."

"But what *is* this force? What does it want with me, with Alexander? And why does it scorn you?"

Agnes shook her head. "It doesn't *want*. It just *is*. It isn't a thinking being that can be mollified or bargained with. If you did believe in the soul, it would best be described as the soul of the land itself. Generations of this family have tried to fight with the land, to reshape it for their own use—"

"And I've done the same," Norah said, the realisation tightening a knot in her stomach that wouldn't budge. Her thoughts caromed wildly from the memory of dark smudges beneath her fingers and furrows in paper to strange and echoing cries on the wind. Each attempt to master her surroundings had been met with disaster and yet she had pushed on, heedless of the warning. "And you tried to stop me. Oh, Agnes..." She leaned toward the other woman, her anger subsumed by this new wash of guilt and fear, and Agnes seemed to take this as permission, for she closed the distance between them in a couple of strides to stand by the bed. The firelight shone through her thin shirt, her body cutting a lean silhouette beneath the raw fabric, like a Grecian goddess rendered in black on ochre. Despite her mistrust, and the lingering feeling that she had been played for a fool, Norah felt the beginnings of a quickening within her. Still she hesitated, resisting the urge to surrender to

Agnes's commanding presence. "I thought I was going mad," she murmured. "And yet you kept your secrets."

"I had no choice."

"There was every choice," Norah said, frowning. "That I nearly died before you would share the truth…" She watched Agnes's expression, so familiar now with each small twitch and blink that she could see the remorse seep in like a reluctant tide. "I cannot endure that again."

"I couldn't save Alexander," Agnes said. "I gave everything I could, and all it did was sharpen his despair to a point. He's been on that roof before. I know it's hard to see him as he is now, but he's more at peace like this—quiet. Calm. But you… whatever it takes, *I will not let that happen to you.*"

There was something in the way she spoke those final words that vibrated in Norah's marrow, like an echo of the voice, the sheer *will* she'd heard in Agnes's command to MacCulloch in the stable, to Alexander on the roof. She did not say 'I promise'. This went beyond a promise. It felt like an oath from a fairy tale: magic, unbreakable. Perhaps it was.

"Let's leave," Norah said, reaching for Agnes, drawing her closer, gripping her sharp hips. She leaned up to press her lips to the spot between the other woman's breasts, murmured the next words there. "We could go anywhere. Surely it would be better for Alexander, for *us*, to leave Corrain far behind." She drew in a deep lungful of air, the sting of brine mingling with the caress of Agnes's scent in her nostrils, a reminder of where they had been, where they now were. A wave of pain and fatigue flowed across the desire kindling in her belly, but could not douse it.

"My family have always lived here." Agnes's hand found Norah's nape and rested there: cool, familiar. "There's a tether to this place, for me. It needs my protection."

The words rang hollow, somehow, and Norah drew back to meet Agnes's gaze. "The land seems perfectly capable of protecting itself, from what I've seen," she observed, the rowan's dark presence looming in her memory.

Agnes bowed her head. "Aye, maybe so. But…" Though it wasn't like her to start an utterance she couldn't finish, she seemed at a loss for anything further to say. Instead, she reached behind herself to grab the collar of the shirt she wore, pulling it off over her head without preamble, her damp hair tumbling down her back in its wake. As in every other way, their unclothed bodies could not look more different: Agnes was hewn marble, stone-cut planes and hollows, small-breasted, long-limbed. She reached for Norah, and time distilled. As Agnes sank onto the bed, Norah opened to her, sharp meeting soft, dark sinking into light.

CHAPTER TWENTY–THREE

THERE WAS AN irony inherent in the fact that the first time Norah woke to find Agnes still sharing her bed should be the occasion on which said bed was far too small for two. Agnes was pressed to her back with her arm pinned beneath Norah's neck. The unsettling result of this was that the first thing to come into focus as Norah opened her eyes was the blue-and-yellow dappled constellation of needle bruises at the crook of Agnes's arm. The sight brought a reflexive revulsion—though she now understood the purpose behind it, it was difficult to escape the memory of the gory procedure she had witnessed. The longer she lay with it, however, the more Norah felt a creeping tenderness, and eventually she leaned in to press a soft kiss to the site. Agnes stirred behind her, and Norah felt lips touch her shoulder in turn.

"I've wanted this," she said, voice thick with sleep. "But I couldn't let you see those marks."

Norah knew it to be only half true. There was a guardedness to their earlier encounters, a question hanging over them that she only recognised now, in hindsight. Agnes had not only feared the exposure of her secrets but also of her heart. But she allowed the tiny lie. All things considered, it was a sweet one.

They lay together as long as they could; which was to say, only a few minutes before Agnes was extricating herself from their sleep-soft embrace, deflecting Norah's pleas with a matter-of-fact recitation of all the chores that awaited her. Not least of these was the routine of tending to Alexander, who needed groomed, dressed, fed, and arranged comfortably before the fire in his room. Norah did propose to assist, both out of guilt and in an attempt to be helpful, but the other woman waved off her offer with a perfunctory acknowledgement. It was clear that however close they found themselves, they still were not equals—Norah was little more than a naive girl when it came to the graft of running a household.

It wasn't just guilt that made Norah want to follow Agnes—nor the desire to be near her, for all that was stronger now than ever. Her true motive was the lurking fear of what might transpire outwith Agnes's presence. Perhaps Agnes sensed this, for she paused at the door to her room. "I'll bring you tea," she said. "Sleep a wee bit longer—don't forget you nearly died yesterday."

Agnes was right, and Norah was too tired to argue. She curled back under the blankets, already cooler for Agnes's absence, and fell back to sleep almost immediately. The little clock at the bedside said it was mid-morning by the time Norah reawakened. As the dust of sleep cleared from her mind, she was reminded that this was not in fact a day like any other. To hear Agnes tell it, her sanity was wearing thin, and would continue to do so unabated until whatever influence the land held over her senses and memories could be broken. She rose and dressed, and went to find her lover, betrayer, and would-be saviour, three-in-one.

She did not have to go far. Agnes was in the kitchen, scribbling away in a ledger of house accounts. The grumbles of her stomach reminding Norah that in spite of the various other pulls on her attention she did require sustenance, she fetched a bowl of porridge for herself, and made a fresh pot of tea.

"So." She tried for a business-like tone but the word came out shrill, and she cleared her throat, poured the tea, and took a seat beside Agnes with her bowl. "What now? What can I do to prevent this madness taking me?"

Agnes reached for her cup and slid it closer, but did not lift it to her lips.

"Leave," she said simply. "The best and safest thing for you to do would be to leave this place, and never return."

Norah furrowed her brow. "I said that last night."

"Last night you asked me to come with you. And I cannot."

"You *will* not, you mean." Agnes did not argue, and Norah's frown deepened. "I won't leave you behind."

"Then we are at an impasse," Agnes returned with a shrug. Norah felt a momentary flare of irritation, but then Agnes reached and touched her hand where it lay on the table, and just like that, all was forgiven.

"So we both stay," Norah murmured. "What does that mean?"

Agnes gave a quiet sigh. "I don't know," she said at length. "I have tried to help the land to heal. I thought perhaps if it was left alone—no sheep, no industry—it would… well. Leave the people alone."

"The sheep," Norah said, pouring some milk into her porridge and giving it a stir. "If we send them away, will it…" She couldn't quite bring herself to speak it aloud; for all that she believed Agnes's claim it still sounded like utter madness when she tried to put it into words.

"The best thing we can do for this place is leave it be," Agnes said. "This part of the world was never meant to be tamed. Whether we can put back to sleep what was awakened by the eighth baron… I don't know."

"Awakened? What is that supposed to mean?"

Agnes frowned down at the ledger in front of her, pulling her lower lip between her teeth to chew it. She pushed her chair back and rose to her feet in one smooth movement.

"Eat up," she said. "I'll show you."

Norah had ridden the little cart before, the day MacCulloch had taken her to see Corrain for the first time. Today's journey was longer, and her legs shook as she climbed down at their destination. Agnes had taken them a good hour inland along narrow farm tracks leaving the coast behind until there was only scrub and grassland gently undulating away in every direction. There were hills here—nothing compared to the lofty Highland bens but enough that the wee glen they'd entered had completely obscured the building until they were almost upon it.

It was a squat rubble-built construction, with two levels of arched open windows. It had no roof or floors; the only wood remaining unscavenged was the skeleton of a large water wheel set in the burn that wound along the lowest furrow of the dale. Around them were other signs of industry—low drystane walls, rusted machinery remnants, and a single 'adit'—a horizontal shaft driven at a shallow angle into the hillside. Norah trod with care around the perimeter of the building—Agnes had warned her that there were vertical shafts too.

"They called it the Burg after the broch on the next hill over. When William Barland bought the barony he had the land surveyed. He thought there was iron here, so he sank a pit."

As soon as Agnes had told her where they were going Norah had felt a wave of dread; if ever there was to be a locus for the malevolent forces it would surely be here, where men had breached the earth in search of riches. And yet as she circumnavigated the gap in the hill, braced for unsettling hallucinations or the sense of a malign presence, there was… nothing. The dark shaft emanated no alien revulsion, no seething betrayal, and she heard no whispers in her ear. It was simply a hole in the ground, empty and still, and somehow that was the worst of all possible outcomes.

The discovery should have lessened the thready hammer of her pulse, but it did not abate, even as they moved back up the burn towards the carcass of the wheel. It was rotten and worn now, the wood darkened from decades of water seepage. Norah felt the sudden urge to tear it all down: the remnants of the building, the wheel, the twisted scaffolding. Even these skeletal remains felt too incriminating to leave standing, a confession and a condemnation all in one.

"This was a crushing mill," Agnes said as they ducked inside the building. "They'd break up the ore here and then ship it to their furnaces down south." It was strange to hear those words used for her own home—to Norah, 'south' meant England. But they were a long way from the Ayrshire collieries where the Barlands had made their fortune.

Norah turned in a slow circle to drink in the building's cavernous interior. "This couldn't have been the most profitable venture."

"No, neither it was," Agnes confirmed. "There was ore, but they had a terrible time getting it out of the ground. Collapses, floods. Men died. The pit was only open a few years."

"Why did he try? Why even bother? He'd made his fortune. He already owned several pits, proper ones."

"Well, this is it. This is the thing. He didn't *need* to. He just *wanted* to," Agnes spat the words like they tasted bitter. "There was iron to be had, so he wanted to have it." She gestured to the walls around them. "This was the start, I suppose. The moment the land took against him. My grandmother used to say that the Barlands would pay what they owed. When I was wee I always thought she was talking about what they'd done to the people—cramming everybody onto crofts, shipping them off. But I begin to think that's not what she meant at all. When William Barland dug these holes, he somehow… struck a nerve."

Norah chewed her lip thoughtfully, her gaze travelling over the pitted stone and rusted metal left behind. There was a profound relief in having these questions answered at last, and yet not one of those answers came with solutions to the problem at hand. "What happened to him? The eighth baron?"

"Did he disappear through a crack in the earth one day, d'you mean?" Agnes chuckled. "Heart attack, I think. This place didn't have decades to get its hooks in the way it did his son and grandson."

You take what is not yours. But as you change the earth so too are you changed: as you twist the land so too are you twisted.

"I see." Norah again wanted to plead for them to absent themselves from the land, for Alexander's sake if nothing else, but despite her apparent amusement there remained something hard and uncompromising in Agnes's expression. Was she *glad* of the Barlands' punishment? It barely bore contemplating and yet the thought, once summoned, was hard to shake. That resolute set to her shoulders, the tilt of her chin. For a moment, Norah was back at the stone circle, watching strong, lean hands cut open a lamb and wash with its blood. Was it truly a fantasy, or was it the land remembering a protector, one who had exacted revenge on its behalf? She shivered, wrapping her arms around herself. "I think I'd like to leave, if that's all right."

"Of course."

It began to rain as they turned the horse back towards Corrain, a thin, soft layer of moisture that didn't so much fall as float about them, soon diffusing into a thick, damp mist. It weighed heavily on Norah's shoulders, reminding her of the press of the sea and her desperate flight from the house the day before. There was that same wash of grey around them, so that it was impossible to tell distance or even elevation; with each rise they crested, Norah became more and more convinced that this was when they would tip over off the end of the world.

She wasn't the only one who felt it. Their usually even-tempered draught horse fretted, Agnes muttering and tutting as she fought to keep them on the path. The going was slow, as they didn't dare pick up too much speed for fear of missing a turn on what was comparatively open countryside. The cart crawled forward, yet even that felt risky; each passing minute brought them closer to Corrain House once more.

Norah first saw the movement out of the corner of her eye. She turned sharply, praying it was nothing more than mists stirred by the wind, but instead of dissipating the motion continued, gathering coherence until she could make out the vague shadow of a figure moving in the grey. She had heard of such a phenomenon before, walkers startled by their own shadow in the swirling mists, but this singular figure reflected neither she nor Agnes, safely seated in the cart. As Norah watched another figure coalesced, then another, all vaguely human in form and trudging onwards through the drizzle; the sight drew icy fingers down her spine though she could not say why. At last she turned to Agnes, wanting at once to ask for her reassurance and yet at the same time fearing what she'd say. Agnes did not look at her, but she did speak.

"You're safe with me," she said. "We just need to keep heading straight."

Their horse snorted and tossed his head, though Norah had no idea whether he could sense the ghostly figures. Certainly Agnes's hands were steady on the reins, brooking no argument, and the cart continued onward, flanked by more and more of the spectres. Every time Norah would glance away they seemed to move closer to the cart, crowding in, though they remained dim and distorted, like she was viewing them through warped and grimy glass. Yet something within her knew them as human—in some way at least, whether in spirit or merely memory. Dark hollows on their faces suggested eyes, mouths, but if they wore a particular expression, whether anger or hurt or hunger, she couldn't say.

She half expected to hear whispers or howls in the air around them, but instead there was only a dead still, and as at the pit this was somehow more unnerving, winding something tight within Norah until she felt ready to snap at the slightest provocation. She shifted closer to Agnes on the bench, and though Agnes could not take her hands off the reins, she did lift her elbow and lean to press it to Norah's side in a sort of slow nudge. *You're safe with me.*

They ought to be back by now. They had not turned, could not have circled back, and yet Norah felt sure they had been going too long through this endless blank white. She was so disorientated that she gasped when Agnes pulled the cart to a halt.

"We're at a gate," she said.

The mist was thick with the spectres. They had stopped with the cart, milling closer. Norah gripped her arm. "You can't."

"It's all right. Just stay here."

It was all Norah could do to pry her fingers away from Agnes's arm to release her. Agnes jumped down and rounded the horse. Within a few feet she was as indistinct as the figures, and Norah's heart hammered in her throat. What if she never came back? Suddenly the cart began to move: Agnes was leading the horse. Agnes was still here with her.

Norah drew in a deep breath and then expelled it, then another, willing the dread to lift. Slowly she realised that it wasn't just her own ragged gasps that rent the air: all around her there was a collective inhalation and exhalation, a sound so consuming and abyssal that her own breathing felt shallow and fragile by comparison. It wasn't until the scent of brine pricked her nostrils that she could resolve what she was hearing—not the breath of the spectres but the ocean's roar. Somehow they had found the sea, and Norah grasped the seat tightly, remembering the steep drop over the cliff, the sharp rocks beneath.

The cart came to a stop. Had Norah lost time again? There had been more gates on the way out. The figures kept moving, drifting onwards through the mist. There was no wind and yet they were borne onwards as if a breeze propelled them inexorably towards their end. Somehow she knew, through memory or instinct, that the edge was near, and gasped as the first spectre reached it and then melted away. More poured after it, dozens of figures slowly sublimating—one moment there, the next consumed by the drop. What did it mean?

Agnes's face surfaced from the fog beside her, looking up from the ground. She reached out a hand. "We're back," she said, and then, "it's all right."

Norah hovered nearby in pensive silence while Agnes unhitched and stabled the horses, led them back inside, made them tea. It was Agnes who broke the silence.

"D'you see, now, why I cannot simply leave?"

Norah blinked. "I can't say that I do," she said. "What I just saw gave me reason ten times over to do just that."

Agnes pressed her lips to a line. Then, "What the Barlands did to the land, perhaps it can be undone and perhaps it can't, but in any event I need to be here—to bear witness. To see that justice is served."

Norah's confusion deepened. "'Justice'? What does that mean, 'justice'? You've only ever spoken of a duty of care. Where does justice come into it?"

Agnes was silent, and in that silence Norah picked once more over the shattered fragments of the past days and weeks. Alexander Barland sitting in his chair, pale and absent. Alexander Barland at his most vital and desperate, up on the roof. *Let me go, please, let me go.*

"You're keeping him here as a punishment."

Agnes looked up sharply. "This is his home; where else would he be?"

"Oh, don't be obtuse," Norah snapped as the pieces clicked into place. "That wasn't a fit of madness on the roof, was it? It was a moment of lucidity. He wants to die, and you won't let him." If one had asked her about the relative morality of suicide six months previously Norah would no doubt have responded dutifully that it was a mortal sin in God's eyes. But here and now God felt very distant, and the other forces at play seemed to muddy matters considerably. "If his suffering runs that deep is it not his right to end it?"

"His *right*?" Agnes bristled, drawing upright and squaring her shoulders. "What right did his grandfather have to run my people off their land? To burn our houses and send us to die at sea? What right did his father have to rape my mother, to keep her in this house and use her when he pleased and throw her away when he didn't?" Norah gasped; this was not a surprise, not truly, but to have it stated so baldly felt almost like a physical blow. "Nobody gave him the right to take her from me but that's exactly what he did, and long before she died, too: there are more than just medicines growing in that courtyard and my mother knew exactly how to use them. And then this man…" Agnes pushed to her feet, away from the table, as though she felt the need to put more distance between her and Norah. "This man decides that his troubles—the land his family stole, the fortune they stripped from the earth—they're just too much to thole? No." She shook her head. "I have to live with what the Barlands have done. The very earth has to live with it. I could not let him simply remove himself from that pain."

"He was haunted by the pain of those people, of the land!" Norah countered. "Driven mad by it! And rather than allow him an escape, you yoked him to this house, to you, so that he may suffer more? And then you had the gall to tell me you were helping him, soothing him." Agnes's voice had been tight and cold, vibrating with barely controlled emotion, but Norah's was as hot as a burning ember. "You are many things, Agnes Gunn, but I never took you to be cruel."

Agnes gave a start at this, her expression flickering momentarily before returning to its stony mask. "I do what I must."

"No." Norah was standing too, now, the table acting as a physical manifestation of the sudden barrier between them. She gave a ragged sigh. "I think you believe that," she said. "But that only tells me that you are as poisoned by this place as he is. Whatever the right or wrong of what Alexander wants, what *you* seek, this punishment, that cannot be something you truly want on your conscience. This… force, whatever it is, you are no more immune than anybody else to its vile influences."

"You're wrong."

Tears sprung up into Norah's eyes at the sheer impassivity of the woman before her, her unerring ability to retreat back into enigma, to become unknown and unknowable. But she *had* known Agnes. She had seen Agnes's warmth, her strength, her heat. She would not lose her to this. "I'm not," she said. "I won't believe that. It's this house that is wrong. But if you won't come away with me I must find a way to make it right." A chill settled across Norah's shoulders and sent a shudder down her spine, as though she had been cast suddenly into shadow. Dark branches loomed in her mind, ever present, ever lingering just out of sight, grasping, rotten. Something hardened within her. However this had begun, whether it was a hex cast from a hilltop or an elemental force awakened beneath the earth, the malign influence of this place was centred on the tree squatting at the very heart of this cursed tomb of a house. For better or worse, if Corrain House was to be their home, hers, and Agnes's, if they were to stay, she meant to defend it, and end this once and forever.

YOU DREAM, AND *in that dream you walk the length and breadth of your cursed stone coffin, whispers and darkness following in your wake. The rooms are empty and infinite, the corridors a twisted maze.*

Outside lies the endless seething earth. You feel it now: the revulsion. You feel the floorboards warp and twist as the land bucks beneath them, refuses to be broken. The avenging earth will not be vanquished and it cannot be appeased. It will not be quietened until you are gone, until this house has crumbled to stone and ash and the people within are nothing but a rotted memory.

The stag stalks by your side, its heaving sides of wood and iron, its eyes flaming coals. You feel strong when it is with you, repulsed but unafraid.

It whispers to you. It tells you that you have power if you will only grasp it. It tells you that you can end this. It tells you that you are the needfire: you are the cleansing flame that can burn out this plague that blights you, you can hack away that diseased limb and cauterise the stump. A flame ignites behind your breastbone. Your veins are glowing tendrils. The stag bellows and the land cries out as you spread your arms and lift your burning eyes to the stars above. You will not be consumed.

The stag lies.

But in your desperation, balanced on that blade between your world and the dark, teetering at the edge of the yawning chasm of the hungry earth, you choose to believe it.

CHAPTER TWENTY-FOUR

THE AXE STRUCK home with a thud that reverberated up Norah's arms, jarring her to the core. She was not a fragile woman by any means—quite the reverse, much to her mother's chagrin—but she was nevertheless unused to activities such as this.

After that morning's visit to the Burg Mine Norah had felt fit for very little, utterly drained by the experience with the misty apparitions that had stalked them home and the argument with Agnes that had followed—not to mention the lingering fatigue from her near-death excursion on the beach. But upon retreating to her chamber and lying down her mind refused to cooperate: sleep would not come. She was too distressed, too angry, and too determined to find an answer.

Agnes could not help her. Agnes, in fact, appeared to be labouring under the misapprehension that nothing could be done, that she and Norah and Alexander must all remain in this purgatory, awaiting the slow erosion of their sanity until nothing was left but hollow shells that ached for a death that Agnes would not permit. The idea that this was her true will was unthinkable: she must be under the influence of this place, just like her brother, just like Norah. Agnes had tried appeasement without success—no matter how lightly they trod the land it raged at them. The solution must lie in a counterattack. But how did one attack the very ground beneath one's feet? The answer did not come to Norah until she rose to visit a pensive Alexander in his stale, dark room.

Through his window she spied the courtyard, and there the rowan tree stood, its wizened hands outstretched, the one physical manifestation that seemed to hold a power of its own over Corrain House and the people in it. In that moment, Norah's resolve sharpened to a point.

THE ROWAN HAD no leaves to shake as Norah hacked away. At first her efforts seemed to have no effect whatsoever, barely even denting its surface as her blows bounced and skited off its hard trunk. Slowly but surely, however, Norah's swing improved, and the blade began to find its mark, knocking ever-thicker blackened wedges from its surface, her chopping echoing all around the courtyard.

She wasn't sure how long she had been going when she was stopped short, mid-swing, by a frantic rapping of knuckles on glass. She straightened up to look: on the western edge of the courtyard, Alexander was standing at his bedroom window on the second storey, knocking and knocking. His eyes were wide with fear, head shaking fervently.

At that moment, all around Norah, the house gave a great shake, as if it was a creature trying to rid itself of something small and biting. The screams followed a moment after.

A bone-deep terror seized Norah. She *felt* rather than heard the long, deep groan of earth and stone beneath her feet, a sound that vibrated beneath what the ear could discern. The shouting continued, coming from the direction of the cliffside scaffold, and she dropped the axe to the ground, running from the courtyard. She had intended to make for the nearest side exit, but on passing by the library's open door she heard an almighty cracking and could not help but look inside. The library floor bulged and twisted before her eyes, the boards at first swelling up like the hull of a ship, and then bending the other way, all at once, like a great shuddering sigh. As Norah watched from the doorway, they bowed and warped and at last gave way, the whole corner of the room caving inward and ripping large chunks of the plasterwork from the wall with them, as effortless as tearing a leaf from a book. The whole room began to tilt, bookshelves toppling and propelling their contents into the newly opened hole. The men's screaming was louder now and Norah realised it was coming from beneath: from *inside* the pit that had just opened.

The last time there had been screaming from the cliff, Norah had panicked and waited to be shepherded down the stairs by Agnes, but she was not that helpless woman anymore. It was she, at least in part, who had brought this upon them; she who had tried to fight back against the land, the sea and the elements. She could not close her eyes against this any longer.

Norah ran towards the service wing, stopping only to scoop up an armful of clean linens from the scullery before exiting through the side door there. The day had begun mild and still, but the skies opened now in a sudden torrent and she was soaked through in moments. She did not encounter anybody else along the way, but when she rounded the corner of the house she saw MacCulloch peering over the edge of the cliff, his spade still in hand. Her stomach twisted with distaste at his presence, but there was no avoiding him under the circumstances.

"What's happened?"

"Looks like a collapse—and a chunk of cliff's fallen away. Some of the scaffold's broken too," MacCulloch said, gesturing over the edge. "There's a couple of men on the scaffold still. One's fallen, don't think he's going anywhere. Can't see the others."

Norah edged closer, near enough to peek over herself. She could not make out much of the scaffolding from this angle, but the collapse was evident enough, large heaps of rock and debris scattered across the sand below—and among them a body, still and mangled. The sound of the ocean faded to a muted bellow, the rain the barest brush across her skin;

she had done this. A man was dead because of her. Was it cheerful Davey, so quick to smile and reassure, so willing to pit himself against this doomed venture? Her blood ran cold.

"We have to help them!" Norah pulled back to fix her gaze on MacCulloch, wishing she could command the same blind obedience with her declarations as Agnes did. "We'll need ropes, and something to secure them against—the horse, get it, bring it over here now."

MacCulloch lifted his eyebrows in obvious scepticism, but nodded. "Right you are, my lady."

He loped off, leaving Norah alone on the cliff edge. She knelt down, the wet mud immediately soaking through her skirts as she leaned over the edge. She shouted that help was coming, but could not make out anything in the incoherent moaning that drifted up from below, distorted by the rain. For a moment she considered whether the rescue efforts would be better off performed from the safety of the beach, but a quick glance was enough to show that the tide was rapidly coming in. Soon the sand would disappear, concealed by waves and completely impassable without a boat. The crew must have been nearly finished for the day. How she wished they had left early, just this once.

Scrambling to her feet, Nora turned to find both MacCulloch and Agnes approaching, the sturdy draught horse between them. The rain battered down, churning the grass-poor ground to mud and making each step treacherous. There were piles of equipment and building materials here and there—props, stone blocks, metal girders, and—hallelujah—a few coiled lengths of rope. Norah rushed to retrieve them, fumbling the wet rope with fast-numbing fingers, her shoes almost losing purchase on the rain-slicked ground.

Securing a rope to the horse's harness was the work of a few moments, though it felt like hours. MacCulloch seemed to Norah to be altogether far too relaxed in his movements, and it was all Norah could do not to yell at him to hurry up.

They created a large loop in the end of the rope and guided the horse nearer the cliff, MacCulloch at its head, Norah and Agnes with the line between them. They tossed it down, watching the rope disappear into the driving rain. Would the men be able to find it? Were they fit to use it? Norah uttered a prayer, once more dropping to her knees in the cold mud to peer over the edge. She could hear the men shouting to one another but with the sound of the rain and the incoming tide now crashing on the rocks at the base of the cliff she couldn't make out a single word that was being said. A man hove in sight, edging along a half-collapsed section of scaffolding, and made a grab for the rope, wrapping it around his forearm and yelling indistinctly upward.

"Someone has the rope!" she turned to shout excitedly to Agnes and MacCulloch, and MacCulloch made to lead the horse away from the cliff. At first it wouldn't budge, pawing at the ground, clearly spooked, but when Agnes moved to its head and took the bridle from MacCulloch it seemed to calm a little and she was able to coax it forward. Once they got moving the rescue was executed quite quickly—the horse was used to pulling far heavier objects and before long the labourer was rolling over the clifftop and onto the grass. It was not Davey—Norah vaguely registered him as a lad called Callum, from Crosskirk, a few years older than Davey and a frequent abettor to his jokes and pranks. He seemed physically unscathed save for a cut to his forehead, bleeding profusely and mixing with the rain to stain his brow orange. He sat up as Norah crouched beside him, massaging his arm where the rope had burned it.

"Are you all right? What happened? Who else is down there?"

Callum looked up at her, eyes wide with panic and confusion. "It was so fast I couldnae tell you," he said. "We were packing up when a prop slipped—just slid free, smooth as you like. Don't know if it was the rain or..." He shook his head. Agnes and MacCulloch had backed the horse up and were already throwing the rope over once more.

Callum reached for Norah, grabbing her arm with a sudden burst of urgency. "Manson's on the scaffold, but the rest of the lads, they're under the house," he said. "The stone facing collapsed and wedged between the scaffold and the cliff face. They're trapped."

Trapped. Norah shuddered. It would be a good eight or nine hours before the tide was low enough to approach the house from below, and given the cold, the men would soon start to suffer—not to mention the toll from any injuries they'd sustained. She nodded an acknowledgement and patted his hand, flashing him what she hoped was a reassuring smile before she rose and hurried to Agnes's side.

"There's one more on the scaffold, but the rest are trapped beneath the house," she said, leaning in close to the other woman's ear to be heard over the splatter of the rain. "We can't bring them out this way."

Agnes acknowledged this with a nod, and was about to respond, but at that moment a fresh tension pulled the rope taut, and she turned her attention back to the horse. In a few minutes, Manson too was at the clifftop. He was in better shape than the other man, pushing immediately to his feet and rounding on Norah.

"I hope you're satisfied, my lady!" he yelled. "There's blood on your hands today."

Norah was too shocked to respond, but Agnes stepped in almost immediately, leaving the horse with MacCulloch to insert herself bodily between Norah and the angry foreman. "That's enough," she said, "we don't have time for this."

"Time isn't the problem," was Manson's rejoinder. "There's no reaching them. They're going to die under that house."

Under the house. Suddenly Norah remembered the buckling floors and tearing walls in the library, books and shelves alike sliding into a cavernous hole. "The library. The floor caved in… we may be able to get to them that way, if we're quick, and lucky."

Manson's eyes widened, and MacCulloch's too. The groundskeeper shook his head. "Hang on, hang on," he said. "The whole room must be fit to collapse; it's not safe."

Agnes set her jaw. "Then we'd better get a shift on," she said.

CHAPTER TWENTY–FIVE

THEY GATHERED WHAT ropes and tools they could from the staging site and hurried inside. Callum they deposited in the kitchen with a rag pressed to his head and strict instructions to stay put, while Manson continued onward with them, muttering darkly. Norah led the way, her pulse an urgent drum. With every beat the foreman's words ran over and over in her mind. *There's blood on your hands today.* She could not deny it, but perhaps if they were fast enough, and the house held long enough, they would not lose anyone else.

It was a desperate hope, but desperation was all she had.

The library had shifted further after she'd quit it; the entire floor sloped downward to the crater in the corner. The walls were holding for now, though sheets of plaster had been shaken off in the collapse, exposing the stone behind. Splintered boards and broken plaster littered the floorboards, the air full of dust and moisture from the driving rain outside, and it was so dim that at first they did not see them.

Roots. Creeping from the pit, dividing and subdividing to spread out across the floor, up the walls, strangling bookshelves and weaving above and beneath the warped, cracked floorboards. The smell was sickly and fungal. Norah could *feel* them growing, that sub-audible hum that made her want to vomit.

Norah felt a grip on her arm preventing her advancing into the room. Agnes wore a grim look, intent like an animal poised to flee.

"What in hell…" MacCulloch began to back away, but Manson put an arm out to block his way as a voice joined the groaning and creaking of the suffering library. A long howl of very human pain from inside the pit.

This seemed to break Agnes's trance. She turned to face the men. "We want strong arms on the ropes. Callum's taken a dunt on the head; he's not fit. We'll need you both." She looked to MacCulloch and Manson.

Manson nodded numbly, but MacCulloch's mouth twisted. "Oh aye? I fail to see why I should be risking my neck on this business."

"Because these men will die if we don't do something!" Norah exclaimed, whirling to glare at him. "So get down there, or I'll send you down myself—*without* a rope!"

The groundskeeper's eyes narrowed. Then he glanced sidelong at Manson, who seemed scarcely less angry than Norah in that moment and ready to cuff him. He leaned in, his sour breath in Norah's face as he spoke. "I'll be owed for this," he said. "Be sure I'll collect."

Norah's stomach clenched, but she refused to let her disgust—or her fear—show on her face. There were worse threats than Jamie MacCulloch in this room.

It was an unthinkable thing, to pick their way through the mess of broken wood and tangled roots that now blanketed what remained of the library floor, and yet somehow the four made it to the caved-in corner of the room. The smell was stronger here, like loam and rot. Norah gagged.

There were few good places to tie the ropes—Norah considered securing them around the nearest whorls of root but had visions of the tendrils shifting and recoiling like animals, and quickly reconsidered. In the end they looped the ropes around the legs of a desk wedged against the wall, Manson and MacCulloch holding the other ends so they could lower and raise them quickly.

Both Norah and Agnes sank to their knees and crawled towards the edge of the pit, the boards shifting and groaning beneath them. They could barely make out the interior of the chasm, all jagged rocks and scattered debris, and, of course, the dark and sinuous shape of the rowan roots wending upward.

"Can you hear us?" Agnes yelled, squinting down into the dark. At first there was nothing, and then a call—not too far away, but muffled. It was a cry of pure anguish.

"Euan's deid! He's deid!"

Agnes cursed. "That you, Davey? You all right?"

Norah could hear sobbing, but the reply came. *"Aye."* She felt a flood of relief, but it was soon dammed as he continued, *"Ah'm stuck! There's a gap, but it's too tight."*

Agnes and Norah shared a look. They would have to send somebody down there. Manson would volunteer in a heartbeat—he had already shown great dedication to his crew—but he was older, thicker-set. If there was any chance of someone wriggling through the debris and coming out unscathed, it would have to be—

"MacCulloch," Norah said.

"Oh, no. Not a chance." The groundskeeper took a step back, abandoning all pretence of attending to the rope. "This is an idiotic venture, and I'll have no further part in it. They knew the risks of the job. I'm no' dying for this." With that he turned and moved towards the door.

"Wait!" Norah half expected to hear that strange vibration in Agnes's voice that made it impossible to resist, but on this occasion it was a simple plea.

"I'll go," she said. "But we need you on the rope."

Dread drenched Norah like a fresh shower of rain. "Agnes…"

"It's all right." Agnes's hands went to her waist, and soon enough she'd unbuttoned her skirt and dropped it to the floor without ceremony, standing in a white cotton petticoat and drawers. She eyed the hole, then reached for the rope. "I'll climb down," she said, wrapping the rope around her waist and tying a knot, "but keep this taut in case I slip. MacCulloch. Are you with me?"

The man scowled, but nodded, taking up his station once more by one of the ropes.

"Norah, I need you ready to throw me whatever I need—a spade, a pick, we won't know 'til I see it. Can you do that?"

Norah wanted to scream, to wrap her arms around Agnes, to refuse to aid this foolhardy endeavour, but when she looked at the other woman, strong and resolute, her dark eyes shining, all she could do was nod. Agnes Gunn did not need to use her will on Norah, did not need to ply her with herbs. She had captured her, heart and soul, and Norah could no sooner gainsay her than she could stop the tide. "Be careful, be canny," she whispered, and turned to affix the remaining rope to the handle of one of their lanterns. She would not send Agnes into the darkness unaided.

With a firm nod, Agnes turned and began to descend into the hole, which swallowed her hungrily, even with the lantern lowered alongside on the second rope. As her head disappeared beneath the jagged floorboards there came an almighty growl—Norah gasped, convinced the intrusion had triggered yet another cascade of dirt and rock beneath them and sending desperate prayers that they might be spared. The room shuddered, though it did not tilt further, and as the sound of the battering rain outside grew even louder she realised that it was a storm rolling in, its thunderous roar shaking the very walls of the house.

Minutes ticked by in which all there was to be heard from below was some purposeful scuffling. The rope went slacker as Agnes reached the bottom. It seemed almost anticlimactic: the pit was perhaps only fifteen feet deep in total. But then the depth was not the issue.

"Davey? Davey, shout to me, let me know where you are!"

"*Here!*" A muffled response. Davey sounded slurred, and Norah wondered if he was bleeding or had hit his head like Callum. From up here she couldn't place its direction at all but apparently Agnes could, for she disappeared beneath the overhang of the floor, clambering across the uneven surface of split rock and earth and the remnants of the massive props that had so badly failed.

"Fool's errand, this," MacCulloch scoffed then. "That lad's done for. Even if he weren't, that witch won't get him out. We ought to leave them there and help ourselves—this floor won't hold much longer."

"How dare you," Norah spat, keeping her gaze fixed on that small, soft halo of light at the bottom of the pit. "You're sour because she's braver than you'll ever be."

"Oh aye, is she? She's happy enough to leave people to their fates when it suits her. Just ask his Lordship." Norah could hear the smirk in his voice and had to fight the twist of discomfort his words prompted. What was he talking about? Just lies, surely, a bluff to cover his own cowardice and fear.

"Shut your mouth," Manson said, sounding as impatient for news from below as Norah felt. "And be ready. You're right about one thing—Davey disnae have lang."

Norah thought she could hear rocks being moved, and the library floor gave a worrying lurch. She gave a yelp in spite of herself.

"Agnes?"

"*I've found him!*" Agnes called. "*I need a compress—can you throw down those linens?*"

Grateful for a prompt and the chance to do something, anything, Norah sprang into action. The linens she balled into clumps and sent down in handfuls; too many, surely, but she could not countenance the thought of the workman— or Agnes—injured without anything to staunch their bleeding. "Hurry!" she urged, fingers wrapped around the splintered edge of the floorboards, heedless of the threat. The wind whistled through the gaps in the wall, spattering rain across the floor in slick puddles.

Further instructions followed as the minutes ticked by—a shovel, and then a belt, which had to be requisitioned from Manson's own waist. That didn't bode well, and sure enough, the next call was the last thing they wanted to hear.

"He'll need hauled up on a rope. He's lost blood and he can't stand. I'm going to make him a sling, but be ready."

What followed was an excruciating stretch of time—it could only have been minutes, but felt to Norah like unending hours. Agnes detached the lantern from the second rope, and fashioned a sling from sheets. On her signal they began to haul Davey up, but the way was not smooth and with each bump or jolt the young man would howl in pain. The sound mingled with the moaning of the wind until it seemed that the very earth itself was keening in pain. Norah bent over the pit, trying to see what was going on in the flickering light from the lantern far below, but out of the corner of her eye she caught the writhing and reaching of the roots around them.

Norah scrambled to her feet and tried to get the measure of the situation. Manson was holding Agnes's rope, pulling up the slack as she climbed her way back out of the pit. MacCulloch was on the other rope, his weight leaned back into it, straining with the effort of hauling the injured man up out of the hole. Though her strength could only be a fraction of his, this appeared to be the only area where Norah could be of help, and with the library now coming alive with oily black tendrils, time was of the essence. Biting back her distaste, she took up the rope behind MacCulloch, grabbing it as tightly as she could in her cold, damp hands, and leaning her full weight back into the effort.

Slowly, steadily, the burden lifted, and their combined strength might have been enough but for the workings of the elements. It was impossible to find purchase on the floor, warped and splintered as it was, and the spreading puddles of water forestalled any attempts to brace their feet.

"C'mon, put your back into it," MacCulloch growled, struggling with the rope, "or are you useless at this an' all?"

Norah felt near to collapsing, but wouldn't give him the satisfaction of her failure. Gritting her teeth, she redoubled her efforts, blocking out Davey's howls of pain, the roar of thunder, everything but the sound of her own breathing. They were close—so close—and her heart lifted to see Agnes emerge from the pit dishevelled but seemingly unharmed. She breathed a sigh of relief.

Then there was a flicker of movement, a dark thing thrashing in the shadows near their feet, and MacCulloch swore and lurched forward. He let go of the rope, still cursing, and Norah was jerked forward, Davey's full weight suddenly in her hands. She slammed into the groundskeeper, knocking them both to the ground, and screamed as the rope tore over her palms and then slithered over the edge of the pit.

There were a series of sickening crunches as Davey's prone form tumbled into the rocky hole. His pained moans stopped dead, the gale taking up his cry. Norah scrabbled to the edge, but there was no question of his having survived. She caught a half-sight of a twisted, broken mess of limbs in the lamplight below and swallowed a throatful of bile. He was dead—a sacrifice to the earth, a victim of her hubris and the house's malign influence. He was dead because of her.

"You stupid bitch…" MacCulloch pushed to his feet, boots sliding on the slick board, and turned to her, still half-stooped. One arm he was cradling to his chest. In the other hand he held a shovel. His face was a picture of hate, his voice thin and high with pain. "You fat carline."

Norah scrabbled back on hands and knees, knowing she deserved this punishment and yet resisting her fate with every fibre of her being. MacCulloch advanced over the uneven floorboards, lurching as if drunk. He lifted the shovel.

"*No.*"

The word came from behind Norah and this time it *was* the Voice, that strange timbre only Agnes could affect. MacCulloch stopped short in shock and lost his footing. As the library lurched again, its floor caved in further, and the boards beneath the man's feet gave way. The shovel flew from his hand and he flailed for purchase, his hand finding a beam and anchoring there. With his injured arm he tried to reach up, but it would not obey—he could not even lift his hand high enough to grab the handhold.

Norah stared down at him, frozen in place. His face was twisted in pain and fear, and for once, pleading. She watched as he struggled, trying to command his injured arm to move, to support his weight, and remembered his threats and self-satisfied smirks. She watched as the fingers of his good hand began to slip from the beam and remembered his sour breath and hissed secrets. She watched his lips form a desperate, silent plea, and she remembered his violent outbursts and extortion.

And then she watched him fall.

The library continued to shudder and twist, and it was this that spurred Norah into action; she scrambled back from the pit that had swallowed MacCulloch faster than she thought possible. Spades and picks slid towards the depression, bookshelves groaning under the stress, and as the wind howled and the rain lashed the windows, the three survivors fled.

CHAPTER TWENTY-SIX

THE KITCHEN, FURTHER back from the cliff and in its own wing as it was, felt safe, at least for the time being. Agnes immediately turned her attention to Callum, fetching water and rags to clean his head wound. Manson sank mutely into a seat and said nothing. Norah had scarcely more presence of mind than he did, the moment of MacCulloch's fall, of the chaotic events that preceded it, playing over and over in her mind. They had failed. *Worse* than failed: fewer people left that library than entered it. There was no going back now even to retrieve the bodies: the roots had begun to spread, already making inroads to the rest of the house as they escaped through its gloomy corridors.

As the panic from one emergency faded, a new concern gripped her.

"Alexander."

Agnes glanced round. "It's the other side of the house. He'll be all right for now."

"All right?" Norah gaped at the other woman, though she barely had the energy to stand. "Whatever force has taken against him—and me—is no longer content to act against us in our minds. It is *coming* for us, Agnes." Manson betrayed no shock at this pronouncement, but then he had been in the library. He had seen the hungry earth, the seeking roots. His expression was worn and tired, and Norah felt a pang of guilt. This was her fault. Perhaps she had not lit the fire that burned beneath Corrain House, but she had certainly fanned the flames. And she would not let Alexander perish in it.

"We need to leave. Tonight. We'll take the cart, go to Thurso, and in the morning begin the journey to Glasgow." She could barely believe what she was saying, but there was no other logical choice. "The family must have residences in the city where we could say. My mother will take us in until we can make the arrangements."

Agnes put down her threaded needle, poised as she had been to stitch the cut on Callum's head, as matter-of-factly as if it was a sock needing darned. She pursed her lips, eyes narrowing. When she spoke her words were carefully curated and a tiny corner of Norah's mind dreaded hearing that Voice, that *will* that Agnes could exert when she had decided a thing must happen. "Norah, you don't know what you're asking. The situation is complicated. We're safe at this end of the house for now. Let's take a wee minute to—"

"*We cannot stay here.*" Norah tried to inject her own will into the words; she just sounded exhausted. She *was* exhausted. Her hands burned as if she had grasped a scalding poker, and every muscle in her body ached. She had no strength but for the iron-clad conviction that staying in Corrain House another day would be the end of them all. "I will not stay here," she echoed more quietly, head sagging. "And I will not abandon Alexander. I'm going to prepare him for the journey."

And with that, she turned on her heel and trudged away, not waiting for Agnes's assent or protest. If the other woman wished to tie her fate to the house, so be it. Norah would be free.

Being in Barland's bedroom was almost like stepping into another world; the wind still howled outside, and the rain lashed at the windows, but with a small fire burning merrily in the hearth it felt almost protected from the earlier events of the evening. But Norah could not shake the sensation that something writhed beneath the floorboards; in between the cheerful crackling of the fire and the sound of the rain there was a deep thrumming pulse, the tell-tale heartbeat of something much larger and much older than anything mortal within Corrain House. If it was a safe haven, it would not stay that way for long.

"I've come to help you pack," she narrated briskly, and to her surprise Barland stirred, lifting his head and fixing her with a stare that seemed almost alert. Already unnerved from the library, the deaths, Norah suppressed a shudder and moved purposefully over to the dresser, pulling out stacks of neatly folded underthings and shirts and mounding them on the bed. There would be a valise somewhere, she was sure, or if she couldn't locate one then her own portmanteaus would suffice. She couldn't imagine packing her art supplies and sketchbooks now—the pages were tainted with images of the rowan, the house, the sea.

"We'll be going into Thurso," she said as she moved to the wardrobe, "in the cart. It's a miserable night but there's nothing for it. We'll make sure to bundle up." The wardrobe smelled of mothballs and dust, and beneath that, an earthy stench, like stagnant water and decay. The aroma and the pain in her rope-burned hands made Norah retch as she sorted through trousers and jackets, but she ignored the discomfort and selected the plainest, warmest garments she could find. From behind her came a noise and she whirled, startled, but it was only Barland shifting in his chair and muttering something indecipherable. He lifted a hand and tugged at the sleeve of his shirt, which she could see now was stained with something dark and crusted.

"Yes… yes, of course, you'll want to change," Norah observed, and selected a shirt from the pile on the bed. She approached him, suddenly shy; despite their wedded status she had never done anything as intimate as changing his clothes, leaving such tasks to Agnes's able hands.

His smell was mingled sweat and vervain and carbolic soap, but as she leaned closer, reached to tug his shirt out from his trousers, she caught another scent below it, pungent and ferrous. The shirt tried to stick to his skin as she removed it, and as she pulled it off over his head it became very apparent why.

Alexander was wounded.

Wounded badly, in fact: right in his middle, just beneath his ribs, was a large, deep puncture. The blood crusted around it was dark, almost black in the dim firelight. Norah gasped when she realised it went straight through him, a matching hole on his back just to the side of the sharp ridges of his spine.

How was he still able to sit? Why was he not bleeding profusely? This was a far more serious wound than could be remedied with a simple transfusion and yet it was barely seeping—not even bandaged.

"Alexander, what happened to you? What—what *is* this?"

The chamber door clicked shut behind her.

"I told you it wasn't the first time he'd been up on that roof."

There was an air of defeat to Agnes's tone that Norah had never heard before, a sort of resigned despair.

Norah frowned at the words, glancing away from him to Agnes's pale face and then back again. She smelled blood, wet earth, and bark, and suddenly remembered her fevered drawing from the garden—the rowan tree, black limbs spread, a single figure impaled on the crown. "No," she murmured, shaking her head. "This is... I don't believe it." And yet, after all that she'd seen, all that she'd experienced, how could she not? Alexander had died—was dead—and Agnes had used something, some charm or hex, to bring him back. Her agitation seemed to bleed out, infecting him, and he shifted, moaning, reaching up to draw long, pale fingers across the wound. "How *could* you?" she asked, pivoting towards Agnes.

"I decided he had not finished paying the price," Agnes said simply. "You were wrong about me. I tried to tell you." She sounded wretched. The moonlight dancing across her tear-bright eyes. "This was me, Norah. I did this. Not the rowan, not the earth. This is who I am. I'm sorry."

Norah gave a bark of a laugh at this. As if this was something that could be atoned for with words. "It's not to me you owe the apology," was all she said, even as she felt her heart crack.

Barland's muttering grew in pitch, and suddenly he was on the move, loping on unsteady legs for the door. Agnes moved to stop him, but Norah intervened, grabbing her wrist, ignoring the pain from her raw palm.

"Don't you touch him!"

Barland fumbled with the door for a moment, and was gone, off at a run along the corridor with a sudden, impossible burst of energy. Agnes broke Norah's grip and set off in pursuit, and so Norah was obliged to follow. Fatigue ate at her with every stride: her layers of clothing were still soaking wet from the storm and her lungs burned, still recovering from her near-drowning. Both Alexander and Agnes made better progress, their long legs eating up the boards beneath them, and Norah was so intent on keeping up that it wasn't until she found herself dodging roots and missing floorboards that she realised where they were headed.

The library was no longer a room.

The whole corner of the house was crumbling, and where the cave-in had been the room now simply stopped: no floor, no walls, the ceiling beginning to fall in chunks from above. The gale whirled around them, carrying a brackish spray of rain and seawater with it. Alexander stood at the edge of this new precipice, skeletal white against the dark sky beyond. His whole body was straining against some unseen force, and it took only a glance at Agnes, who stood near the door, her burning stare fixed upon him, to know what that force was.

"Agnes." Norah was panting, her hair plastered to her feverish forehead. Every fibre of her being rebelled from stepping any nearer to that empty space, and yet she forced herself closer, until she could feel the rain against her cheeks. "Let him go. Please. You know you must."

"I can't." Somehow Norah could hear her over the wind, even though she would not look away from the man—the revenant—on the edge. "Norah, even if—" She sucked in a breath. "Even if I want to, can't you see that we need him, now more than ever? After tonight there will already be so many questions we cannot answer—the house, the deaths, what Manson and Callum have seen. Without him we have no home, no future, nothing."

The gale tore a laugh from Norah's throat. "If in the end this is all you are, Agnes Gunn, I have no home and no future, with or without him. There is a woman I want to spend my life with, but it is not this woman, the one who pursues revenge over everything else. Do you truly want this, more than peace, more than *me?*"

Agnes's eyes widened, flickered with uncertainty, hope. The figure swayed on the edge. "There's just so much. Those dead men, their families, every gossiping hag who's been calling me and mine devils and witches for a hundred years or more. It's too much." As if to emphasise the gravity of their situation, the house around them gave a great groan, and the sounds of falling masonry and cracking wood echoed from the hallway.

"Then let's forget it." Norah reached out and took Agnes's hand, watching Barland's pale silhouette teeter on the brink of the cliff. Agnes's fingers were cold, clenched. Norah fit her palm around them. "Let's leave it all behind. It doesn't matter. None of it does. Only you, and me. We'll disappear, become different people, and the stories will just be that—stories. Leave the land to look after itself. It doesn't need us. It never did."

Finally, Agnes looked away from her quarry, turned her gaze on Norah. "You'd lose everything," she said. "Your mother. Isa. You'd never see any of them ever again."

"It doesn't matter. I have all I need," Norah said, and she squeezed the other woman's hand, ignoring the sting. "But only if you end this, right now."

Agnes exhaled, and in that exhalation, a catch in her throat became a sob.

There was a movement in Norah's periphery: Alexander. He had turned his back to the yawning ocean and was now watching the two women, heedless of the rain beating down on his bare shoulders.

"Alexander." Releasing Agnes's hand, Norah stepped forward, feeling oddly serene despite the yawning drop just beyond. The wind whistled around them, tugging at her hair, her clothes, whispering invitations to the waiting sea. "We never got the chance to truly know each other. I'm sorry for that. You didn't deserve this—any of it."

The revenant shook his head. "I don't know if that's true," he said. "But I am glad it has ended. Thank you." He glanced beyond Norah to the woman behind her, and Norah watched him struggle for words, the muscles of his face tensing with conflicted emotion.

Then he turned and stepped off into nothing.

From behind Norah resounded a mournful, keening cry. Agnes had dropped to her knees, suddenly as limp as a marionette whose strings had been cut. It was as though in his own way Alexander had a hold over Agnes too, a hold that had now released all at once, once and for all.

Norah rushed back to her side, kneeling and taking her hands once more. The house seemed to echo her lament, its timbers crying out as the wood warped and cracked, and Norah tugged Agnes to her feet, pulling her back as animate roots slithered across what remained of the floor, questing for the doorway.

"Quickly love, we need to go," Norah murmured, guiding her into the corridor, where the ground lay littered with plaster and riven canvases, faces and landscapes torn and slashed by the violent quaking of the house. The air carried the scent of burning wood and fabric: somewhere, an oil lamp had smashed and fire had begun to eat away at the inside of the house even as the rain and wind and sea assaulted its exterior. The hallways seemed almost to have remade themselves into a labyrinth; as they fled the library their route twisted and turned like a path through a forest. Agnes would not run, too stunned, too distressed, and Norah was obliged to guide her along by the elbow, picking their way over the uneven, rootbound terrain. She didn't register the way they had taken until they rounded a corner and Agnes halted suddenly, pulling them both up short.

Up ahead was the ninth baron. Where so many other paintings had fallen from their hooks or been punctured and torn by the encroaching vines that climbed the walls, the portrait of Alexander's father hung untouched. Around the bend beyond pulsed a gentle orange glow: the fire.

"We'll go the other way," Norah said, wrapping her hand around Agnes's arm, but Agnes shrugged it off, stepping forward.

Then Norah heard it. The cracks and pops of wooden joints. The hot breath and wet lungs. Long, pronged shadows crawled up the wall as the stag emerged into view. Its fleshless wooden ribcage heaved with each rasping inhalation, viscera glistening black beneath. Its amber eyes glowed like embers. Its warped antlers were huge, blood-slick, spanning the whole width of the corridor in a bony web.

When Agnes stepped forward, in front of Norah, she was at once Agnes and not Agnes. In that moment it was as though standing there occupying that same space, that same tall, sharp frame, was the woman from the stone circle, reaching through decades of suffering and loss to lend Agnes an unspoken ancestral strength. Úna Guinn had welcomed the flames, but Agnes would not burn. Agnes never looked away from the beast in front of them. She reached to the side, lifting an oil lamp from its wall hook. As her fingers curled around the handle Norah's stomach clenched with shock to see that her hand was a dark, livid red, charred flesh blackened and peeling, but the witch was unfazed, gripping the lamp tightly and giving it a single backward swing to build momentum before launching it at the stag. Somehow, it flew right through it, instead hitting the Baron's portrait with a smash. It did not catch immediately, but the fabric hanging on the wall beside it did, the oil-soaked fabric going up with a roar. Norah watched, fixed in place, as the Baron's face bubbled and eventually ignited.

The angry earth cannot be vanquished and it will not be appeased.

The stag was burning too, now. It gave a deep, hoarse roar of pain and anger, and lowered its antlers to charge. It pawed at the ground; stirred by the movement, black tendrils of root and vine writhed around its hooves and ankles, tangling it tight. The stag bellowed again, bucking at its restraints, staggering forward one step, then another. All the while its gaze pinned the women, hunger and rage burning as brightly as the flames licking its body. With each second that passed the corridor grew hotter, closer with smoke; with each second the stag was entangled further, the roots charred but still grasping, still strong. The stag tossed its head, thorn-sharp antlers scoring the walls, the ceiling. Its legs began to buckle beneath it, its body blackening and crumbling like charcoal on a dying fire. Smoke poured along the corridor, heavy and thick with the scent of burning flesh and wet wood. The Barland stag was dead, the embers of its remains entombed by roots that in turn burned and crumbled into ash.

The woman who turned to face Norah was Agnes again. Perhaps there had never been anyone but Agnes—perhaps even up at that stone altar, lingering at the edge of her sight, burning in her dreams, it had only ever been Agnes. Her hands, the red-raw burns already fading, curled into fists.

"Can we go now?"

Norah could see her clearly now: powerful, yes, a witch, perhaps, but a woman beneath it all, angry and heartbroken and scared. Regardless of what had twisted her—the angry earth, the pain of her family's legacy—she had broken the cycle, let the anger loose to burn the rotten timbers of Corrain House and wipe it from the earth. She had chosen to let it all go and in that moment Norah chose *her,* knowing it was no guarantee of anything but the chance to make a new start, finally free, finally together.

Their escape went by in beads of lucidity strung together with pure panic. The realisation on arriving in the now overgrown kitchen that Manson and Callum were already gone—hopefully of their own accord. Shoving dirty and freshly laundered clothes alike into a sack in the scullery. Finding the horse still tethered by the back door, mercifully unharmed and only somewhat spooked. Half running, half sliding down the slope to the cliff path, their retreating figures cutting dark silhouettes from the glow cast on the ground as fire fought rain to burst from the windows and doors of Corrain House in a final purification.

The rain was so heavy it stung Norah's skin as she scrambled down the cliff path; the walk to the tiny kirk on the hill had never felt so long.

It was dark and cold when they finally stepped inside, but it was blessedly quiet and still, and for that Norah was grateful. Agnes had regained her senses in their exodus from the house, and the two women moved in tandem, taking candles from the stack by the door and scattering them about the kirk, filling the space with soft light and at least a ghost of warmth. As soon as the final candle had been lit Norah went to Agnes, wrapping her arms tightly about the other woman's lean frame and leaning her head on her shoulder. Agnes smelled of earth and sweat and soot, but unsullied, untouched by the stench of decay that had risen from the pit.

Agnes soon began to weep again, deep, wrenching sobs, clinging to Norah like flotsam from a shipwreck. She cried instead of speaking, and Norah somehow understood it: the guilt, the grief, the *release* from years of darkness and lies. Her own guilt sat in the pit of her stomach, a stone that she knew not even time would erode. They would have to bear that remorse: separately, and together. They would have to move onward even as some part of them always remained here, at Corrain.

Eventually Agnes's sobs dried to a trickle and they parted, though neither woman was minded to move more than an arm's length away from the other. They shed their wet, dirty clothes, arranging them over the pews to dry in the modest heat from the candles, and pulled blankets from the sack to arrange in a makeshift bedroll on the carpeted altar. As soon as they lay down Norah felt exhaustion enfold her, and she fought it off only long enough to press a kiss to Agnes's jaw and wind their fingers together, so that Agnes could not leave without her knowing. The wind sang past the windows, and Norah fancied it carried with it the mournful exhalations of Corrain House's final dying breaths. The cleansing rain battered the name-etched windows and the steep-pitched roof, but Norah closed her eyes and saw only an endless starry sky.

EVEN NOW, AFTER everything that had happened, Norah could not help but smile at the act of waking up lying naked on a church altar, another woman pressed to her back, legs and arms woven with her own. Agnes was still deeply asleep, and did not stir even as Norah eased out from her arms and rose, grabbing one of the blankets to wrap around her shoulders.

On the altar sat a little pile of objects from where Agnes had emptied her pockets before bed, and it gave Norah a tiny private thrill to pick through even the mundane possessions of this woman she had so long wanted but only now felt she was truly beginning to know. A few pence. A metal thimble, worn and tarnished and too narrow for Norah's finger (for she tried). A spool of thread, though its needle had presumably been left back on the table in the kitchen of Corrain House.

A sleek black fountain pen. This Norah picked up, weighing it in her aching palm, pressing the pad of her thumb to the sharp point of the tiny garnet inset on the end of its cap.

Pen in hand, Norah went to the window.

ACKNOWLEDGEMENTS

"WE NEED TO have a call" is not something any author wants to hear from their agent when they're not expecting news.

It was January 2023, and our wonderful literary agent Amanda Rutter was departing to become an editor. We were delighted for her of course, and she was determined that we would not spend long without representation. Trouble was, we had spent a year wrestling with *The Needfire* and were barely 30,000 words deep. We had nothing new to send out.

Up stepped the Friday Scream Team, the best gang of cheerleaders a Lesbian Gestalt Entity could hope for. Raine Wilson and Dave Goodman (coiner of the hashtag #yearncore) let us feed them the remainder of the book on a fevered conveyor belt a few thousand words at the time, and the whole gang went way above and beyond the call to provide much-needed feedback, sense checks, and encouragement as we entered the trenches again. There too was our fellow Pitch Wars graduate and friend Chelsea Dotson, whose marginalia gave us life as she tried to work out who she could trust among our tiny, morally ambiguous cast.

When we first surrendered this manuscript to John Baker, the one-man hype machine destined to become our new agent, we made a solemn vow that we would tell nobody that the back half of it had been drafted in about three weeks (it would grow by over ten thousand words in revisions). This vow Morag broke immediately after signing our agency contract with the vigour and frequency of the dedicated humblebraggart. Thank you to the many saints who tolerate her nonsense on the daily. That includes Erin.

The Needfire, unlike its namesake, sparked from many different sources. Morag's childhood scrambling around the hillsides of the Isle of Arran, running across ruined crofts and bronze age forts and stone circles, the evidence of centuries of human settlements on a land that refuses to be tamed. Erin's environmental education studies, her trips to the highlands and islands with professors like Pete Higgins, whose habit of calling sheep 'meadow maggots' hooked deep into her brain and made it onto the pages of this book. Our chats about the Clearances with Ruaraidh Halford MacLeod, clan historian and the father of a dear friend, who told us about the etchings by evicted crofters on the windows of Croick Church, a striking image which we also borrowed for the novel. And of course our love of the Gothic, which Morag at least traces back to her Grandfather's enduring love of classic literature and film, and which he passed onto her. Sadly he isn't here to see her published (though it's possibly just as well given his rather presbyterian sensibilities - some scenes would no doubt have prompted a strongly-worded missive).

At time of writing we have yet to agree on a dedication. Too many people helped us get here. Faith, our very first fan, who true to her name believed in us from day one and continues to read every word we write even when we traumatise her with a Murder Tree. Our Pitch Wars mentor, Keena Roberts, and the rest of the Pitch Wars gang, our earliest fellow travellers on this journey. Our many interconnected writing communities—the Inklings and the Edinburgh SFFers and all the rest, with their irrepressible humour and unfailing support. Amanda and John and Julie Gourinchas, who somehow managed to be precisely the right advocates in the right places at the right times. And of course our thoughtful, patient, whip-smart editor Amy Borsuk, and the whole team at Solaris who have welcomed us into their beautiful home with such warmth and enthusiasm. Thank you to our families, who listened to our stories of the mad journey we've been on and still rooted for us, and to the friends who toasted to our successes and commiserated in our challenges.

Thank you all. This book is for you, whether you want it or not.

FIND US ONLINE!

www.rebellionpublishing.com

/solarisbooks   /solarisbks

/solarisbooks   /solarisbooks.
                     bsky.social

SIGN UP TO OUR NEWSLETTER!

rebellionpublishing.com/newsletter

YOUR REVIEWS MATTER!

Enjoy this book? Got something to say?

Leave a review on Amazon, GoodReads or with your
favourite bookseller and let the world know!